blueberry point Romance collection

Lilac Crush
Love, Lies and Fireflies
Promise Me October
Her Northshore Christmas

D. E. MALONE

Blueberry Point Romance Collection
ISBN 978-1951516-14-7 (e-book)
ISBN 978-1951516-15-4 (paperback)
Copyright © 2022 D.E. Malone
All rights reserved.
Cover designed by Blue Water Books

For exclusive content and book news, subscribe to D.E. Malone's *Welcome to the Sweet Life* newsletter.

LILAC CRUSH
A BLUEBERRY POINT STORY

D.E. MALONE

blueberry point Romance collection

Lilac Crush
Love, Lies and Fireflies
Promise Me October
Her Northshore Christmas

D. E. MALONE

Chapter One

An easy fix.

Three little words. That's all it took to carry Grace Callahan back almost twenty years as she stood at her kitchen counter. She set the last of the batch of chocolate oatmeal cookies inside the Tupperware container and clicked the lid into place, listening to the voices.

Grace shook her head at the foolish thought as she padded across the room, cracked the door, and peered down through the ornate rails of the circular wrought iron staircase into the carriage house below. That voice couldn't belong to who she thought it did.

Trey Merrick, the lead grounds person at Blueberry Point Lodge, set some tools against the wall. Next to him, another man unloaded a stack of empty plastic planters from his arms, setting them beside the tools. A ball cap concealed his face, but Grace would bet her next paycheck, meager as it was, that it was him.

Kendon Wright.

The memory of his face—the sun-kissed skin, the dreamy, inquisitive hazel eyes, and a minuscule scar marking his chin—emblazoned itself in her mind again when the voice floated into her studio apartment. That, and the image of a sprig of lilacs, presented to her on an overcast June day.

It seemed like another life. In hindsight, maybe it was the life Grace *should* have chosen.

"That's not going to cost an arm and both legs, is it?" Trey joked.

"Nope. Only one of each," the other guy said.

It *was* Kendon. There was no mistaking his voice now.

The men chuckled, their merriment echoing in the vast space.

"Let me take a closer look at it, then I can give you a rough estimate," Kendon said.

They walked over to the staircase, which caused Grace to have a mini heart attack. She eased the door closed again, leaving it open a crack. A face-to-face meeting with Kendon would be bad enough, being caught eavesdropping would be downright humiliating.

Below, the men huddled together as they examined the steps leading up to her apartment, their voices now hushed. Kendon ran his hand along the rail, his gaze lifting. Grace inched the door closed a little more, careful not to rattle the vintage knob that was looser than it should have been. She caught a glimpse of his face when he surveyed the stairs.

Grace sighed and glanced at the clock on the wall above the kitchen table. Her shift started in seven minutes. Not that Darcy Stetman, the inn's owner, watched the time. She was the most casual employer Grace had ever worked for. But she didn't want to take advantage of Darcy's goodwill. This job was the only thing between an empty refrigerator and a full one until something permanent popped up.

Grace could be across the lawn and inside the inn in less than a minute, but risking a meeting with Kendon twisted her stomach in knots. She dreaded the chance of running into him, of having to rehash what she'd been up to these last nineteen years. The time spanning high school graduation until now seemed like a blur. A messy, unhappy period of her life for sure, and one she'd left behind in Pittsburgh. She'd come to Hendricks to escape. Now she questioned her choice of returning to her hometown to heal.

Closing the door, Grace leaned her forehead against it, thinking.

She could call Darcy. Tell her her stomach was upset— totally true. She'd come as soon as she could. This last week had been spent giving each room a deep cleaning as Darcy and her husband, Sean, readied the historic sandstone brick mansion for their first guests next month. And Grace's list was long; she didn't have time to spare with excuses.

Grace eyed the door on the other side of the room,

which led to the outside stairs, her usual route. But that would mean walking past one of two windows on either side of the carriage house. And since the overhead door was wide open, well, there was no way Kendon wouldn't spot her.

Just go. You can do this.

She gave herself a decisive nod as she pushed away from the door. Grace swept her hair back, knotted it at her neck with a hair tie, and grabbed the container of cookies she'd made for Darcy.

Outside, she welcomed the ever-present scent of the firs and cedars, a reminder she no longer lived in the city. The inn's lawn met the rocky shore of Lake Superior a short distance away. White-capped waves tossed on the water. It was a chilly April day, but the promise of warm weather was on the horizon.

Grace took a deep breath. Part of embarking on this new journey alone was facing obstacles head on. Running into Kendon was a small challenge compared to the drama she'd gone through with the divorce.

She clung to the wooden rail and took each step gingerly so the stairs wouldn't creak and give her away. If she could make it far enough across the lawn, Grace might pretend she didn't hear if Kendon spotted her and called her name.

She made it to the bottom of the stairs and hurried past one of the windows on the side of the carriage house. Grace walked quickly, looking straight ahead, listening for the sound of his voice. The more distance she put between her and the carriage house, the better.

Ahead, Blueberry Point Lodge loomed on the sloping lawn. It was a majestic inn, all chimneys and tall, paned windows. She'd been washing those windows one by one these last two and a half weeks. She couldn't complain. There were worse jobs than gazing out at the lake with paper towels in one hand and a bottle of Windex in the other.

The brick patio and French doors leading into the inn's dining room beckoned. Once she had a hand on the door handle, Grace let out a heavy sigh. She slipped safely inside and shut the door behind her, now chancing a look toward the carriage house. Inside its wide opened doors, Trey's canvas coat was the only contrast she could make out from this far away.

"Morning, Grace."

Startled, Grace whirled around at the sound of Darcy Stetman's voice and pressed a hand against her chest. "I didn't hear you come into the room."

Darcy grinned. "Sorry to scare you."

Grace's boss pushed in a dining room chair at one of the round tables in the immense room as she walked toward her. Breakfast had ended an hour ago. The scent of sausage and sweet pastries still hung in the air.

"Sean says he can hear me thumping around down here from the third floor sometimes." Darcy waved her hand. "Even if he's embellishing, you're the first to claim I'm capable of sneaking up on someone."

"My mind is all over the place today. An elephant could catch me by surprise." She handed Darcy the container of cookies. "Here's dessert for you and Sean tonight."

"Your cookies are amazing—thank you." Darcy lifted the lid. "The smell of oatmeal cookies always takes me back to weekends in my grandmother's kitchen."

Grace turned to look out the window again. "Say, is that Kendon Wright with Trey in the carriage house?"

Darcy came over to stand beside her. "It is. Know him?"

"Yes. We went to high school together."

"Nice guy. Super talented. Did you date or were you just good friends?"

Grace moved away from the door. Relief loosened the tension in her shoulders now that she was safely out of sight. "Only friends. What's he doing here?"

"He's a welder. An artist. You know, making sculptures out of scrap metal. He's doing a few pieces for the gardens around the property."

"How nice." An artist. She could see that in Kendon.

"He's also talking to Trey about repairing that staircase in the carriage house."

She nodded. That was all she needed to know. Staying out of Kendon's way would be tricky, but she'd manage. At least he was avoidable for the time being.

Grace brushed her hands together. "Should we get started?"

"Would you like a cup of coffee first?" Darcy nodded to the tea cart at the other end of the room.

She glanced again through the doors. The men were nowhere in sight.

"I've had enough for now, but thanks." She laughed, even though there was nothing funny about Darcy's question. Even she could hear the nervous ring in her laughter. *There's nothing to worry about, Grace.* "Maybe a rain check?"

Darcy touched her arm and pointed to one of the pocket doors of the dining room. "Of course. This way."

Grace shed her jacket as she followed Darcy, leaving the dining room to hang it in the hallway closet near the side porch.

"I thought we could get started on the bedrooms upstairs. Linens arrived yesterday for a few of the rooms," Darcy said. "I'm excited to see them."

They walked toward the kitchen, where Grace gathered cleaning supplies in the utility closet, dropping them into the plastic bucket hanging from her arm. Darcy pulled out a vacuum. Together they climbed the grand double staircase to the second floor as the grandfather clock in the foyer chimed.

A brilliant light shone through the floor-to-ceiling windows in the upper foyer. There was a plush love seat and a Queen Anne coffee table in front of the windows and a large assembly of potted ferns, palms, and fiddle-leaf figs. When the sun blazed, the foyer was a perfect napping spot Darcy had told her when she'd given Grace the grand tour two weekends ago.

"Now that we'll have guests soon, I won't be able to use this as my little private oasis as often as I'd like," Darcy had joked. Grace understood Darcy's infatuation with it. Coupled with the lake view and warm surroundings, Grace wouldn't mind it as an escape either.

Darcy led her into the Tamarack Room, Grace's favorite

room. As homey as her studio above the carriage house was, Grace had fallen instantly in love with the peacefulness of this bedroom with its moss chintz curtains and full wall mural of the forest. When she bought her own home someday, she'd decorate it with this room in mind.

"I'll be working in the Granite Room. Why don't you start in here?" Darcy said as she pulled the curtains open a little more. "Call me when it's time to put on the linens."

Grace carried the bucket filled with cleaning products into the bathroom, thankful for the solitude of working alone. She could more fully digest the fact that she was in the same town as Kendon again.

Kendon.

It'd be wrong to think he hadn't crossed her mind. The shame she felt since their last meeting plagued her for months when she left Hendricks after graduation. It never really left her mind completely. She'd been young, stupid, and completely under the spell of Jeff Callahan, her now ex-husband and Kendon's best friend.

She took her frustration out on the enamel surface of the claw-foot tub, spraying and scrubbing until the finish shone like white marble. Time slipped by as Grace worked on the other fixtures, and finally, the floor. A small, steady drip from the sink faucet caught her attention. She'd mention it to Darcy but could fix it herself. The spout probably needed a new aerator was all.

"Hello?"

On her hands and knees, Grace gasped.

No!

"Are you in here?" A little rap sounded on the other side of the door.

Grace rocked back on her heels, and for a split second, foolishly glanced around the bathroom for an alternate escape route.

Nonononono—so not ready for this!

She jumped to her feet, the wet sponge still in her hand, as Kendon inched open the door.

"Sean told me it was you when I saw you cross the lawn earlier. I thought I'd—"

Grace whirled around with the water-soaked sponge and met Kendon, sponge to chest.

"—say hi," he finished, looking down at her hand. A dark spot bloomed on his red flannel shirt. The *drip drip* of the sponge splattered onto the tops of the paper sleeves he wore around his work boots.

She felt as if her breath had been sucked from her chest.

Here was Kendon, looking not much older than he had almost twenty years ago.

And Grace was sure she'd aged enough for the both of them.

Chapter Two

The sting of humiliation ignited and blinked out just as quickly when Kendon Wright came face to face with Grace.

Grace Callahan.

Who would have thought he'd run into her again?

"Kendon. This...this is a *surprise*."

He wondered why she'd ducked and hurried away from the carriage house earlier. Had she even known he was on the grounds? Surely the memory of their last encounter hadn't simmered these last nineteen years.

"It is. How have you been?"

She stared at him wide-eyed, like a frightened rabbit. Grace Callahan had changed. Subdued, almost melancholy, that was how he would describe his first impression. The shadows underneath her eyes were a telltale sign. So was the wavering smile. Life hadn't been as charmed for her as he'd predicted. A story for another time, perhaps.

Grace lifted a shoulder and looked away. "Oh, you know. Good, I suppose."

"How long have you been in Hendricks?" Sean had confirmed it was Grace when Kendon caught sight of her hurrying across the lawn earlier.

"A few weeks," she said, avoiding his gaze. Did she feel guilty for not reaching out?

"You've been out East this whole time, right?"

"Yeah, near Boston." Grace nodded. She smoothed the long mass of chestnut hair flowing over one shoulder, bunched together in a black rubber band. "Then Pittsburgh."

He searched her face for more answers. He got the sense she wasn't about to share more than what she'd already given him.

Grace shrugged again, the items in her plastic bucket shifting. "And now here I am," she said with a weary smile.

He wanted to ask in the worst way if Jeff was with her. Sean had been discreet about giving away details, which Kendon supposed was honorable. Tenant privacy beats hometown gossip.

"Sean told me you're living in the carriage house. So, you're home for a while?"

She tried to move past him in the doorway, except it turned into an awkward dance with each of them trying not to crowd the other. Once out of the small space, Grace turned toward him again, visibly relieved. Kendon sensed she felt cornered. Like prey.

"We'll see," she said with a nervous laugh. "I'm taking

it day by day you could say."

He should go. This was more awkward than he imagined.

"Well, like I said, I just wanted to see how you're doing. Maybe we can catch up since I'll be on the property for the next week at least." He moved toward the bedroom door to leave, which made her put more distance between them.

Grace nodded. Her expressive blue eyes darted around the room. "Maybe."

"Okay. Nice to see you again."

This time her smile was a little more genuine, like the old Grace. Now that he was on his way out the door.

"Yes, it is. See you later, Kendon."

KENDON PULLED OUT OF THE LONG GRAVEL drive of the inn and turned onto Highway 61 toward Hendricks later that afternoon. The town stretched along the lakefront for a few miles, sporadic businesses tucked away from the road amongst the cedars and tamaracks—the two-pump gas station, an artist's studio, Lee Nuy Accounting—until the Hendricks sign marked the city limits. Hendricks was one of a handful of towns between there and the Canadian border forty-five minutes away. The winding highway hugged the lakeshore, sometimes following it close enough that you could throw a rock into the water from the shoulder. Other times the lake disappeared behind the trees. He'd had the same view for all of his thirty-seven years and he never grew tired of keeping company with the Big Lake.

While he drove, Kendon's thoughts returned to Grace and how she'd changed. She was still pretty in that don't-look-at-me, unpretentious way that he'd always found disarming. And Grace hadn't lost the inquisitive spark in her eyes either. Not completely anyway. He remembered how she never just looked at him, she *drank* him in. At least that was how he would have described Grace in high school. But now? Now she seemed like she was trying to save herself from drowning.

They'd been best friends in high school—Jeff Callahan, Grace Downing, and him. Attending a church youth camp in northern Wisconsin the summer before high school brought them closer together. They'd spent two weeks together praying and singing, fishing and boating, cementing a bond based on the fact that they were the only kids to attend from Bethel Lutheran Church that summer. That, and teaming up for the nightly five-legged races with the other campers. There was something to the solidarity of tripping over each other's feet and skinning knees with dozens of other high schoolers that made the transition from summer camp to the hallways of high school a natural one in terms of their three-way friendship.

Grace was always the quiet, somewhat shy girl in their class. He hadn't thought much about her until he went off to camp. But once Grace started feeling comfortable around him, she was like the new girl in school. Exotic. *Interesting.* And she loved to laugh at pretty much everything. Kendon loved that about her, especially since he never felt like a particularly funny guy. With Grace, Kendon might as well have been Jerry Seinfeld.

He slowed when the sign for Ford Hardware & Lumber came into view. Kendon needed that new MIG welder he'd ordered. A job as big as that carriage house staircase called for a new one. He'd been nursing his old welder long enough, so he'd asked Chase Ford to find him one to his specifications.

Anyway, Grace, Jeff, and he were inseparable after returning from that camp. Grace never seemed to feel out of place when he and Jeff swapped stories about their love for Star Wars, hockey, or girls. In fact, she was pretty helpful in the last department, dropping a good word for him and Jeff when it came time to ask someone to a dance. Grace was definitely not a girl's girl, though. She was comfortable mucking around in the Sage River when he and Jeff took their poles up the trail on fall weekends to catch trout. She could outrun Jeff which infuriated him to no end. Maybe a little too much, Kendon had always thought. And she was a whiz in math, which was to his benefit since Algebra II almost sent him to summer school junior year. He had Grace to thank for keeping him square.

Kendon pulled into Ford's parking lot, maneuvering into a space near the front of the store, and shut off the engine. He sat there for a minute, thinking about Grace's reaction when he'd seen her.

The tired shadows underneath her eyes.

The darting glances.

She'd been almost skittish.

Grace wasn't the old friend he remembered. Their last encounter after graduation wasn't ideal, but it didn't warrant her shunning him like this.

Something had happened to Grace Callahan, and he intended to get to the bottom of it.

Chapter Three

The next morning Darcy recruited Grace to help her move furniture from one of the cabins on the property before the carpet installers arrived. The sun had barely blinked over the horizon before her boss led Grace, steaming coffee mugs in hand, from the brick patio off the dining room and across the back lawn toward the first cabin.

They'd started with the lighter items first—a coffee table, a side table, two dining chairs. But when Darcy tossed the decorative pillows from the futon to the floor, removed the mattress, and attempted to lift the bulky frame, her dark eyes widened with surprise.

"I didn't realize it would be this heavy," she said with a frown

They managed to turn it on its side while Darcy lamented the fact she'd put off the task until the last minute. Moving the piece across the room was a slow process. Tilting it to navigate the front door of Loon Cottage, one of two cabins on the grounds of Blueberry Point Lodge, was an even slower ordeal. If it landed on one of their feet, Grace bet the moving session would be over in a hurry.

"It's oak, isn't it?"

"I think so," Darcy said. "Sean and his brother, Matt, carried everything inside. I should have asked for their help."

Grace had moved her share of furniture. First, from Hendricks to her and Jeff's townhouse in Boston. From Boston to a condo in Pittsburgh until they renovated a nineteenth-century row house in the historic Lawrenceville neighborhood. Jeff didn't spare a penny on updates and amenities during the four years they'd lived there, including the furniture, even though it was beyond their budget. Grace left all of the too formal mahogany room sets in Pittsburgh. It was more Jeff's taste than hers anyway.

Ahead of her, Darcy maneuvered one end through the door. Grace could only follow the motion of the futon because she couldn't see beyond it. Darcy grunted.

Grace tried to peer around the futon. "Careful. You okay?"

"Maybe? I think adrenaline is masking the pain at this point," she said when Grace caught her eye around the side. Darcy winced when the weight of the piece knocked her sideways on the porch. She almost lost her footing.

"I'm almost through the door. Let's set it down."

"Good. I need to catch my breath," Darcy said.

She was smaller than Grace by several inches, almost petite. But Grace had seen Darcy lift a five-gallon water jug without effort and cart a wheelbarrow full of landscaping bricks around the gardens last week. The woman was no stranger to hard work.

After a pause to reconfigure their grip on the futon, they moved it to the far end of the porch. Darcy sat on the top step and patted the spot beside her for Grace to sit.

"I might have to ask the installers to move the futon in the other cabin," Darcy said. She sipped the now cold coffee from her mug. Grace had discreetly poured hers into the landscaping next to the porch. Cold coffee wasn't her favorite.

"But they charge for that, and we're over budget on this place as is," Darcy continued. She sat up straight, arching her back.

"Can Sean help? We can move what we can from the other cabin and wait for him."

Darcy checked the time on her phone. She grimaced. "That won't work. He has errands to run first and a doctor's appointment. The carpet installers will be here before nine."

"We'll have to get it done then." She stood and brushed her pants off. Darcy didn't look like she was in a hurry to follow. "Are you sure you're okay?"

Darcy looked up at her with her brows pinched together. "I will be. Must have tweaked something." She slowly rose from her spot, pressing a hand against her back.

Grace waved at Trey Merrick, who was on his knees in the flower bed circling the gazebo as she and Darcy walked to the other cabin. The grounds of Blueberry Point Lodge were lush with spring flowers thanks to Trey. He labored over the gardens daily, bringing them back to life despite an old leg injury. Grace often noticed him sitting in random spots around the property, wincing while he rubbed his leg. He was friendly but kept to himself. She respected his privacy in the same way he avoided asking her questions when their conversation veered into personal territory. He'd become a comforting presence during the short time she'd lived in the carriage house.

She and Darcy moved a few of the less bulky pieces onto the long, wide porch of Lark Cottage, leaving the futon alone this time. It grew increasingly obvious that Darcy had hurt herself. When she lifted a flower arrangement from the dining room table, she gasped sharply.

"I think I'm done for the day. I'm sorry, Grace. Do you think you can finish by yourself?" Darcy leaned over the table, supporting herself with one hand on her back, the other hand gripping a chair.

"Of course! It shouldn't take me too long." Grace hated seeing Darcy in such pain. "Do you need help getting back inside? Should we call Sean?"

"I'll be fine once I lay down." Darcy dragged her feet as she made her way to the door. "Thanks so much, Grace."

Grace watched her boss slowly make her way to the brick patio, ready to step in if Darcy looked like she wouldn't make it. But once Darcy ambled through the door and was out of sight, Grace turned back to the room, surveying its contents. The dining table would be tricky, not because it was heavy, but awkward. As was the full-sized mattress in the bedroom. Still, she could do it.

She'd eased the mattress and box spring out onto the porch and was back in the bedroom, ready to remove the bed's side rails when she heard the *thud* of heavy footsteps on the porch. Grace got up from the floor and peeked into the living area.

"Grace?"

Her heart flipped again at the sound of Kendon's voice. Was this going to be a regular occurrence with him working at the inn, seeking her out every day?

"I'm here." Resigned, she met him at the door.

Kendon took up almost the entire door frame. He'd taken off his ball cap, and now his sandy, thick hair was askew from the hat and the fierce wind whipping across the lawn from the lake. He looked disheveled yet handsome. Gone was the fresh-faced teenager she'd said goodbye to so many years ago. Standing in front of her was a man who'd filled out in all the right places, from the slightly weathered complexion with a faint shadow of new whiskers on his jaw to the broad muscled shoulders that were hard to miss underneath his shirt. Grace caught herself staring for a few seconds too long.

"Darcy texted me to say you might need some help?" he said, stepping inside.

Grace crossed her arms. "I've got everything under control here. But thanks."

He looked around the room. "Are you sure? It looks like there's still quite a bit—"

"Really. I've got this." She tried smiling to let him know she could, in fact, finish by herself. The last thing she needed was to work closely with Kendon. There were too many questions left unanswered, and she preferred not to be drawn into that conversation today.

The whine of a diesel engine cut into the silence inside the cabin. Grace crossed over to the sink, looking through the window in time to see the Lakeshore Flooring truck bumping along the gravel drive. It stopped in front of the carriage house. Grace grumbled under her breath.

"Wonderful. They're here." She turned back to Kendon, who stood there watching her with a slightly amused expression.

"Looks like I'm your guy."

Grace swallowed. "I guess you are."

They worked in silence, perfectly in sync. Kendon would look to Grace, she'd point at the next piece, and they'd bring it outside like they were partners in a synchronized furniture-moving performance. A chest of drawers was the last item they moved onto the lawn when the two carpet guys showed up.

Grace let them know they could start on the closest cabin and to call Darcy if they had questions. Then she turned back to Kendon, who'd parked himself on one of the dining room chairs in the grass.

"They can take it from here. Thanks for helping." She

hoped Kendon would give one of his perfunctory nods then return to do whatever he'd been doing before Darcy recruited him.

"No problem," Kendon said, looking a little too comfortable and not in any hurry to leave. "What's on your agenda today?"

She caught a momentary glimpse of seventeen-year-old Kendon, sitting across from her at Frozen Planet Ice Cream Palace, their go-to hangout after school. He'd always wanted to know how she occupied her time when they weren't together. At first, she'd thought he was a tad nosy. Then she'd come to realize that he cared by the way he hung on her every word. Kendon thought she was *interesting*.

Grace glanced back at the inn, her mind blank. The way Kendon studied her, *really* looked her over, made her self-conscious and tingly at the same time.

"Oh, you know. Same thing I've been doing since day one—cleaning."

"Is this permanent? I mean, will you stay on once the inn opens?" he asked.

Grace hoped for something more than a cleaning job. A job that would challenge and excite her.

"I'm keeping my options open." A safe answer.

Kendon rubbed the tops of his thighs before he stood and stretched. "Let me know if I can help in any way. And I'll be on the lookout for job openings." He lifted his hand before he started toward the carriage house again. "I'll let you get back to work. Have a good day, Grace."

Grace stared at his retreating back. "You too."

Looking at him, a spark of affection spread through Grace. He still seemed like kind, thoughtful Kendon. Maybe she should make an effort to return his kindness. At the very least by not looking for the quickest escape route the next time they ran into each other.

Chapter Four

Kendon closed the door of the Lakeshore Weekly office behind him, stepping out onto the sidewalk in downtown Hendricks two days later. He'd popped in to see his sister, Lexi, and ask her to lunch, but he'd just missed her. The office assistant told him Lexi was on a photo assignment with a group from New Mexico canoeing the Boundary Waters for charity or something. She was always on some adventure with her camera. Good for her. It was her dream job; she'd told him as much when she landed it a few years back.

Instead, he headed toward D & G Market down the block, intent on grabbing a bite to eat in the cafe before heading back to Blueberry Point Lodge. The two-block walk would do him good. Cottony clouds drifted overhead. He caught the smell of fried fish from O'Grady's Restaurant on the lakefront, making his mouth water. He passed shops with their doors open and tables of sale items moved onto the sidewalk. Spring on the North Shore was his favorite time of year.

Inside the market, Kendon stood over the deli case, wavering between buying a turkey wrap or the Roast Beef Wrangler, when he noticed Grace down the aisle. She studied the lighted pastry case, a white paper bag in hand, a sour expression creasing her brow. The sandwich could wait.

"I have the same trouble and usually grab one of everything."

Grace jumped when he spoke but gave him a small smile. "They're out of my favorite. I'm not sure what I want as a second choice."

"What's your favorite?" He looked into the case. It was nearly depleted.

"Creme-filled long Johns. With chocolate icing." Grace chewed her lip. "They only have regular chocolate-iced ones."

"Hmmm, an easy fix."

Kendon raised his finger to get the attention of Burt, who worked behind the bakery counter. The middle-aged man, wearing a white paper hair covering just above his ample eyebrows, lifted his chin when he saw Kendon summon him.

"What can I do you for, Kendon?" He rearranged the hair covering, then looked to Grace and back at Kendon again.

"We're in need of a creme-filled long John. Can you make one from a regular long John?" He tapped the glass door of the pastry case.

Burt opened the door of the case to take one from the tray. "Sure can. Gimme a sec."

At the back counter, Burt took his frosting injector, poked it into one end of the pastry, then the other, filling it with creme. Then he slipped it into a bag and handed it to Grace, who'd watched quietly until now.

"Thank you so much," she said to Burt. He nodded before going back to the bread slicer.

A little smile lit up her face as she peeked into the bag. "I never would have thought to ask for that."

"You know what they say about desperate times..."

She laughed. It was good to hear that again.

Kendon shuffled his feet. "I came for a bite to eat. Want to join me?"

Grace's face fell, the uncertainty back. "I...I should get back."

"I eat fast. C'mon, we can sit at the counter by the window and talk about people as they come in."

She nodded, her smile lighting up her eyes. "Like old times."

She followed him while he grabbed the roast beef sandwich and a bottle of Hank's root beer. When she didn't find anything else to eat, he looked at the pastry bag in her hands.

"Is that your lunch?"

"It's more than I usually eat," she said.

She'd always had a sweet tooth, he remembered. He also recalled how she never brought a lunch in high school, choosing instead to sit at the table with Jeff and him, nursing a chocolate milk while she listened to them bicker about who owed the other an extra monster cookie that week. Or the chances of whichever sports team was in season to win that weekend. Listening was a close second to laughing for Grace.

Kendon could feel the rapid beating of his pulse as he paid for their food then led her over to the little seating area past the deli. There were only a few tables, plus a long lacquered pine counter against the window. Facing the parking lot, they could see customers coming into the store. Beyond that, the shops on Main Street. He pulled out one of the tall stools. She did the same, sitting down next to him.

But once they were settled, Kendon realized he was too self-conscious to eat being in such close proximity to Grace again. He took a halfhearted bite of his sandwich then set it down, opting to pop the top from his bottle instead for a sip of root beer.

"So, how do you like living in the carriage house?"

Grace stared through the window. She wrinkled her nose as she smiled.

"It's darling. And so convenient. I was a little desperate to find a place," she said. "Things sure got expensive around here since I've been gone."

Kendon chuckled. "Everything anywhere is more expensive than it was nineteen years ago."

When she stiffened, Kendon regretted reminding her how long she'd been away. He gripped the neck of his bottle, thinking carefully about his next choice of words.

"Hendricks isn't what it used to be when we were young. That's good and bad. The city people found us.

That has driven prices up." He took another bite of his sandwich, then folded it back into the wrapper. He'd finish it on the way back to the inn.

"Luckily, Darcy and Sean offered it to me for next to nothing," she said. "I'll have to find something eventually, but it took the pressure off."

"How'd you know it was even available?"

She looked down at her hand on the tabletop and chewed on her lip. "Ingrid Callahan let me know."

Ingrid. Jeff's mother. And Grace had said Ingrid let *her* know. Not Jeff and her. Only Grace. He wanted to ask what happened. He'd heard they'd married, bought a place in Boston. If they ever came back to Hendricks to visit his parents, he wasn't aware of it.

"Jeff and I aren't together anymore," she said, as if reading his thoughts.

The bottle was halfway to his mouth when she said it. Kendon froze before he noticed she was looking at him.

"We've been divorced for a few years."

Kendon nodded. "I'm sorry."

"I'm not." Grace gave a nonchalant shrug as she opened her bag to pluck out the pastry. "We weren't a good match. At all."

He almost laughed at her candidness. Or maybe it was relief that they weren't together anymore. *I could have told you Jeff was wrong for you. You only had to ask before running off with him.*

"Ingrid has helped me a lot actually. I didn't expect that," Grace said, raising her brows when she looked at him again. "You know, after divorcing her son and all."

"That's a little telling, isn't it?"

Grace huffed. "You don't know the half of it."

"Ingrid and Henry were always pretty cool people. I remember wishing they were my parents on more than one occasion. And I have pretty great parents."

He picked at the paper label on the root beer bottle, wondering what else he didn't know about Jeff. Back in school, Kendon had known Jeff the longest out of anyone. Their mothers had been grade school best friends too. Ingrid coming through for Grace didn't surprise him. Ingrid and her husband, Henry, had always been warm, welcoming people. They had to be, running Blueberry Point Lodge for years before they'd sold it to the Stetmans. He'd heard the Callahans decided to sell once Henry began having health problems. It was only through the grapevine that he'd heard that, having lost touch with the couple after his and Jeff's falling out. He'd run into them around town on occasion, but they were busy with the inn, and work had always consumed him. Kendon figured they knew the messy details of their son's broken friendship with him. When Kendon shifted in his seat, Grace sighed loudly. She still had the spray of freckles across the bridge of her nose. He found it hard not to stare.

"I'm sorry. Listen to me going on about him. You and Jeff were close. I don't mean to bash him," she said, looking away again.

"You're joking, right? I haven't talked to him since you two left town. We were close at one time, sure. Not anymore."

"Then this conversation isn't making you uncomfortable?" she asked with a frozen smile.

"Not at all. It's...it's news to me. You coming back here after all this time. I figured you guys had two-point-five kids by now. The picket fence and cocker spaniel."

Her face fell momentarily before she smiled again. "Once upon a time, that's what I pictured. I'm not such an idealist anymore."

Kendon desperately wanted to put a more positive spin on this conversation. They sat in silence for another minute while she finished her pastry. His mind whirled with memories from high school. Good ones. Memories that wouldn't cause her any more pain.

"Remember when Ingrid picked the three of us up from school that one day during sophomore year? When we got sent to the principal's office for 'loitering' near the faculty parking lot?"

Grace's smile blazed like a star. "Didn't Mrs. What's-Her-Name not realize the science teacher sent us out to his car with armloads of...what?"

"Mrs. Herman was the narc. Mr. Pennecia was the science teacher. I think there were old beakers or something in those boxes. Wasn't he taking them home to recycle?"

"Right," she said, snapping her fingers. "Mrs. Herman thought we were breaking into cars. And Mr. Pennecia had disappeared for a parent conference or something, so he couldn't even vouch for us. Not until the next day at least."

"Good times." Kendon drummed his fingers on the

countertop. He glanced at her, noting her wistful look as she stared through the window. "Ingrid was the only one of our parents around to pick us up."

"As if mine would ever have considered coming," she said with a grimace. It was true. Grace's parents hadn't been the best example of familial love.

"Isn't it great what the Stetmans are doing to the inn? I mean, Ingrid and Henry kept it up so well, but now it's got a whole new personality." Grace rested her chin on one hand. "I love that place. More good memories."

Kendon remembered the hide-and-seek games at Blueberry Point Lodge that he and Jeff and their other friends used to play during grade school. They'd spend Sunday afternoons when the inn was free of guests, long before Grace entered the picture, dashing from room to room on three floors. The attic ballroom had been unfinished and eerie until the Callahans renovated it for more living quarters. Once the Stetmans bought the inn, he'd heard it was improved even more.

"How many nights did we spend sitting on the rock wall by the water?" He shook his head and chanced another look at Grace. It was still hard to believe almost twenty years had passed since high school.

Grace giggled. "Countless. I think I still have a scar on my elbow from when I slipped off that one night," she answered. "Such simple times."

Those were his favorite times together with Grace, even though Jeff was there too. He remembered the sensation of his and Grace's arms accidentally brushing or their hips pressing against each other's from sitting so close. He'd dwell on that particular night, going over what was said, how she'd looked at him, the clenching desire in his gut, until the next time it happened. They'd sit there in the dark, looking at stars, listening to the water lap at the rocks, and he wished they could stay there until the sun came up again. A chill ran up his neck thinking about those times again. Kendon glanced at her hand resting on the table, her long, slender fingers, and wondered what she'd do if he enfolded her hand in his own. He almost laughed. She'd run off and not bother with him again, that's what. *One step at a time.*

"I should get back to the inn," Grace said, slipping off the stool. She crumpled her bag and hitched her purse onto her shoulder.

"Me too," he answered, even though he had another twenty minutes.

"Thanks for the donut," Grace said. "And your long John hack—brilliant."

"Maybe I've missed my calling as a pastry magician."

"If that's even a thing, it would be a good side hustle," she said with a smile.

Kendon waited until she left the store so he could watch her cross the parking lot. Was he too optimistic to think she'd warmed up to him a little over the last three days?

He was a patient guy. After all, he'd waited for nineteen years, hadn't he?

Chapter Five

Sleep hadn't come easy last night, but Grace didn't think her restlessness was enough to wake up with a whopping headache. The incessant pounding in her head when she opened her eyes proved her wrong though. She lay in bed, staring at the white swirls on the ceiling, wondering how she'd make it through the morning let alone the day feeling like this. But when the pounding changed to sporadic intervals, Grace sat up, slid into her slippers and went to investigate.

The noise came from inside the carriage house. She cracked open the door leading to the iron staircase and the racket grew louder. Kendon was at the bottom of the steps, his back toward her, pounding on the rail. The muscles in his back worked underneath the t-shirt. She shook her head to erase the image of him from her mind, but that was silly. Kendon and his muscles weren't easily dismissed.

He'd wormed his way into her thoughts these last few days. And their impromptu lunch yesterday hadn't helped. If it weren't for their shared past with Jeff, Kendon was the type to put her instantly at ease. He listened. He understood. Even after all these years apart, being with him felt comfortable. She'd liken the feeling to curling up on the couch, wrapped in her plush fleece throw with a bowl of buttered popcorn, and bingeing her new favorite series on television.

Only, a series ended. Kendon was here to stay.

Grace eased the door closed, careful not to rattle the knob mechanism too hard. But she wasn't careful enough. The broken knob, already loose in her hand, disengaged completely and hung from the hole. On the other side of the door, Grace heard the outer knob clatter onto the landing.

Wonderful. So much for being discreet.

She pulled the knob off and peered through the hole in the door. It wasn't large enough to see down to the carriage house floor. Maybe Kendon didn't hear it with the noise he was making.

Seconds later, a knock. "Grace?"

Grace's hands flew to her cheeks. *No!*

She turned in a circle, not wanting to face Kendon with tangled hair and pajamas she should have relegated to the rag bag long ago.

The door rattled. The cylinder of the outer knob poked back through the hole. Kendon knocked again.

"Grace, if you're in there, I need to have the door open to fix this."

She glared at the doorknob. Hadn't Darcy told her to avoid that exit altogether? The stairs were under repair, the landing needed attention, and the doorknob was one of those antique brass ones with the ornamental designs, loose in its housing. In other words, this was her own fault.

"I'm here. Come in."

The door swung open. Kendon stood there, eyes wide. He gave her a once-over and pursed his lips before averting his gaze again. Reading his reaction confirmed her suspicions; she was the fresh-out-of-bed version of a hot mess.

"I was about to peek out and say good morning and it broke off in my hand." *You big liar. Why can't you just admit you were spying on him?*

"It's on my list to fix," he said, looking down at her side of the door. She handed him the knob.

Kendon looked irresistibly rugged in the dark yellow shirt. The color complemented his hair, which brushed his collar. She liked him with longer hair. Maybe a little too much.

"Didn't Sean and Darcy tell you not to use this door? With the stairs under repair and this doorknob, it'll be less of a risk if you use the other door." He paused after he'd inserted the housing back into the hole and flashed a smile at her. "Not that I don't want you poking your head out to say hello."

"Noted."

He did a double take when he caught her studying him a little too closely again. Grace felt her face flame.

"What do you have going on today?" he asked.

"I'm morning Darcy...I mean, I'm with Darcy this morning." *Good grief.* She needed to go back to bed. "I'm riding along on one of the Sturgeon Widows Tours this afternoon. Darcy says there's an opening for a guide next month."

"That's something that interests you?" he said, leaning against the door frame, jiggling the knob.

"I worked at a private museum in Boston for a while until I got on with the National Park Service. I love history. Narrating tours would be a dream job." She'd have to find another job to supplement since she couldn't live off of what a seasonal tour guide position would pay. Especially if she wanted to eventually buy her own place.

"I might have another prospect for you," Kendon said.

"Oh?"

His brows ticked up. "At the lighthouse."

"Clearwater Lighthouse?"

"The one and only."

The iconic structure sat on a high rocky bluff on the west side of town. An old shipwreck lay underneath the shallow waters offshore. It was visible on cloudy days if one stood on the sunken stone patio near the picnic area on the lighthouse grounds. The area had a notorious history of swallowing ships, and Grace had loved those stories as a kid. Her fascination with local history had carried into adulthood. She'd planned to pursue a history degree after Jeff finished his studies, but that plan had gone off the rails.

Grace crossed her arms. "I'm listening."

"The current caretaker and his wife, Jed and Trudy, are moving to be closer to their son's family. They leave at the end of next month. I don't think the people involved with the land trust that oversees the lighthouse have found anyone to replace them yet."

Could she live in a lighthouse? The idea intrigued her.

"Does that interest you at all?" Kendon asked.

Rental properties in Hendricks were hard to come by. What few apartments were available cost more than she could afford. Her time in the carriage house was short-term since the studio would soon be open to guests. Darcy had told her so during their first conversation.

"How do I get in touch with them without showing up on their doorstep?"

He chuckled. "I guess that's a 'yes.' Tell you what—let me give them a call. I'm sure they'd love to give you a private tour. If you don't mind, maybe I can come with and make the introductions."

"Would I mind? Not at all! That would be perfect." Having Kendon along might save her the awkwardness of having to talk too much.

Kendon would pick her up later after her bus tour and when he finished a small project on the other side of town. He rigged the doorknob for the short-term so she wouldn't have a gaping hole there. When he closed the door behind him, she listened to his footsteps echo on the metal staircase.

Grace lost track of the time she stood in front of the door, thinking. Kendon resumed his work on the stairs, judging by the sharp sounds of the hammer on metal. Ever since he'd started working in the carriage house, Grace found herself unable to relax, knowing he was close by.

It wasn't the notion of living in a lighthouse that occupied Grace's thoughts at the moment. No, it was spending more time with Kendon later in the day.

More time *alone*.

Chapter Six

Grace was ready and waiting in the driveway when he arrived back at Blueberry Point Lodge later that afternoon.

Kendon cleared his throat as Grace got into the truck. "Trudy will be there. Jed had to run to Duluth for the night."

"Did you tell her about me?" Grace asked. "That I'm looking for a place?"

"Yes, I did. She said to ignore the mess. They've already started packing."

She huffed. "It's nice of her to show it on such short notice."

"Trudy is a close friend. I've done some work there over the years. She and Jed are both sweethearts."

Kendon looked straight ahead as she buckled herself in. He risked getting caught with his mouth open if he glanced at her. She'd styled her hair differently. Secured it with a barrette or something. It accentuated her cheekbones and eyes. Grace had always liked to hide behind her hair, and she had a lot of it so it didn't take much effort. She'd dressed up too. Gone were the faded jeans and oversized sweatshirts he'd seen her in these last few times. She'd chosen an ankle-skimming skirt and light blue cardigan. He wished he could get away with studying her at his leisure. The quick glances when they talked or when her attention was elsewhere only whet his curiosity.

Ten minutes later, they turned onto the gravel road leading to Clearwater Lighthouse. Its white tower and red lantern room at the top loomed ahead. The building was one of the most photographed lighthouses on the Great Lakes.

Trudy met them on the small concrete porch, which lead into the public portion of Clearwater Lighthouse. Kendon had seen the labyrinth of small rooms showcasing the history of the lighthouse and the shipping on Lake Superior many times. Framed newspaper articles and other art decorated the walls—maps of shipping routes and photographs and sketches of wrecks, travel logs, lighthouse keepers, and their families. Other artifacts were encased under glass display cases, like navigational equipment and clothing. He and Grace followed Trudy through a heavy oak door leading to the living quarters.

"How long have you lived here?" Grace asked once they stood in the living room with its low ceiling of exposed timbers and white-washed walls.

Trudy, a small woman with a proud stature, pushed her

enormous red eyeglass frames onto the bridge of her nose. She squinted, thinking.

"Eleven years? Jed keeps better track of those details than I do."

"What's involved with being a caretaker here?" Grace asked. She scanned the room, from the cracked plaster walls to the polished oak floors under their feet, covered with a faded Persian-style rug. Kendon couldn't tell what ran through her mind as she took in her surroundings.

Trudy brushed off one of the side tables with her hand and straightened the lampshade. "This lighthouse is fully automated, so it's a lot less work than it used to be. The land trust keeps someone on hand to oversee the technical aspects of the lighthouse. Jed and I maintain the living quarters and conduct tours."

"So, you're not required to do anything overly technical?"

"Jed is pretty handy. He's able to troubleshoot plumbing and heating issues here, but as far as maintaining anything related to the lighthouse controls, like the lantern room, no," Trudy said. "If you're not inclined to take care of issues yourself, I'm sure there could be someone on call."

Trudy led them through the two bedrooms and a kitchen, which looked like it hadn't been updated in decades. She asked if they wanted to see the lantern room, noting "you can see Split Rock Lighthouse in Two Harbors on a clear day."

Grace glanced at Kendon and then gave Trudy a slight shake of her head. "I don't think that's necessary today."

She grew less talkative as the tour progressed. Kendon had tried to catch her eye more than once, but she kept her head down or her attention focused on Trudy, a tight-lipped smile ready when the older woman spoke to her.

They walked down two stone steps into a small sunlit room with windows on three sides. The interior walls were made of wide stone slabs coated with white enamel paint. Trudy explained this was her favorite reading room when the weather allowed it.

"It's unheated, but the stone walls hold in the warmth. Sometimes I feel like a loaf of bread baking in here, even when it's chilly outside. It's really quite delightful."

Kendon looked over at Grace expecting her to agree with Trudy too, but she'd walked over to one of the windows, looking out at the overgrown shrub blocking the lake view.

Trudy joined her. "It's a lilac. If the weather is warm when it blooms, I love to open the window and catch the scent. I'll have to trim it back a bit after the blossoms fade. They should pop open in the next week."

"I love lilacs," Grace said softly.

Kendon stared at Grace's back, an awkward memory floating up from his subconscious. She gazed at the scenery until Trudy opened the door to lead them outside. Grace crossed her arms as she followed Trudy, keeping her eyes on the stone steps.

"Do you have any more questions for me?" Trudy asked when they gathered near the small flower garden next to a diminutive stone building, an equipment shed, Kendon guessed.

Grace thrust out her hand. "I don't think so. Thank you for the tour, Trudy. It was so nice of you to meet with us."

Her abruptness surprised Kendon. Trudy's eyes widened slightly at the quick handshake too. Grace hurried away from them toward Kendon's truck.

He thrust his hands in his pockets and smiled at Trudy. "Thanks for your time. It was nice of you to accommodate us on such short notice, like Grace said."

She patted him on the shoulder. "It was no trouble, really. I don't think I adequately sold the place to her, though, did I?"

Grace was already sitting in the passenger seat. "It's not you; trust me."

Trudy looked toward his truck with a sympathetic smile. "I'm surprised that poor woman came back to Hendricks at all. Nothing but misery for her when she lived here. That family of hers—" Trudy pursed her lips— "they were something else."

"I don't think I ever talked to them."

"You do remember her father being in and out of jail, don't you? It was like that ever since he was a teen. Grace's mother, Kim, was a timid, quiet type," Trudy said. "I'm sure he ran all over her and the kids when he was around."

Kendon scratched his head, glancing at the truck. He didn't like talking about Grace's family when she was close by. "They're long gone now. That's probably why she chose to come back."

He barely remembered the Youngs, but he'd heard the

rumors. And Grace never talked about her family, so Kendon didn't push it. They'd lived on the edge of town in a little blue bungalow with a rusted-out frame of an old Chevy truck in the side yard.

He'd been inside her house once during high school. Grace had forgotten a homework assignment in the fall of their junior year, so he'd had to drive her home once she arrived at school on the bus. Her parents weren't there, she explained, so they couldn't bring it to school. Kendon had waited in the driveway for ten minutes while she went inside to grab the assignment. Already late for the first bell, Kendon got tired of waiting and went to the door to hurry her along. He knocked a few times, but she didn't answer so he went inside. Standing in the living room, the conditions in that house had shocked him with the sheer volume of stuff piled on the floor and furniture. She'd met him in the hallway, red-faced and frowning. He remembered Grace pushing past him, navigating the narrow path through the junk-filled living room to the front door. She never said a word about that day, and he felt too embarrassed for her to ask.

Kendon wished Trudy well and walked to his truck. Grace was digging inside her bag when Kendon got behind the wheel again.

"A quaint place, wasn't it?"

Grace hadn't stopped scrounging around for whatever she looked for. "It was."

"But you're not interested?"

"I don't think so. Being out here all alone and not being a handy sort? It scares me."

"I'd be around to help. I mean, if there was an emergency."

She looked over at him with a skeptical look. "You're busy enough without running to my rescue."

"I'd hardly call it rescuing. Lending a hand, maybe? To a friend?"

Grace crinkled her nose. "Thanks, but it's not for me. I should get back to the inn."

"You still have work to do? It's late." Was she trying to avoid him again?

"There's a program at the inn tonight that I'd like to catch," she said.

"Oh?"

Grace waved her hand dismissively. "About the gardens. Trey's giving a little talk to the garden club."

He tossed another question around in his mind, trying to figure out the best way to ask.

"Grace?"

Grace stopped rattling around the contents of her bag and looked over at him. "What's up?"

"Why'd you come back here? To Hendricks."

Grace closed her bag and set it on the floor by her feet.

"Why?" Apprehension clouded her face. The same nervous Grace was back from when he first saw her the other day.

"I'm curious."

She looked past him through his window toward the lighthouse. "Did Trudy say something?"

"No."

Grace chewed on her bottom lip as if she were carefully

formulating her response. Guarded. That was the word Kendon would use to describe Grace since her return.

"I like it here. It's home," she said with a shrug.

Her answer was too simple. There were so many other unspoken reasons, Kendon suspected.

"What do you like about Hendricks? I mean, you've been gone for almost twenty years. Your brother and sister don't live here. The town has changed."

"Why is this important, Kendon? What does it matter why I came back?" There was a note of irritation in her tone now.

"You kind of took off back then, like you couldn't wait to leave this place behind you. Even though I thought..."

Grace slumped. "You thought what?"

"I thought we were closer than...than it turned out."

She leaned against the headrest. "It was abrupt, I admit. Jeff pressed me to move with him and it was spontaneous. Besides, there wasn't anything to—"

"—hold you back? Right. I get it."

"Oh, Kendon. I remember. Don't think that I don't."

"What do you remember?" Again, images of that day flashed in his memory. Grace leaning against Jeff's red truck in the driveway of Blueberry Point Lodge, a purple duffel bag at her feet. His pathetic offering of flowers. The hollow sensation in his chest overshadowed it all.

"What you said to me that last day," she said. "When you came to Jeff's to see us off."

He swallowed hard. Kendon had thought he'd had a chance up to that point. But it was a fantasy. He hadn't acted soon enough. The old bitterness he felt that day settled in the back of his throat now. Time had dulled the hurt.

"What happened to you since you left, Grace?"

She looked ahead again as her eyes grew glassy. Grace tried to blink them away. She sighed before she haltingly told him about leaving Hendricks that summer after graduation.

Jeff had been accepted to Boston University for architectural studies, then continued on for his master's in historical preservation. The plan was for him to establish his career on the planning commission for the nearby town of Warthman, then she'd go to school. Jeff grew increasingly distant as he immersed himself deeper into his work, and money was tight. She'd applied twice for an undergraduate degree, been accepted twice, only to hear Jeff say it wasn't a good time.

They'd had a small wedding out East with only their immediate families attending. Then after a surprise pregnancy and the subsequent miscarriage, and holding down jobs she wasn't passionate about while Jeff's work consumed him, her reality started to take its toll. Anxiety had never been on her radar, but she started having panic attacks. Her doctor prescribed medication and recommended a therapist.

Kendon listened, his jaw aching from clenching it. The white-hot anger he'd felt toward Jeff surged again.

"I'm sorry you went through that. I wish I would have known."

"What difference would it have made?" A lone tear left a wet trail on her cheek. Grace swiped at it angrily. "I've put it behind me." She laughed. "I guess it doesn't look like it at the moment, but trust me."

"That still doesn't answer my question."

"Which was?"

"Why did you come back to Hendricks?"

Grace nodded slowly as her hands twisted in her lap. "I already told you; it's home. And I didn't know where else to go."

He wasn't sure he believed that. If her roots brought her back to Hendricks, she might have visited at least once during the last nineteen years. "For what it's worth, I'm glad you decided to come back."

His hand covered hers before he realized what he did. A gesture of comfort, that was all it was. But as soon as they touched, a *zing* ran up his arm.

Grace felt it too. She'd been tapping her foot with nervous energy like usual, but she froze. She stared down at their intertwined fingers.

"I am too," she whispered.

He could barely breathe. Grace was so close, so temptingly close...

"Do you ever wonder...if you picked the wrong guy?"

Grace's hand stiffened. There was the barely noticeable intake of her breath. After a moment, she slid her hand out from underneath his and patted his affectionately.

"All the time." A forced laugh escaped her. She reached over to turn the volume up on the radio when the piano riff of a rock ballad started. "I love this song," she said.

Kendon stared at the dash, hearing the music but not comprehending what had just happened. Taking her hand wasn't the worst mistake, but it certainly made her uncomfortable. And what a stupid thing he'd asked, putting her on the spot like that. *Idiot!* Embarrassed, he started the truck and backed away from the lighthouse. Next to him, Grace was back to sorting through the contents of her bag, quietly humming along with the song. She'd always been an expert at shutting down uncomfortable conversations. And judging by Grace's reaction, her choice of husbands was high on the list of taboo topics.

Chapter Seven

*M*aybe you picked the wrong guy.

Grace hummed along with the song on the radio and watched the scenery outside the window while her mind raced.

Was Kendon just being Kendon, the tongue-in-cheek, keeping-things-light Kendon she remembered from high school? Or did she detect a shred of hope in his words? How had he *wanted* her to react?

Beside her, Kendon drove with one hand on the steering wheel, while the other rested on his thigh. She studied his hand from the corner of her eye, the long, sinuous fingers, the tanned skin, a flaky callus on the underside of his thumb. Kendon tapped his index finger in time to the music. His hand on hers had felt safe and dangerous at the same time. The simple gesture had made her heart pound.

The five-minute drive from the lighthouse to

Blueberry Point Lodge took forever. Grace wanted to be within the quiet confines of her apartment so she could think.

"Maybe we could grab lunch again sometime soon," Kendon said as they turned into the driveway. "Or I could pick up something from Red's and meet you in the dining room."

"Sounds nice, but I'll be pretty busy the rest of the week."

He chuckled. "Too busy to eat?"

"Darcy usually has lunch waiting when we break. It saves time."

"She works you hard, huh?"

Grace knew him well enough to tell that his smile disguised disappointment. "I don't mind."

He nodded as his expression changed. The smile disappeared. His eyes lost their luster. It hurt her heart to see him physically disconnect from whatever hope he'd held.

"I'll need access to your apartment tomorrow," Kendon said as soon as they pulled up in front of the carriage house. "The decking needs to be replaced on the landing after all and the threshold of your door too."

She nodded, her hand already on the door to escape. "I'll leave the door unlocked."

"It will take me most of the day."

"I'll be busy too. Inside the inn." Grace opened the door. One foot on the ground. Almost there.

"Then I probably won't see you," he said.

She slid out of her seat then bent down to see inside

the car. His brow wrinkled as he searched for another song.

"See you, Kendon."

"Later," he said as he stayed focused on the radio.

Grace closed the door and walked around the side of the carriage house, feeling his eyes on her until she was safely out of sight. She hated herself for being standoffish. But getting close to Kendon again felt different this time. Their friendship seemed to be morphing into something more, and Grace wasn't sure she was ready for what that entailed.

* * * *

LATER THAT NIGHT GRACE SAT INSIDE THE cedar gazebo along with Darcy and a dozen other people from around town as Trey Merrick wrapped up his talk about the gardens he designed around the property. It was a trial run of a program he'd give to guests once the inn opened. At Darcy's request, Grace had baked lilac lemon cupcakes, one of her most favorite recipes. The clear plastic container sat beside her on the bench, the warmth of the cupcakes clouding the cover.

"Does anyone have any questions for Trey?" Darcy asked. She leaned over to Grace and whispered. "Let's pass those out now. My mouth has been watering for forty-five minutes."

Hers was too. She'd been too busy to pull together dinner for herself, first making the cupcakes then taking a call from Bethany Ransom, a friend of Darcy's. The woman had a little backyard studio apartment up on River Rock Road to rent, one she'd been staying at on her grandmother's property. They'd made an appointment to meet so Grace could tour the inside.

A man sitting across from Grace raised his hand with a question for Trey.

"You mentioned there were old gardens when the previous owners bought the inn. Had they all been revived or did you uncover even more when you started working here?"

Grace took the lid off the cupcakes and walked around to hand them out while Darcy followed with napkins and plates.

Trey took a cupcake from Grace when everyone else had theirs.

"Most of the gardens had already been restored when I got here. There were old rose bushes on the south side of the house that needed some TLC," Trey said. "And the lilac bushes by the carriage house had been smothered with overgrowth. That area had been the biggest challenge. Especially with this not working in my favor." He slapped his thigh. A car accident last year was responsible for his limp and reliance on a cane at the moment, he explained to the group.

Grace sat down again. She'd used some of those lilac blossoms at the bottom of her steps to make the simple syrup and frosting for the cupcakes. Darcy let everyone know this and most were surprised to learn lilacs had edible petals. It was one reason they were Grace's favorite flower.

A woman named Chelsea swooned after her first taste. "Delicious. What color were the blooms that you used for these?"

Was there a difference in the taste? Grace had no idea. The question caught her off-guard.

"They were white."

A dab of frosting dotted the woman's lip. She licked it away. "I was going to guess purple with a tinge of blue. It symbolizes happiness."

The woman sitting next to Chelsea chuckled. "These are definitely making me happy."

"What does white mean?" Darcy asked.

"New beginnings. Purity," said Chelsea.

Grace was all for new beginnings and happiness. She couldn't go wrong using either color.

"I'd love to copy the recipe," Darcy said.

"I'll have to rewrite it. Ingrid Callahan made these cupcakes for my birthday one year and they were so good, I demanded she write it down. The card is so stained now I wouldn't be able to read it if I didn't know it by heart."

"Memories make the best recipes taste even better, don't they?"

Grace smiled. "They do."

"I didn't realize you and Kendon had been close when you were young," Darcy said.

"We didn't really become friends until high school. Then we...lost touch."

His face blazed into her mind when Darcy said his name. Grace gazed at the carriage house, to the spot where he'd been parking his truck next to her car for the last week. Of course his spot was empty now. Strange that she found comfort in the fact that it would be back tomorrow.

The string lights hanging from the perimeter of the gazebo's roof blinked on, illuminating the faces of the handful of guests who still had questions for Trey. Grace looked beyond the gazebo toward the inn which glowed in the waning light. The torchlights were lit around the brick patio. Two attendees had wandered over there and settled into the chaises. They wrapped the wool blankets around their shoulders that Darcy had set out. Grace remembered Ingrid draping a blanket over her shoulders on nights when she, Jeff, and Kendon hung out on the patio. So many of her memories were tied to Blueberry Point Lodge, some of the best times of her life.

"He's such a great guy, Kendon. So talented." Darcy said. "Have you seen his metal sculptures yet?"

She hadn't.

"They're amazing. The library has two in the landscaping near the front door. I've commissioned him to make a bear and a heron for the garden near the entrance," Darcy said. "If you ever get a chance to peek inside his workshop, it's worth it."

His talent didn't surprise her. Whatever Kendon wanted to do, he'd always found a way to make it happen in his quiet, determined way. And he had always loved the outdoors and working with his hands too. Grace could picture him in his shop, wearing goggles with a welding torch in hand, sweating over a pile of discarded metal. She smiled to herself.

"So, the lighthouse wasn't for you?" Darcy asked.

Grace started, her thoughts still on Kendon. "I liked the living space well enough, but it's a little too desolate out there."

Darcy wrinkled her nose. "Really? It's only ten minutes from town. Me, I find it peaceful. If I were still single, I'd live there in a heartbeat."

Again, the reference to her single status hit home. Grace silently scolded herself for being so sensitive. It had taken her the better part of two years to become comfortable with living alone and taking care of herself. Her marriage to Jeff had been all about Jeff first with her needs a distant second. Divorcing Jeff was a welcome change, but sometimes a reminder that she was really on her own still stung.

"I think you'll like Bethany's place better then," Darcy continued.

"Yes, thanks for the tip. I've already talked to her. I'm looking at it on Friday."

"It used to be a garden shed, but her grandmother had it renovated years ago," Darcy said. "To wake up every morning surrounded by Donna Marconi's beautiful gardens would be like living in a wonderland."

The last of the guests had left the gazebo. Darcy excused herself to collect the plates and napkins. Trey took the last cupcake when Grace offered it to him.

"Cupcakes from lilacs? That'd be a big 'no' for me if

they weren't sitting under my nose here," he said. "I don't even have a sweet tooth, but these are calling my bluff."

"Thank you." Grace snapped the lid on the empty container.

"Poor Kendon missed out," Trey said, inspecting the cupcake after he took another bite.

Grace had turned away, ready to call it a night. The idea of a warm bath and cup of tea called to her.

"I'm sorry?"

"Kendon said he'd be here tonight when I talked to him this morning. He must have changed his mind," Trey said with a shrug.

"Something must have come up." Grace suspected that something was her. After brushing him off earlier, Grace didn't blame him for not wanting to see her again today.

She said good night to Trey and walked across the shadowy lawn toward her apartment. Above, stars hung in the sky. The moon had begun to rise, its face peering through the trees. Grace climbed the stairs, feeling a weariness settle into her bones even though she'd been sleeping soundly, given her busy days inside the inn. She paused on the landing, looking out over the lake. Moonlight touched the surface so it was easy to follow the motion of the waves. Grace swallowed. Below, the white lilac blossoms caught the moon glow too.

New beginnings.

How fitting that her favorite flower would be so closely aligned with her life now.

Coming back to Hendricks was her chance to start over. She hadn't thought that staying at Blueberry Point

Lodge would dredge up so many memories though. The sooner she found her own place, the better. She could put those memories back where they belonged—behind her—including her friendship with Kendon. Continuing to see him only encouraged him that there might be something more, something she wasn't ready for, if ever.

It was too bad really, him being linked to Jeff in her mind. In another time, another place, maybe they'd have a chance.

Chapter Eight

The day after he and Grace toured Clearwater Lighthouse, Kendon stood on the landing inside of the carriage house with Sean Stetman, surveying the decking underneath their feet. It looked solid enough on the surface. But once Kendon rigged the ladder underneath it yesterday and got a look at the underside, his suspicions were correct. The supports showed decades of decay.

Kendon rubbed the stubble on his chin. "Doesn't look good for keeping this under your budget."

Beside him, Sean made a face.

"I was afraid of that all along." Sean ran a hand through his hair. "What are we talking?"

"The four timbers alone will run you a few hundred bucks. And I'd have to reinforce with steel tubing since those beams support the staircase."

"So, ballpark. Over a thousand?" Sean asked.

"Easy."

Sean grimaced again. "This project was a stretch as it is. Had to talk Darcy into it."

"Luckily, you have that outside entrance."

"No kidding. We can still book the space. This exit will have to be off limits for the foreseeable future is all," Sean said. "Really, it's just a fire escape anyway."

"We'll put the decking replacement on hold then. I do need to pick up another doorknob set at Reil's. Then I'll be finished here. The set I bought came without the mounting plates."

"I can go," Sean said. "Was heading that way anyway. I can be back in a half hour, tops."

"Here, take my truck. I have you parked in." Kendon tossed Sean his keys. "The doorknob set is on the seat. Meanwhile, I'll tear off this old threshold and put on the new one." Sean disappeared through the overhead doors downstairs. Seconds later, the crunch of gravel underneath Kendon's truck tires echoed inside the vast space.

He kicked the rotted wood strip separating the apartment from the landing. There were at least four different colors of paint peeking through its chipped surface.

Kendon eyed the door leading into Grace's apartment. He pressed his ear to it, listening for any hint she was inside and not still at the inn. It was late. She'd returned home before four o'clock each day since he'd worked here.

But of course Grace wasn't here. She'd made a point yesterday of telling him so. *Sorry I'll miss you,* she'd said. And he'd spotted her scurrying across the lawn well before her shift started earlier this morning. It was obvious she wanted to avoid him by the way she waved at him over her shoulder without breaking stride.

He picked up the new threshold where it rested against the wall and pushed open the door. The scent of a fresh-baked cake hung in the air. Something floral too. He breathed deeply and stepped into the apartment.

Sparsely furnished but homey, the room radiated Grace's presence even when she was absent. The sun cast stripes on the walls through the vertical blinds. Plush red pillows lay on the gray suede futon. A white sweatshirt hung over one of the bar stools at the kitchen counter. He stepped farther into the apartment and laid a hand on the soft fabric. A book lay on the side table, face down, next to a mug. Kendon took it all in, feeling Grace in every detail.

A Mason jar of white lilacs on the counter caught his eye. They were in bloom now around the perimeter of the carriage house. Kendon walked over and lifted the blooms under his nose.

"Hello?"

The jar almost slipped from his grasp. He looked up to find Grace standing inside the apartment at the other door, confusion wrinkling her forehead.

"I-I didn't see your truck outside. I thought you were gone," she stammered.

Of course. She'd stayed away until she thought he was safely out of sight.

"Sean borrowed it to run to the hardware store for me. There was a…a part missing for the new doorknob."

"Oh," she said, holding on to the door behind her. "I can go if—"

He put up his hands. "Grace. Please. This is your place. You don't need to leave."

Grace looked around as if it just dawned on her there was no place to hide. The only out-of-sight retreat happened to be the bathroom. Hopefully she wasn't *that* desperate to get away from him.

"I have some work to do on my laptop," she said. "Promise I won't make a peep."

Kendon nodded. Lifting the new metal strip he held, he waved it like a truce flag. "I'll have this on in no time, then I'll be out of your hair. I can come back and do the knob tomorrow."

Grace gave him a tight smile as she settled onto the futon with her laptop.

But it proved impossible to concentrate knowing she was behind him. Every time he lined up the screw into one of the predrilled holes, ready to drive it into the floor, the screw wobbled out of place. His hands shook. His thumb slipped off the drill lever. Something got in his eye and he blinked like mad before he finally had to set the drill down to wipe it away. All because Grace was behind him on the futon, and not paying him any mind, he was sure of it.

"Kendon?"

He stopped his struggle with the drill and looked over his shoulder. Grace probably noticed his ineptitude and was going to ask if he could finish everything tomorrow.

"Yeah?"

"I'm sorry for yesterday," she said.

An apology was the last thing he expected. "What for?"

"For being dismissive."

He sat down on the floor, his back against the wall so he could face her. Even after a day of cleaning, Grace radiated freshness. She never made much effort to enhance her looks with makeup. Her natural beauty was enough. Kendon couldn't take his eyes off her now if he tried.

He lifted his shoulder. "You have a lot on your mind."

"I do, but I'm not so busy that..." she said as her voice trailed off. "I want you to know I appreciate all your help."

Kendon looked down at the floor. What had he done besides hint that she should have chosen him instead of Jeff? And within a week after seeing her for the first time in almost twenty years no less. She'd returned to finish healing from her divorce, not to hunt for another romantic partner, especially him. Involuntarily, he chuckled at his stupidity. He didn't have much finesse in the romance department.

"What's so funny?" Grace asked. She set her laptop aside and got up from the futon. She crossed the room to stand in front of him.

"You don't owe me an apology, Grace. If anything, I shouldn't have said that stupid thing to make you uncomfortable."

She blinked. "What stupid thing?"

"About you picking the wrong guy. I didn't mean for you to take me seriously." It was all so wrong, this feeling he didn't know her anymore. Looking up at her, Grace seemed like a stranger wearing his former best friend's face.

"I didn't," she said flatly and held out her hand.

"What?"

"Give me the drill," she demanded.

Confused, he gave it to her.

She kneeled next to the threshold where he'd fumbled with the screws minutes before. Without pause, Grace set a screw into one of the holes and deftly drove it into place.

Bzzzt...done.

Same scenario with the other screws.

Bzzzt. Bzzzt. Mission accomplished.

He squinted at her while his pulse ramped up like his power tool. Grace's jaw was set as she handed the drill back to him. *Where was Sean anyway?*

"Thanks."

She gave him a curt nod while she settled onto the floor across from him, crossing her ankles, leaning back on her hands.

"Looked like you were having some trouble." Grace brushed something off her leg. "I'm checking out another rental tomorrow, by the way. Bethany Ransom's place."

He nodded. "Her grandmother Donna is a character. Likes to give me a hard time. The sharper her tongue, the more she likes you."

"So I've been told." Grace's brows pinched together. Her lips moved like she wanted to say something else, but she struggled with the words. "Tell me, have you ever made a bad choice?"

He huffed. Another surprise. "I, uh, all the time. Just this morning, I decided to use almond milk in my coffee instead of regular cream."

Grace didn't crack a smile. "I'm serious."

Obviously.

"I mean, you were always the voice of reason." Her tone softened. "The calm to Jeff's crazy. Never got in trouble. You were always cool, quiet Kendon."

Cool, quiet Kendon. That made him sound like an air conditioner.

He swallowed. "So, you mean 'life regrets'?"

"Yes," she said, her focus on him now laser sharp.

Sure, he'd made mistakes, a few big ones, plenty of small ones. He'd made the mistake of hanging in the shadows, watching her and Jeff's friendship change into something more. Kendon had waited too long. Maybe it had been for fear of being shut down or laughed at. Or that by breaching friend status, it broke an unspoken code of conduct among the three of them, which obviously hadn't bothered Jeff. Maybe because he hadn't felt he deserved Grace. She'd chosen Jeff after all, not him. He wasn't about to offer up that bit of wisdom though. Especially after she'd already made it clear her life wouldn't have been better by choosing him over Jeff.

He brought his knees up and encircled them with his arms, lacing his fingers together. "Sometimes I regret not getting out to see the world like you did, I guess."

"Moving away didn't exactly serve me well," Grace said with a humorless laugh.

"No, but at least it made you realize that you wanted to come back here. It gave you perspective."

He'd lived for a few years in Rochester when he worked for an industrial parts manufacturing company. But he didn't count that as a worldly experience. Five hours away, same state. Hardly a transformative endeavor.

Grace chewed on her lip, again looking like something heavy weighed on her mind.

Outside, a car door closed. Sean was back.

"That would be your new doorknob." He pushed himself off the floor.

Still, Grace sat there, legs out, craning her neck back to look at him. "You're still as hard to read as ever, you know that?"

"Sorry. It's not intentional. Need a hand?"

Grace considered his outstretched hand for a second before she took a long, loud breath and was on her feet in an instant. He pretended not to see her hands coil into fists at his offer. She shook her head.

"I'm good, thanks," she said.

Time and again, she'd made that clear.

Chapter Nine

The next morning Grace stood inside the garden apartment in Donna Marconi's backyard. Her granddaughter, Bethany, a bright-eyed, willowy blond, swept her hand along an empty bookshelf as she gave Grace some background on the former garden shed.

"Gran had the shed remodeled when I moved back from Marquette. She'd broken her hip, so I came home to help with her recovery. We're both pretty independent and opinionated so...how do I say this?" She looked at the ceiling with a smile as she wiped her hand on a dish towel. "We mutually agreed that we couldn't live under the same roof."

Grace laughed. "At least you were both on the same page." She liked Bethany's forthrightness.

"Don't get me wrong. I love Gran. She's such a force. My biggest cheerleader next to my husband," said Bethany. She put her hands on her hips and looked around the room before settling her attention back on Grace. "So you're probably looking to find a place as soon as you can?"

"The sooner, the better." Grace took in the honey-hued wood floors and the giant picture window which faced the backyard. From this vantage point, the back of Donna Marconi's house wasn't visible. Plenty of privacy. "Darcy didn't give me an exact date, but I think the inn will open to guests later next month."

"I'm so excited for them," Bethany said. "Darcy and Sean have worked so hard for this."

She'd only been at Blueberry Point Lodge a few weeks now, but Grace agreed.

Bethany walked toward the little galley kitchen separated from the main room by a kitchen counter. "I hated to leave this place. It's darling and cozy, and if you don't know Gran, she'll be your new best friend before too long," Bethany said. "But once Nate and I married, we moved to his house over on Water Street. This is ideal really for only one person."

Grace forced a smile. "How long have you been married?"

"Two months."

"Congratulations." Grace's smile broadened at Bethany's obvious delight. "I remember Nate's family. They moved away while he was still in school, right?"

"Yes," she said, shaking her head. "He was so obnoxious back then. I completely ignored him."

Grace chuckled. "But now you're married."

"Isn't life funny?"

Grace swallowed.

"Feel free to open cabinets and closets if you want to take a closer look," Bethany offered. "I don't want to rush you, but I do have to get to the studio for a class." She slipped on her jacket.

She followed Bethany into the tiny kitchen and peered into the empty cabinets above the back counter. As long as the doors weren't falling off their hinges, it suited her needs. Grace closed the last cabinet.

"It's perfect."

"I'm happy you like it. Gran is pretty particular who she'd let live here," Bethany said with a sidelong glance. "The only real negative I can think of is parking in the street. Not a big deal in the summer but honestly, you'll hate snow by December." Bethany shrugged.

Grace grinned. "I'm not afraid of a little snow."

Bethany's brows shot up. "A *little*? How long have you lived out East?"

"Not long enough that I've forgotten what a North Shore winter looks like."

The apartment was smaller than the space above the carriage house but the details were more charming. And she loved the paint scheme: sunny yellow walls in the living area. Muted apple green in the bathroom. A line of decorative tile ran the length of the backsplash in the kitchen depicting different flowers and ferns. It was like Donna's gardens had spilled into the room. She'd have to make do with less storage, not that she had much.

"If you're sold on taking it, I'll let Gran know. We can work out the details whenever is convenient for you."

Bethany showed Grace to the front door. "I can guarantee you won't be lonely here. You're within walking distance of everything."

Grace paused at the door. "I'll let you know. Thanks so much."

INGRID CALLAHAN STOOD IN THE DRIVEWAY NEAR the carriage house talking with Darcy when Grace arrived back at the inn a short time later. Her former mother-in-law placed an aluminum pan of something warm in Grace's hands as soon as Grace greeted her.

"Just a little blueberry coffee cake," Ingrid said as they hugged. Grace caught the familiar scent of lavender. "I love to bake but can't risk keeping it all to myself. And you know Henry."

"Thank you, Ingrid." Grace kissed her on the cheek. "I wish I knew you were coming. I would have come home sooner."

"It's so nice to see your face again," Ingrid said when they separated. "And I miss our phone chats. Promise we'll get together for coffee now that you're back in town."

Despite Grace's broken relationship with Ingrid's son, Grace could feel the woman's warmth through her hug.

"I'd like that very much. I'm so glad you stopped by." Grace realized how much she missed actual human touch. It had been a while since she felt the effects of a genuine hug. "Though I didn't realize you knew I was back in town."

"You know how small towns work. I probably found out you were back in town before you actually realized you were coming," Ingrid said with a chuckle.

Grace peeked under the foil. The coffee cake smelled delicious, especially since she hadn't eaten yet. "You're right. I've been out of the loop for too long. Can you come in for a bit, see the apartment?"

Ingrid's eyes twinkled. "Oh, I hoped you would ask."

They made their way up the outside stairs. Grace unlocked the door and held it open for Ingrid to go in first.

The older woman gave the studio apartment a quick appraisal. "My goodness. The Stetmans really livened this up. It's charming."

"Isn't it? Too bad I have to move. And you can't beat the view from here."

Grace remembered how it used to look long before Darcy and Sean took over. This had been a glorified storage space. The diamond-paned windows and the exposed beams on the ceiling gave it character and something to work around once the Stetmans decided to turn it into a living space last fall. Grace especially loved the brick wall behind the futon. An enormous vibrant oil painting by a local artist hung there, depicting the lake and horizon in exaggerated tones of blue, lavender, and orange. She took the coffee cake over to the counter. Ingrid followed.

"I heard you toured the lighthouse," Ingrid said.

Grace smiled. Of course Ingrid had heard. She imagined it came straight from Trudy's own lips. She didn't know Trudy well, but Ingrid had a third ear when it came to talk around town, something Grace learned firsthand from sitting at Ingrid's dining room table so many days after school.

"I did."

"What an interesting experience that would be," Ingrid said.

"It would be for the right person. Would you like some coffee?"

"That would be wonderful," Ingrid said, settling onto a stool.

Grace prepped the coffeemaker then sliced into the coffee cake. She set a slice onto a plate for Ingrid and one for her. As the coffee brewed, Grace filled her in on seeing Donna Marconi's rental unit and her moving plans.

"I figured the lighthouse would be perfect for you though," Ingrid said. "Giving tours. Surrounded by all the history."

"Honestly, it's too overwhelming."

"What is, living at the lighthouse?"

Grace's thoughts had returned to the lighthouse more than once since she'd visited with Kendon. A *dream come true*, she'd thought upon hearing it needed a new tenant. All boarding expenses paid and a stipend for giving tours. Twenty-something Grace would have jumped at the opportunity, back when she still believed in taking chances. When she wasn't beaten down by dashed dreams and a narcissistic husband. Getting back her swagger would take some time, but for now, baby steps.

"Living alone. I mean *alone* alone." She slid Ingrid's

mug toward her after filling it. "At least at Donna's I wouldn't be so far from everyone."

Ingrid gave her a sympathetic look. "Oh, honey. That's not the fearless, sure-footed Grace talking that I used to know."

Grace pressed her lips together and held Ingrid's gaze for a moment. She sighed. "I know."

"What are you afraid of exactly?"

Grace couldn't put her finger on it. Being invisible maybe? She'd never been particularly outgoing, but she found herself craving human interaction the longer she stayed in her unhappy marriage. Jeff socialized enough for both of them. Between his client dinners, conferences, and the wide circle of friends he'd made through the racquet club and rotary, Jeff had rarely been home.

"I'm not quite sure, Ingrid. It...the marriage...it took a lot out of me." She looked toward the door that led down the circular staircase, thinking of Kendon.

Ingrid shook her head and looked exasperated. "I'm sorry."

"It's not your fault, for heaven's sake."

"Maybe if we hadn't...I don't know. It drives me crazy, wondering where we went wrong by him."

"That's not it. I'm sure you and Henry were wonderful parents. You were to me, at least."

Ingrid's blue eyes glistened. "You deserved so much more."

Grace lifted her shoulder. *It is what it is.*

"We're here for you—I am, Darcy. The ladies at church would love to see you again. There are so many new faces.

And Kendon too. I'm sure he's glad you're back," Ingrid said from behind her cup, sipping it demurely.

Grace narrowed her eyes at Ingrid. There was a conspiratorial undertone in how Ingrid said his name.

"What?" Ingrid set her cup down.

"Oh, nothing."

Ingrid left her stool and wandered over to the picture window to look out across the lake.

"I'll never forget that day you two left," Ingrid said. "I think a piece of my heart stowed away with you two in the backseat of that Bronco."

"We were so young." Grace topped off their mugs before joining Ingrid at the window. "It seems like another life."

"I'll tell you what—poor Kendon had another piece of my heart. If you could have seen him staring after you two when you drove away," Ingrid said, crossing her arms. "I think he stood there for a good five minutes after you were gone."

Ingrid's words sank in as they watched the waves pummel the beach in the distance. The sun shone, but the wind had a nip to it.

"I still get a lump in my throat thinking about the look on his face," Ingrid said.

Grace remembered a similar feeling as Kendon stood next to the Bronco, ready to see her off. By that point, Jeff and Kendon were no longer speaking. Grace figured it was because Jeff reneged on their plans to apprentice for Kendon's family construction business. The plan had been for Kendon and Jeff to start their own company, flipping old houses in the Twin Cities, once they got the experience. But Jeff had bigger aspirations, which he didn't share with Kendon until a few weeks before they left Hendricks. And it included taking Grace with him.

Kendon had leaned on the open window, his face so close she could feel the warmth of his breath when he spoke. *For you*, he'd whispered as he pressed a single stem of white lilacs into her hand. But Jeff had seen the flowers and scoffed. *What are those for?* he'd asked as they turned onto the highway. *Does he think a fistful of weeds will make you stay or something?* He'd tossed them out the car window even before they got to the city limits.

Now Grace wondered if the flowers had been a hint for something she'd missed.

Maybe you picked the wrong guy.

Ingrid wrapped an arm around Grace's shoulders, bringing Grace back to the present. With an affectionate shake, Ingrid smiled. "You left, but now you're here."

Grace grinned back. It was impossible to ignore Ingrid's infectious good cheer.

"I am. It's nice to be home again." She rested her head against Ingrid's as they stood side by side. Grace wished she hadn't waited so long to visit with Ingrid. It had been two years since Ingrid and Henry traveled east. Even though the divorce had been finalized, the couple made a point of taking Grace out to dinner. They were as close to parents as she'd ever known.

Ingrid faced Grace and took her hands. "Maybe returning to Hendricks is less about coming home and more about moving on from Jeff," she said.

"Sorry, Ingrid. I'm not following."

Ingrid squeezed her hands. "It's not *what's* here for you but *who*."

Grace nodded. Ingrid's hopeful expression made her smile.

Maybe I picked the wrong guy.

Chapter Ten

Kendon slowed to a walk and leaned against the wood post next to the Powder Rock Trail to tie his shoe. He glanced toward the empty parking lot and beyond that, Highway 61. It was agony, this running thing he'd resolved to turn into a habit. So far he'd been at it fourteen days, with four days off in between, and he resented every minute.

But running was a distraction to keep his mind busy. For too long his days had consisted of work, home, sleep, then back to work. He only deviated from that on weekends when sometimes he ended up at Bernie's Garage to work on one of his larger commissioned sculptures. He'd fallen into a rut. So he'd ordered new shoes, one of those fitness watches, and clocked himself as he alternated taking each of the trails around Hendricks. Maybe he'd be in running shape by October for the

Sturgeon 5K. He almost laughed at that. Him a runner? What a joke.

Kendon trudged along the highway for a half mile until he turned onto Timber Creek Road toward home. While he walked the last block, Kendon's thoughts drifted to Grace as they had so many times since she'd come back to town. It was his hope that once he finished his work in the carriage house, she'd want to stay in touch. But it had been almost a week and nothing. Maybe it was too painful, seeing him. Maybe he and Jeff were too closely linked in Grace's mind.

On his way up the driveway, he checked the mailbox before he collapsed on the porch steps to clean his shoes before he went inside. After a few minutes of picking out mud caked in the treads, he cracked his shoes together a couple of times, brushed his hands on his pants, and walked up the steps.

Kendon stopped midstride.

A Mason jar filled with lilacs sat on the rubber doormat. A note was tucked underneath the jar. Kendon picked it up, unfolded it.

I think you're right. G.

His heart tripped over itself before it took off at a gallop. Kendon spun around, hoping to see her parked across the street, sitting there watching him. But the street was empty.

Kendon reread the note several times after picking up the jar and walking into the house. He set the flowers on the dining table as he pulled out a chair to sit.

I think you're right.

If that meant what he thought it meant, what he *hoped* it meant, of course he was right. He'd known she picked the wrong guy even before Grace told him she and Jeff were heading to Boston. Kendon had wished she'd regret the decision and show up on his doorstep even years after she and Jeff took off. But Kendon had always been a dreamer, not a doer in matters of the heart.

It was time to change that. Before he wasted another chance.

He fished his phone from his pocket and called Grace's number before he talked himself out of it.

Two rings.

This was crazy.

Three rings.

Pinning my hopes on a jar of flowers.

Four rings.

Yet here I go, risking my heart.

"Hello?"

Kendon jumped, already resigned to her not answering. "Grace. Hi."

"What are you doing?"

"Sitting here looking at your flowers. Thank you."

"You're welcome."

There was an awkward pause and Kendon wondered if this was a good idea, calling her before he'd formulated some semblance of a conversation in his head instead of stumbling around like he was doing now.

He leaned against the chair and closed his eyes. *Don't make a fool of yourself.* "So, what are you doing?"

"Talking to you," Grace said.

He heard the humor in her voice. "Besides that."

"Sitting outside. It's a gorgeous day, isn't it?" she asked.

Sure enough, there was birdsong in the background. It sounded close enough that it could be outside his window.

"It is." *C'mon, Kendon. Untie your tongue.*

"Wanna join me?"

She was kidding, right? What a question. He'd drive to the Twin Cities in a heartbeat. He'd catch the soonest flight to anywhere. All Grace had to do was ask.

"Sure. Where are you?" A shudder coursed through him at the prospect of not just seeing her, but seeing her *soon.*

Grace chuckled. "Look through your patio doors."

He drew a sharp breath and glanced across the room toward his deck. A view of the small, wooded backyard was somewhat obscured by the arborvitae surrounding the house. But he didn't need to see farther than his picnic table outside the door. Grace sat on the bench facing him, legs crossed, wearing an impish smile. She waved and mouthed *surprise.*

Kendon crossed the room and threw open the door.

"Grace."

Her smile took over her whole face. "Before you think I'm stalking you by leaving flowers at your door and hanging out on your deck, I saw your truck and thought you were home," she said, standing.

"I went for a run."

Her brows arched. "Really. You're a runner now?"

"Sort of." When Grace cocked an eyebrow higher, he waved her off. "It's a like/hate relationship."

Grace continued to stare at him. "Sounds complicated."

He gave her quick once-over. She'd dressed up again. Instead of a rubber band holding her hair back, Grace let it hang loosely around her shoulders. She pulled the peach-colored cardigan around her again when the breeze blew it open. It hardly seemed like nineteen years had gone by looking at her. Kendon stepped out onto the deck and closed the door behind him.

"I have news," she said. The teasing gleam in her eyes was still there.

"Oh?"

"I talked to Trudy. I've decided to move into the lighthouse when she and her husband leave."

"You won't regret it, I bet. What made you change your mind?"

Grace chewed on her lip while she looked toward the sky. A little smile appeared like she'd found the answer up there. She turned her attention back to him.

"I'm tired of being afraid, I guess. Of running from life," she said, hugging her arms against her chest. "My own stupid choices led me to this point, I know. I let Jeff call the shots on everything, forgetting that I had dreams too. His ambitions always seemed to take precedence over mine, and I was too complacent about it."

"I'm sorry."

Grace shrugged. "Time to look forward instead of back. I've been trying to do that and not having much success.

Until now." She sat down again and pointed to the spot next to her for him to sit too. She shifted on the bench to face him. Grace tucked a strand of hair behind her ear.

So, that explained the note. *You were right.* He'd suggested Grace move into the lighthouse. While it was good news, it wasn't what he'd wished for.

"I've changed my mind about something else too," she said softly.

"What's that?"

"About you." She looked up to him, her blue eyes as clear as the sky. Her chest rose and fell with a deep breath. "I know it's a lot to ask. Maybe it's nineteen years too late—"

That was all it took—an unfinished thought but complete enough for Kendon. He leaned forward, cupping her face in both hands, and pressed his lips against hers. There was the initial hesitation as Grace stiffened, caught by his abruptness, but he knew she wouldn't pull away. Not by the way her hands clutched the underside of his forearms, digging a nail or two into the tender skin.

The sensation of this first sweet kiss caught him in a heady whirlwind, pulling him inside out with a need he hadn't known before. Grace's eyes closed as she lay her head against his shoulder and melted deeper into the kiss. His head swam when her hand found its way into the hair at the back of his neck.

Seconds or maybe minutes could have passed for all Kendon knew. That was how intoxicating she tasted.

Grace drew in a deep breath as she pulled away. "Kendon," she breathed.

So many emotions and thoughts knotted together in the middle of his chest.

"I'm in love with you, Grace, I always have been, and when you left, I tried to talk myself out of it, thinking, 'We're just kids, it's not the real thing,' but then you came back and those feelings hit me full force, and I was surprised that nothing had changed." It came out in one long, breathless sentence, and he was only getting started.

His thoughts, bottled up for years, spilled out. Kendon couldn't shut himself up. Meanwhile, Grace listened with a mix of emotions playing across her face. Confusion. Regret. Joy. Incredulity.

Grace took his hands. For a second, Kendon feared she had something to say he wouldn't like. It might kill him.

"You were always the steady one. And Jeff, he wanted to chase the next best thing, and for me back then, that was exciting. I *needed* to leave town," Grace said, her voice a throaty whisper.

"I get it. I didn't resent you for it. It tore me apart, but there was no one to blame but myself. I could have said something."

She sighed. "Maybe I would have been less inclined to stay in a loveless marriage had I known—" Grace shook her head. "No, never mind. That's wrong of me to say."

Kendon knew what she meant. Even if she had known his true feelings, Grace was ready to escape anyway. She didn't want to demean Kendon, thinking of him as a backup plan.

Grace smiled warily. "As hard as it was, the divorce was sort of a rebirth for me. I know that sounds strange, but I haven't realized until recently that I'm becoming someone I actually like again."

He leaned in for a hug. "I'm so sorry you went through that alone."

Her arms went around him as she rested her chin on his shoulder. "But I'm not alone now.

Kendon smiled. *And you never will be again if I have anything to do with it.*

Grace pulled away and looked at him with earnest.

"I'm going to hold you to your promise, you know. Now that I'll be living in the lighthouse."

"What promise is that?"

"That I can call on you for emergencies. Like if the sink starts leaking or the furnace goes out."

He huffed. "I saw the way you commandeered my drill the other day. I don't think you're as helpless as you're letting on."

She sank against him again, looping her arms around his neck, grinning as she rested her forehead against his. "I'm not. I just want to see you as often as possible."

Kendon cracked a grin too. "So, what you're saying is I should expect a daily emergency of some kind?"

"Exactly," Grace said and pulled away to see him fully. "I love you too, Kendon."

His heart might not be cut out for so much all at once. "Say that again."

Grace teased her lips against his mouth again in a slow, agonizing way.

"How about I just show you," she said.

LOVE, LIES AND FIREFLIES
A BLUEBERRY POINT STORY

D.E. MALONE

Chapter One

❦

Farra shielded her eyes from the sun-kissed day to get a better view of Blueberry Point Lodge. Those chimneys—all five of them—soared to the heavens. And all those windowpanes. Good grief.

The word *castle* came to mind. So did *work*. There was bound to be a ton of upkeep on a place like this.

Movement on the second-floor balcony drew her attention. Her childhood friend, Darcy Stetman, leaned over the ornate balustrade and waved.

"Don't just stand there," she called. "Get in here so I can give you a hug."

Farra dropped her hand. "Will the butler greet me, or do I just walk in?"

Darcy laughed. "Sean took the day off," she said. "He's been complaining that his boss works him too hard lately." She pointed at herself for emphasis and rolled her eyes.

Farra continued up the walkway, passing a row of boxwoods and large metal sculptures of a bear and a heron in the small garden on either side of the front door. Her hand was on the doorknob when it flew open and Darcy rushed to embrace her, knocking her back a step. Some things never changed.

The last time she'd seen Darcy and her husband, Sean, was at their wedding in October, seven short months ago. They'd been in the middle of massive renovations to the inn but had made it habitable enough to host their special day and lodge some guests.

Inside the foyer, Farra looked her up and down. "Marriage seems to suit you. You look amazing."

Darcy waved her hand. "It's this house. I barely have time to eat. Something always needs cleaning or fixing or polishing."

"It's only going to get busier. When's the first booking?"

"Five days," Darcy said, her eyes widening. "I've purposefully put myself into a state of denial or else I might start hyperventilating. Let me show you to your room so you can dump your stuff before others start showing up."

"Are you sure you're ready for this?" She took in her surroundings, pivoting in a full circle. The foyer with its double-wide staircase opened up to two large rooms. A bank of floor-to-ceiling windows and two sets of French doors offered a view of Lake Superior that Farra would bet was one of the prettiest on the North Shore.

Darcy giggled. "If it's too much I'll say we're booked."

Farra laughed. "That would be me every day."

She followed Darcy upstairs to the first room with a wall of windows and a four-poster canopy bed.

"This is amazing. I feel like I'm royalty." Farra caressed the lavender sateen coverlet. A coffee mug with the inn logo rested on a stenciled tea tray in the middle of the bed, along with tea bags, wrapped chocolates, and a bar of lavender soap. Darcy's brows shot up when Farra looked back at her. "Nice touch."

Darcy gave her a satisfied smile. "You think? I hope it's not too over the top. I wouldn't care so much about soap and tea, but Sean's mom insisted. Chocolate, on the other hand..."

Farra set her bag on the luggage rack next to a Queen Anne chest of drawers.

"How is Sean handling the prospect of hosting strangers in his house?"

Darcy laughed. "He's fine with it. Funny, I never would have guessed he'd be so on board with running an inn, but sometimes he seems less anxious about it than I do."

"That's cool, collected Sean for you. I'm sure he's a hotbed of nerves underneath the surface."

Darcy ran her hand across the top of the chest of drawers before looking at her palm then brushing it off on her hip. "Right? He's good at hiding it. Me, not so much."

Farra drifted toward the windows, the panorama of the lake drawing her. "An amazing view."

They stood in front of the windows looking out on the grounds. Beyond the property, the lake was a surreal landscape, the sun skirting across its surface. Farra wanted to get outside and walk through the grounds' abundant gardens. It would give her a chance to stretch her legs after the four-hour drive.

"I saw you when you pulled in. I don't think you had that trailer last fall, did you?"

"Bought it shortly after. I decided to give up the lease on my apartment in Marquette and downsize. Now I'm portable."

"Portable. Wow," said Darcy, shaking her head. "I'm a little jealous. And it's adorable, by the way."

"It was a little necessary. I lost one of my biggest sponsorships. The company filed for bankruptcy."

"I'm sorry."

"Don't be." Farra crossed her arms, stilling looking at the lake. "It's helped me focus on what's really important. I've ditched some bad habits."

"*You* have bad habits? Miss Perfection?" Darcy pursed her lips and gave her a skeptical look. "Like what?"

"Hoarding, for one. My apartment was limited on space, but that didn't stop me from collecting stuff. Jack doesn't allow me to save junk."

"Who's Jack?" Darcy looked at her sharply.

"My trailer. I named him Jack Kerouac. You know, after the *On the Road* author?"

Darcy tilted her head back, laughing. "You named your trailer? That's classic."

"I thought you'd appreciate that." Farra drew closer to the window and eyed the cluster of gardens closest to the house.

"Do you take care of your own gardens?"

"No, we have someone for that," Darcy said. "I'd love to, but I don't have the time."

"Whoever it is does phenomenal work."

"He's a friend of my in-laws. He had his own company but ran into some health problems. The work Trey does here is enough to keep him working while he slowly builds some stamina to go full-time again."

"Did you say Trey?" That name. It jarred her memory.

"Yes. Trey Merrick." Darcy glanced at her. "Do you know him?"

"Wasn't he at your wedding?"

"Yes, he was. It was such a crazy, mixed-up day with the weather, I'm lucky I even remember who was in the bridal party."

Farra laughed. "The weather was awful."

Darcy paused. "Now that you mention it, I think I remember you saying you two hit it off."

"We did." She shrugged and tried to keep her expression neutral. No need to go into *that*.

Darcy seemed to get the message since she didn't delve deeper. "He's somewhere here today. If I see him, I'll let him know—"

"That's not necessary. He probably wouldn't remember me anyway."

"No problem." Darcy's forehead creased when she looked at her phone. "I should check on lunch. We'll be giving the tour in a half hour."

"Sounds good. I might look around outside."

After Darcy left, Farra wandered downstairs again and stepped onto the brick patio. She inhaled the scent of fir trees and lake water, delighting in the freshness of the late-spring day. What a perfect setting. Darcy was lucky, though knowing her, she'd worked her fingers to the bone to make it happen.

Farra followed the path across the lawn toward the gazebo and the gardens she'd admired while still upstairs. It was both a rustic and an elegant structure. The northern winter dulled the cedar since their wedding, but it was still stunning. Trellises of honeysuckle and clematis vines climbed in wild abandon toward the roof, making the inside of the gazebo a verdant, private spot.

She loved the pairings of the flowers, which brought her thoughts back to Trey Merrick. It amazed her that he was responsible for the beauty of these gardens. It wasn't exactly fair, her astonishment that he created this. They hadn't had a chance to talk about their respective jobs that night. There hadn't been much time for anything other than a lot of dancing, laughing, and their subsequent escape to the gazebo, which had been interrupted way too soon.

A wave of regret filled her as she thought about Trey now.

She'd first seen him before the ceremony, standing amongst the groomsmen. He knew more people on the guest list than she did, judging by how close he seemed to members of the bridal party. Farra couldn't remember exactly the moment he noticed her too, but by the time the reception dinner rolled around, they exchanged regular glances across the crowded room.

He was handsome in an understated way. No one

feature stood out, but everything melded together in a perfect recipe of maleness. What attracted her the most was the effortless way he moved, almost as if he were a dancer. He crossed the room, his body working in perfect synchronicity, and she could barely take her eyes off him.

Farra stopped in front of a stand of fuchsia peonies and stooped to smell the blossoms. She hadn't seen peonies this color since she was a girl. The flowers brought back memories of a nasty bee sting on the nose. It had swelled and she'd argued with her mom about missing two days of day camp because she thought hers looked like a pig's nose. Farra smiled. Looking back, her nose hadn't been quite that big, but the smallest inconveniences can be like mountains to kids.

Another animal sculpture was tucked amongst the flowers, this time a raccoon. The animal was a hodgepodge of metal parts: golf drivers, rebar, a set of washers the size of half dollars welded together for eyes. It was adorable. Whoever the artist was had as much talent as Trey did with his flowers.

Farra scanned the grounds, hoping to catch sight of him, yet not wanting to be bothered at the same time. After asking to see her again after the wedding, Trey Merrick disappeared. Not one call. She'd tried to find him online, but apparently he wasn't a social media guy. The hurt still stung since she'd really liked him. Granted, Farra had only known him four whole hours, but she'd felt it was the start of something.

Boy, had she been wrong.

Chapter Two

Pruning shears were useless for knocking out buckthorns.

If it weren't for his bum leg, Trey Merrick would be behind the wheel of a brush cutter, bulldozing them to oblivion. The Department of Natural Resources guys might frown at that since conservation experts had more precise methods for killing invasive plants. At least he'd blow off a little steam while doing it. It was only a small patch of buckthorn, but given the condition of his leg, it was an enormous task. He stood at the edge of the wooded lot, feeling like a solitary beaver staring down a forest of redwoods.

Grumbling, he limped across the lawn to the carriage house at Blueberry Point Lodge to sharpen the shears. He needed to sit down for a bit anyway. The pain in his leg kicked up a few notches since he'd overexerted himself. Maybe he'd call it a day after this. Trey was thankful for the flexibility of the job, thanks to his employers, Darcy and Sean Stetman.

As he ran the sharpening tool over the blade, a scrappy little SUV wound its way up the pea gravel drive, a mini travel trailer bumping along behind it. The car's yellow pop of color against the green landscape was easy to spot. Must be one of Darcy's friends coming for the grand pre-opening of the inn. Good for the Stetmans. He couldn't be more excited for them. He owed them big time.

Trey hung the sharpening tool on the rack then held up the blade in front of the window to get a better look at its edge. That should do the trick. He set the shears on the counter and looked through the window in time to see the SUV driver get out.

He squinted. The distance might be playing tricks on his eyes, but she looked familiar.

It couldn't be, yet...it could.

Farra Hall.

She stretched her arms overhead and gave the property a quick glance before she lugged a bag out of the backseat.

Of course she was here. And all the feelings she'd stirred in him during the span of four hours rushed back too. That night he had decided Farra Hall was the type of woman he could see himself with for the rest of his life. It was the most electrifying, wacky, sobering four hours he'd ever spent with someone and it all played out in the crowded confines of the Stetmans' wedding reception. What he wouldn't give to replay that night for a few reasons.

Trey pulled the hedge sheers off the rack and set to

sharpening those blades too. As he worked, her face swam up in his memory and he shook his head. If only it had turned out differently. She was a ball of energy, that woman. He'd hesitate to think it was nervous energy; it was just part of her fabric. In one of the few quiet moments they'd found at the reception that night to talk at length, Trey learned Farra liked to keep busy. Like marathon-running, mountain-biking, white-water-rafting busy. She seemed even more adventurous than him. Well, before his life took a turn for the worse. These days he was lucky to make it through lunch without taking another dose of painkillers.

He looked through the window again and watched Farra carry her bag to the inn's entrance, disappearing around the corner of the house. Trey lifted the tray of dusty miller from the potting table and carried it into the sunshine. More planting was on his schedule for next week, but it would be the perfect cover. Getting a closer look at the woman who looked uncannily like Farra was foremost in his mind.

The flower bed around the gazebo extended in one direction toward a moon garden twenty feet away. A gravel path wound its way from the gazebo steps, through perennials mixed with cosmos, zinnias, and splashes of celosia and butterfly weed to the smaller garden. Trey and Darcy had pored over gardening sites to find the perfect mixture of flowers that caught the moon's glow. He'd found her two cedar arches and an iron obelisk for balance.

Trey set the trays inside the pull cart and drove the

tractor over to the gazebo, parking it so whoever might be looking out of a window in the lodge wouldn't see his struggles. He cursed himself for his stupid pride. Why should he care what someone he'd met once and hadn't seen or talked to in months thought of him? It was silly, he knew. Especially since he was the architect of his own stupid decision not to reach out to her after the wedding.

The late-morning sun lulled him while he cleared remnants of leaves and twigs from winter, then started planting the first flat. Getting his hands dirty was as good as any therapy, he thought. The repetitious, physical work suited him, working alone and at his own pace. He squeezed the flower pack until the dirt plug popped out from the first container. After loosening the soil, he set the flower into the shallow hole he'd already dug.

A shadow passed over him.

"Hi there, Trey."

Trey didn't have to see her to make the connection. Seven months couldn't wipe Farra's voice from his memory. He smiled while his pulse hammered on the side of his neck. The sun behind her blinded him when he looked up. When he shielded his eyes, Farra moved to cast her shadow over him.

"Nice to see you." He leaned back on his arms, stretching out his legs. "It's been a while."

Farra looked at him for a moment and those dimples flashed. His heart skipped a beat. "Darcy mentioned you work here now. I know you're busy, but I wanted to say 'hi.' How have you been?"

"Doing well. I'm between jobs. The Stetmans had work for me, so it all fell into place."

"That's lucky for both of you." She shifted her weight.

"What are you doing here?" It was a silly question. He already knew.

"Darcy invited me for their..."—she looked back at the inn while she flailed her hand in the air like she struggled to find the right word—"...opening."

"Ah. You're on the V.I.P. list."

She gave him a curious look. "I guess," she said. Then, "You don't seem surprised to see me."

Trey glanced down at the plants. He was acutely aware that he was on the ground and she towered over him. What an idiot he was! If he had the foresight to not sit down, knowing she might come to see him, he wouldn't be stuck down there. It was impossible to stand without a struggle, and it wouldn't be pretty. Sitting at her feet instead of flailing about won out, though the humility burned inside.

He coughed. "I saw you drive up earlier."

Farra nodded while her gaze roved over him and then the plants.

"You do beautiful work. I had no idea," she said, bending down to study the plant identification marker next to the Buckeye Belle peonies.

"Thanks. Can't take all the credit though. Darcy and Sean mapped out what they wanted, and I put it into place." He shielded his eyes from the sun again when Farra moved to look at the other peony varieties on that side of the gazebo. He almost said she looked good, but stopped himself. He was afraid his words wouldn't ring true to her. On the other hand, a compliment like that might start something he wasn't prepared for. It was the whole reason he didn't call her after their one and only night together.

An awkward silence stretched between them. He shielded his eyes to look up again, and he caught her frowning at him.

She let out an exaggerated sigh. "Okay. Well, it was nice talking to you."

He wanted to say more, but his thoughts were jumbled. Not one question came to mind to keep the conversation going. At least not sitting on the lawn in the middle of a workday. It was just as well to let her go. His reasons for not following up after the wedding were still very much intact anyway. But the memories surged, begging him to question himself.

"Same," he said.

If Farra heard him, she didn't let on. She marched toward the house with that no-time-to-waste air about her. It attracted him to her before. Now it served as a stark reminder of all he'd lost.

Chapter Three

Farra shut the patio door behind her and stopped to peer through the window. Trey was back to working over the flower beds, his bare arms golden and toned in the afternoon sun. Her heart stayed where it had fallen during their conversation—in her stomach, a little twisted and sad, like a deflated party balloon. None of the magic they'd shared during that night last fall remained. In fact, he didn't seem happy to see her at all. Shoot, he couldn't even be bothered to get to his feet. Instead, he sat on the ground, looking up at her, like he was inconvenienced by her coming to see him.

Voices behind her snapped Farra back to the present.

"We're ready for the tour," Darcy called.

A dozen people, mostly women, congregated in the foyer across the room as more people drifted down from upstairs. Farra took one last look at Trey then joined them.

Darcy bubbled over with pride as she showed off the

inn and recited the fascinating history of the place built by a relative of Sean's who worked in the mining industry in the early 1900s. The house stayed in the family for a few generations until it was sold. Then Blueberry Point Lodge fell into disrepair until someone else bought it and opened a modest inn. Luckily, the Stetmans snatched it up when the house went on the market again. Darcy, Sean, and the rest of the family finished the extensive remodel last month.

While the house was stunning, Farra inwardly cringed again. It must take days to clean. The windows alone with all those tiny panes. And the expense. She counted her blessings for her little trailer. A bucket of water and a few squirts of window cleaner were all she needed once a week. No utility bills to worry about either. Having a home on wheels was especially handy now that she'd lost the OutdoorXcape sponsorship. If she could find another company to support her recreation obsessions, life would be good. For now, Jack was home on the road. It suited her.

After covering the downstairs, including the two rooms converted into one big space for small conference gatherings and wedding receptions, Darcy led them upstairs again. She stopped at the landing in front of the Tiffany-style stained glass window. It was a double pane of a lighthouse and a ship with white sails.

"Commissioned by the first owner for his wife in memory of her father. He was a lighthouse keeper in Presque Isle in the late 1800s," Darcy said. "If you look closely, each individual pane has an etching of—"

Darcy's voice trailed off as Farra's attention was drawn to a side window on the landing. It had a view of the winding driveway leading toward Highway 61. Dust kicked up behind a pickup truck leaving the house, an arm hanging out the window.

Trey.

She was disappointed in herself for giving him another thought. But they'd had such a great time that night—dancing, laughing, and dancing some more—even after the band stopped playing. Farra counted on hearing from him. She only lived across the lake in Bayfield. Well, across the lake seventy miles as the crow flies. It was really three and a half hours driving through Duluth and around the southern shoreline. But still. It wasn't too far to drive to see him again; he seemed worth it. She'd driven farther to adopt Jesse, the mutt for her mother she'd picked up from a St. Louis shelter last fall.

As Trey's truck turned onto the highway and disappeared from sight, she let her mind wander. It had been magical inside the gazebo. The torrential rain from earlier in the day had tapered off and clouds skirted past the waning gibbous moon. Tranquil sounds filled the air—water dripping from eaves and leaves, waves lapping the shoreline somewhere beyond the lawn's edge. Crickets had backed up nature's melodies with their own staccato music.

They'd huddled on the gazebo bench after he'd taken off his jacket to lay across the damp seat. Trey asked about her music tastes, her parents, and whether she was an early bird or night owl.

Definitely a night owl. How about you?

Same, he'd said. *What do you like about it?*

Honestly? Sitting outside on the patio when everything is quiet. Stargazing. Watching the fireflies light up.

He'd been surprised. *"No kidding? I do that too when I can't sleep.*

She'd accused him of agreeing with everything she said just so he could get her phone number. And then she didn't hesitate when he'd asked for it.

"Farra?"

Farra jerked when Darcy nudged her gently. Embarrassed, she mentally shook herself.

"Sorry. I was so engrossed in the story I guess my mind wandered." Her face grew hot as she said it.

Darcy smiled. "I knew you'd love it here. This house has so many stories."

The group climbed to the second landing so Darcy could show them the conservatory with floor-to-ceiling windows facing the lake. There were eight bedrooms, four on each side of a long hall. At the end of the hall, another door led upstairs to the old ballroom. She and her husband lived upstairs, Darcy explained. They'd converted the space into a two-bedroom apartment.

An indoor jungle. That was what the conservatory felt like. Air plants and potted trees leaned toward the windows, trying to capture the light. Farra walked toward the windows, breaking away from the group a little as they gathered around one of Darcy's lemon trees, its sunny fruit a magnet.

The gardens below were a visual delight from up here.

The plot with the cedar trellises she'd walked through earlier was a perfect, verdant circle. The different shades of green, planted in homogenous groupings, gave a spotted impression from her vantage point. More impressive were the three smaller gardens surrounding the bigger one. They were each star-shaped, which wasn't apparent at ground level, nor from her bedroom window earlier.

Darcy joined her at the window.

"After lunch, I'll take you through the gardens," she said to the group. "They're a work in progress, but we have someone tending them now who does an amazing job."

Someone next to Farra said under her breath, "I'd like to meet the gardener. He looked pretty amazing from what I saw of him."

Farra glanced at her. The young woman chuckled under her breath. Her friend nudged her in the side, but gave her a wink and a "no kidding."

"It looks a little like the moon from up here," said a middle-aged man from the fringe of the group.

"That's why we call it the Moon Garden. That, and because the plants bloom after dark."

"Oh, I bet that's a sight. I can't wait to see it," someone else said.

"And you will," Darcy answered. "We have something special planned for you tonight."

The tour finished downstairs in the foyer again. A woman in a white jacket with a silver tray came from the kitchen and passed Farra with an assortment of sandwiches, each tied together with a length of jute cord, sitting on mini palm fronds. Farra smiled at Darcy's attentiveness to details. Darcy should earn high marks for presentation. Her friend always had a knack for first impressions.

Farra found a table for lunch near the windows so she could enjoy a view of the lake. What she wouldn't give to get out there in a canoe. Maybe Darcy had one. She'd ask her later.

"Is anyone sitting here?"

It was the young woman from upstairs who'd made the crack about Trey. She stood over Farra at the table, eyeing the empty spot next to her.

"No one except you if you want it."

"I'm Natalie. Call me Nat," she said, draping her sweater over the back of the chair. "This is my sister, Justine."

Her sister gave Farra a small wave then plunked herself down in the seat next to Nat.

"Friend or family of Darcy and Sean?" Nat asked as she dug a compact mirror from her bag and popped it open. She swiped a rosy swath of color across her mouth, smacking her lips together. Nat pursed her lips together in the mirror then snapped the cover closed. "No, let me guess: a cousin?"

"Nope. Friend." Farra didn't mind having the chance to correct her. She seemed a little too boisterous for her own good.

"Gotcha. We knew Darcy when she lived in Marquette. I lived with her for about a year. Then I got restless."

Farra waited for her to tell the rest of her story since Nat looked at her expectantly. Farra wasn't about to ask for more details. Honestly, she just wanted to take in the scrumptious details of Darcy's lunch. But Nat seemed bent on oversharing her life's history while her sister sat next to her, scrolling through photos on her phone.

"Marquette isn't the best place to meet people, you know?"

"No, I wouldn't know," Farra said, moving her napkin to her lap. One of the catering staff came to the table with a tray of berry lemonades in frosted glasses. Farra took the spear of fresh raspberries from her drink and set it on her plate. She sipped the lemonade while scouting the room. There was an empty seat two tables over. Would it be too obvious if she moved?

"Anyway, we've been in Florida for the past year. So much better, right?" She elbowed her sister.

Justine huffed, still looking at her phone. "I wouldn't mind living here if there were more gardeners around like the one we saw earlier."

Nat's eyes popped when she looked back at Farra. "Right? Did you happen to see him? He was good scenery."

Farra bristled. They were talking about Trey again. It shouldn't bother her, but it did.

Nat didn't wait for Farra to answer. "Anyway, Jacksonville is home for now. We live near Dunn's Creek Crossing in a duplex. The people that own it rent—"

At that moment Darcy announced the lunch buffet was ready and waiting. Farra took a sip of her drink and stood.

Thank goodness. Her tolerance meter for one-sided conversations trended downward after the first minute with Nat. She needed Nat yapping in her ear for the entire lunch like she needed the reminder that Trey stood her up last fall.

And as long as she was a guest at Blueberry Point Lodge, the chance was high for both.

Chapter Four

Trey took a quick shower and changed from his sweat-soaked clothes to a clean pair of jeans and a nice button-down. The therapy session earlier had really taxed him, especially after the almost full day he'd put in at the inn. His therapist gave him a light scolding after she'd seen him limp into the office and throw himself onto the padded table with a groan.

You're going to undo the work we've done if you're not careful, she'd said. But that was easy for her to say. Trey was tired of nursing his leg when the rest of his body and mind was ready to resume the life he'd given up last October.

He buttoned the last of his buttons as his sister Cynda burst into the house and froze, her annoyance wrinkling her forehead. She gave him a quick assessment, deciding she didn't like what she saw, and threw her hands on her hips. Trey knew he should be sitting down with his leg up, but impatience got the best of him today.

He hobbled quickly to the armchair and plunked himself down.

"Before you say anything, Tisha said my range of movement has really improved in the last few weeks." He couldn't look at her directly or she'd know it wasn't quite the truth. "So, good news."

Cynda sat on the ottoman facing him and swatted his good leg.

"You're such a liar. Tisha is the second of three people I have on speed dial. We were friends *before* your leg got pieced back together. We talk."

He grumbled under his breath. "Whatever happened to patient confidentiality?"

"You have me listed as an approved health information contact. Remember that discussion?"

Trey sighed. Cynda was Mom 2.0, only much more hardcore. "Oh yeah."

"'Oh yeah' is right." Her gaze swept over him. "Where are you going?"

"Out?"

"I know that. But where?" She took an exaggerated sniff, then smiled wryly. "Are you wearing cologne?"

"Back to the inn. It's their test drive weekend before they open."

"Good for them. They must be thrilled," she said. "That doesn't answer my other question though."

"About the cologne. Yes, I'm wearing it."

Cynda pushed her hair off her forehead and narrowed her eyes at him. Looking at his younger sister was like seeing a female version of himself. Her hair, which brushed her shoulders unlike his close-cropped style, was a sandy shade of blonde. Same hazel eyes too. And like him, they saw everything. It was hard to sneak anything past Cynda.

"So, who is she?"

He folded his hands across his stomach. "I don't know what you're talking about."

Cynda chuckled dryly. "You think I'm so wooden-headed, don't you?"

He laughed at her description. "No, I don't. I just don't think you need to know everything."

Cynda got up from the ottoman and crossed the room. She took a drink of water from her metal flask, giving him the stink eye over the rim.

"So, you don't need me to stick around and help with dinner?"

"They're serving food there."

"Do you need a ride?" she asked. "You don't look like you're moving so great."

He set the ice wrap on his leg again. He'd become good at using his left foot on the brake and accelerator instead of his right. Driving wasn't too much of a problem normally, but after the heavy workload today, he'd feel it for sure. "Nah, I'm good. I'll sit here another twenty minutes then be out of your hair."

She gave him another skeptical look even as she reached for the doorknob.

"Let me know if you need anything. And behave." She winked at him and left.

Ten minutes was all he could stand, though the short

rest with ice on his leg worked wonders. Now back in the truck, Trey headed toward Blueberry Point Lodge as the early evening sun dipped behind the treeline.

When Sean had invited him to tonight's party before he left this afternoon, he'd done it with the caveat that Trey give a short talk about the moon garden to anyone interested. Trey reluctantly agreed. He could hardly turn the Stetmans down for anything. They'd come through for him in a big way when he healed enough to work.

He pulled into the gravel drive for the second time that day while reciting the flowers he'd planted.

Artemisia...snow-in-summer...Lamb's ears...hydrangea...

The garden was a sight when the moon was full, the light illuminating the white blooms and foliage. His favorite had to be the ostentatious moonflowers. Big as saucers. They didn't like the cold Minnesota springs though, so he'd wait to plant them during the next few weeks. Darcy and Sean's guests were in luck this weekend. The moon wasn't quite full, but there was enough so the garden could put on a proper show for everyone.

He was early. A smaller tent replaced the enormous one the Stetmans had used for their wedding. It still lit up the lawn with its string lights and portable heaters. Trey spotted Bret Hanning tending bar, the only person out here aside from a few of the catering staff working on the buffet. Bret saw him and waved him over.

"What can I get you tonight?" Bret asked.

Trey leaned against the bar to take the weight off his leg. "Just a water for now. Where is everyone?"

"Party doesn't start until six. We've got ten minutes." Bret handed him the water. "How's the leg?"

"Getting better every day."

Bret nodded. "That's really good to hear. I can't even imagine."

Bret was a thirty-something single dad who liked fly-fishing as much as Trey did. Hopefully they'd get to hike up to Sheevy's Lake a few times over the summer and fall like they did every year since Bret moved back to Hendricks a few years ago. Bret talked him into trying a marathon last year. That was so off his radar now, the marathoning. Trey still worked at walking up stairs at his usual gait. He hoped to complete his first hike next month without trouble. Running? No way. He appreciated how Bret pushed him to work harder in his low-key manner. "Gotta get you up and running again, man. I need my fishing guide back," he liked to say. Bret was a good guy.

"You gonna be ready for the Sturgeon Run come fall?" asked Bret.

Trey winced. "Hope to. I'm not feeling it now though. Trying to take it a day at a time."

"Tell you what," said Bret as he moved ice around in the trough with a silver scoop. He nodded toward the lake. "There's the best therapy you could ask for. A soak in that every day would get you better in no time."

"I bet the water temperature isn't above fifty degrees." He'd soaked his feet in the lake plenty over the years in all seasons. Lake Superior was notoriously cold, even at the height of summer. In late spring the water temp was probably closer to forty.

"It's not so bad once your body goes numb," he said, chuckling. Bret lifted his chin toward the inn's patio. "Here they come now. Better claim a table."

The group was larger than Trey imagined. He counted twenty as they drifted through the patio doors and across the brick terrace toward the tent. He hobbled to the nearest table and sat. People still filed through the doors when he looked up again.

"Why are you here anyway?" Bret asked. "I figured you be sunk into your recliner with takeout from Red's and a full night of Netflix planned."

Trey shot him a skeptical look. "What? I don't even have a television."

"I knew that," Bret said. "Man, that bum leg has killed your sense of humor."

"I can't argue that." He sipped his water. "Why am I here? Because Darcy asked if I'd talk about the gardens if anyone was interested. And—" Trey waved toward the buffet—"dinner."

"No kidding. That will be one of the perks of tending bar here. Sure beats frozen pizza. Anyway, are you sure I can't get you something else?"

"Surprise me."

While Bret mixed him a drink, Trey leaned back and watched the group come into the tent. Farra hung near the end of the first group, arms swinging, head turning, taking it all in with that easy, fluid manner of hers that was so attractive. She talked to two women who followed a few steps behind her. If she'd seen him already, Farra was good at pretending she hadn't.

"Here you go." Bret slid a drink across the table toward him. The garnish caught Trey's eye. An orange peel with a strategically placed toothpick shaping it into a heart. Three blueberries on the toothpick too.

Trey plucked it out, holding it to eye level. "Look at you getting all creative."

"That's what I earn the big bucks for," said Bret, his focus now on the group coming toward him.

Trey glanced back at Farra, who was still lost in conversation with the two women next to her. His pulse kicked up in anticipation of talking to her again. He squeezed the peel from the toothpick, ruining the aesthetic of Bret's fruity art, and popped it into his mouth, peel and all. This time he was ready. For what, he didn't know exactly, but as Farra came toward him, he knew he'd better come up with an objective quickly.

Chapter Five

Several guests passed Farra in the hallway, heading downstairs for dinner, wearing skirts and dinner jackets. She grumbled under her breath. Her dark-wash jeans and hooded sweatshirt were too casual, but she'd suspected as much. While the day had been spent touring the house, the grounds, and the town of Hendricks aboard the funky Sturgeon Widows Tours bus, Darcy planned sit-down dinners for tonight and tomorrow too. She'd meant to ask Darcy about the dress code earlier after seeing the full menu cards tucked into the glossy folder she found on her bed, but it slipped her mind. Whiskey Sorghum Brined Pork Chops. Blood Orange Beer Brined Turkey Breast. Honey Chipotle Glazed Sweet Potatoes. She was literally salivating when she finished reading. These were entrees deserving of something more respectable than denim and fleece.

It was a small inconvenience to change. She'd dash

across the lawn, change, and rejoin the party in no time. That was another plus of having Jack on site. No need to fret about packing. Her entire household came with her when she traveled. She'd even suggested Darcy save her bedroom for another guest while she slept in the trailer. *Nonsense*, Darcy had said. Farra wouldn't get the full experience if she slept anywhere other than inside Blueberry Point Lodge. How would she be able to write an authentic article otherwise?

Downstairs, the clinking of pots and servingware in the kitchen carried into the living room as Farra stopped to look over the bulletin board next to the check-in desk. Photos and articles highlighted the inn's progress since the Stetmans started renovations. Most write-ups were from local publications like the Hendricks newspaper, a full-cover North shore magazine, another newspaper from Duluth. Her blog post would be up there by next weekend. She'd start working on it tonight.

After changing into a skirt and sweater inside the trailer, Darcy caught up to one of the groups heading to the tent. The night had a bite to it. She tucked her hands into her sweater pockets while eyeing one of the tall portable heaters. Those threw off serious heat. She'd grab a drink and park herself at a table near one of those for the night.

Darcy and Sean went all out decorating. There were strings of lights and fresh flowers in globe vases on the tables and a wet bar with a menu full of regional wines and craft beer. She smiled at the basket of mosquito repellent, mini bottles of hand sanitizer, and single bags of campfire crunch, all with the BPL logo, sitting in the middle of the nearest table. Darcy thought of everything.

"Hey, Farra."

She turned in the direction of his voice. Trey sat in the farthest seat, almost folded into the shadow of the overhang. The lit mason jar candle made his eyes dance as he smiled up at her. Her heart felt the instant sting of rejection just looking at him. But she could hardly deny he was as good looking as ever.

"What are you doing here?" She cringed inwardly. Questioning why he was invited to mingle with the inn's guests was rude. Farra didn't mean the way it sounded, but guilt still made her look away for a moment. She glanced again at the bar but decided a drink could wait.

"I'm supposed to talk about the gardens later on." He pulled out the chair next to him. "Do you want to join me?"

How could she say no? Trey looked so hopeful, a sharp contrast from earlier in the day.

"Why not?"

She sat down and inhaled. Gone was the suit jacket and green silk tie with little Adirondack chairs on it. Farra remembered thinking what wasn't to like about a guy with patio furniture on his dress wear? And she'd been right. He didn't take himself too seriously, owned his own business, and loved the outdoors. Now, seven months later, her attraction was as strong as ever. The only visible change was that his face had filled out a bit. It looked good on him.

"How are the Stetmans treating you?" He tipped back

his glass, then swirled the ice cubes around before he looked at her.

"I'd give them a five-star rating so far. Darcy was born for this."

"They're good people."

One of the catering staff came by to offer a tray of hors d'oeuvres. Farra took three artichoke mousse puffs and set them on a napkin. Trey filled a plate with one of everything before settling back onto his chair, a grimace twisting his face.

"Are you okay?"

"Yeah. Must have overworked myself today." He popped one of the hors d'oeuvres into his mouth. "Are you still in Bayfield?" he asked after he swallowed.

She shrugged. "A little more now than I used to be."

"Oh?"

"I lost a sponsorship after Christmas that paid a lot of my travel bills. I'm blogging closer to home these days. But it should pick up soon. I've got some feelers out."

"Sorry to hear. Did Darcy tap you to promote their opening?"

"I offered. There's no shortage of things to write about on the North Shore, so I'll have plenty of material even when I finish a few posts about this place. Plus, I know the area well to begin with. She's a lifelong friend. It was a no-brainer."

He nodded, tracing the rim of his glass with a finger. His mouth twisted a little like he wanted to say something but thought better of it.

She cleared her throat. "You said you're between jobs?"

"Yes. I should be back to full time next month," he said, taking one of the bags of campfire crunch and opening it. He tilted the bag until an assortment of chocolate chips, nuts, and mini marshmallows scattered on his napkin. Trey pushed three cashews toward her and she smiled. He remembered.

When she looked at him, he wore a wistful smile. Something passed between them as the silence hung. She wanted to ask what happened. Why did he bother saying he wanted to see her again and then not call? But it wasn't a good time, not with the party atmosphere that Darcy and Sean worked so hard to create. Maybe he wouldn't tell her the truth even if she did ask. Not asking questions was easier sometimes.

Darcy popped over to the table.

"I see you two found each other again." Darcy's attention bounced between her and Trey, but neither acknowledged the obvious. Before it got any more awkward, Farra scrambled to break the silence. She poked at the basket in the center of the table.

"How many hours did you have to scour Pinterest for this centerpiece idea?"

Darcy's face brightened. "Aren't they the cutest? I came up with it myself." She rested her hand on Trey's arm. "The people that were interested in the gardens asked to sit with you during dinner if you don't mind. There are four or five of them. I'm sure you can answer their questions a lot more articulately than I can."

"Sure. Send them my way," Trey said.

"Thanks so much." Darcy waved to someone on the

other side of the tent. Then she looked back at Farra, discreetly cocking an eyebrow. "Hope you're enjoying yourself."

Farra murmured a garbled affirmative. A *whoosh* of heat made her cheeks burn. She hoped Trey didn't catch Darcy's double meaning, but his attention was already on a few people pulling chairs out across the table. Two middle-aged ladies and a couple sat down as everyone introduced themselves. Trey introduced himself and started talking about coming up with the initial design with the Stetmans. He was well into the discussion when Natalie rushed up to the table, breathless.

"Is there room for me here?

There was a shuffling of chairs so Nat could squeeze in at the table. Farra moved closer to Trey so Nat could sit next to her. Nat looked at the chair, looked at Farra, then dragged her chair to the other side of Trey and plunked herself down.

"So you're the resident expert on moon gardens I hear." Nat's smile was so overdone Farra could almost count her fillings.

"So they say."

"I asked Darcy what everyone was gathered around here for. When she said you were talking about flowers, I said, 'Count me in!'" Nat's hand shot up for emphasis.

Farra wondered if Trey minded the interruption, but he just smiled. *Was he blushing?*

"Do you garden?" Trey asked.

Nat's face fell. "Do I garden? I, uh...does buying plastic

succulents at Wal-Mart count?" She laughed, glancing around to see who else thought it was funny.

Farra gently nudged Trey's shoulder. "What were you saying about pairing the flowers?" It was a subtle way of getting the conversation back on track. Farra didn't miss the daggers Nat shot her way.

"Right. What I was about to say is that you have to think about the garden's purpose. Is it something for show? To attract wildlife? Or in this case, to group a number of night-blooming flowers together."

While Trey dazzled them with facts about planting moonflowers and the bottlebrush fothergilla shrubs that smelled like licorice, Farra studied Trey. Something about him had changed. He seemed more laid back, less of the magnetic force he was that night at the wedding. Oh, he was as attractive as ever, maybe more so with the extra weight he'd put on. But he wasn't bursting with energy anymore. Not earlier when she'd seen him, and certainly not now.

"Do the flowers really glow in the dark?"

It was an innocent question. But it sounded inane coming from Nat when it was accompanied by the batting eyelashes and pursed lips. Farra felt embarrassed for Trey, who was forced to look her in the eye.

"They do." He glanced outside and ducked to see the sky, but the tent awnings hung too low. "If it's clear tonight, I can take you out there and you'll see for yourself."

Wait, what?

Nat sat up straight. "I'd *love* that."

"We'd be thrilled to see it too," said the couple across the table.

The corners of Nat's mouth dropped when she realized her intended party of two just doubled in size. Farra almost burst out laughing. She bit the insides of her cheeks in the nick of time.

Nat pressed on. "Can you show us now?"

Near the bar, Darcy rang a handbell. "If everyone could grab a drink if you still need one, we're going to serve dinner in about ten minutes."

Trey glanced back at the group. "We'll wait. It should be good and dark after dinner."

"Good thinking," Nat said. "I'd want to take my time in the garden."

If her tone wasn't gushing like a fire hydrant, Nat's body language practically shouted, "Pay attention to me!" She rested her cheek in her hand and wore a moony smile while she gazed at Trey. Farra wouldn't be surprised if Nat's pupils morphed into blinking hearts any moment.

Farra leaned back in her chair and crossed her arms. She simultaneously wanted to avoid watching this love fest between Trey and his number one fan. But then Nat crossed her legs, moving a little closer to Trey in the process, and Farra decided she didn't have anything better to do than stick around.

Dinner was as amazing as the menu card she'd seen earlier promised. Farra tried to savor the meal, but she was starving. The food lulled everyone into a quiet stupor. The clinking of silverware and the resonant strains of bluegrass playing from the sound system were the only noises amid the hushed conversations. Dessert came way too soon.

Trey crumpled his napkin and set it on his plate.

"So what comes next after the weekend?" he asked.

On the other side of Trey, Nat shifted in her seat while glowering at her. Farra ignored her and looked at Trey.

"I'm going to take Jack up to Sleeping Bear Sand Dunes for a while. Find a spot, hunker down for a few weeks, take some long walks along the beach. I have the write-up on this place to work on too."

He leaned back and dug his hands into his pockets, looking toward the bar. He had such a nice profile. But the grimace was back, his brows dipping low.

"Sounds romantic," he said while he flexed his leg a few times. He winced. Romantic? Peaceful and relaxing—yes, but romantic? Farra studied him. If he was teasing her, she wouldn't bite. He'd made it clear a few times now he wasn't interested in her. That drink called to her after all. She shifted in her seat to leave.

Trey leaned forward. "Listen, for what it's worth. I'm sorry," he said in a rush.

"For what?"

"For not following up."

Again, she wanted to ask him why. It didn't make sense. They'd really hit it off, or so she thought. And what was with the "sounds romantic" comment and all the lingering looks tonight? Was he trying to mess with her head? Farra thought the Stetman wedding was the beginning of something. Sometimes you meet someone and you just feel it; the connection is so strong. She was honest-to-gosh giddy for days afterward. But when she didn't hear from him after three days, four days, and then a week passed by, it was clear that her mutual attraction radar had gone wonky. Why else would he have ghosted her? Some guys liked to reel women in and let them go for an ego boost. Catch and release. And if there was one thing she didn't handle well, it was rejection.

She shrugged. "Not a big deal."

He nodded, not looking at her.

"I mean, it was a fun wedding," she added. "We hung out for a few hours. I didn't count on anything more." She shook her head incredulously. What a silly idea.

On the other side of Trey, Nat's eyes were huge. Her mouth formed a little "O."

Farra stood and drew her sweater closed. It was getting colder despite the tower heater. "Anyway, nice talking to you," she said. "I'm going to get myself a drink."

Trey looked at her with a mixture of humor and uncertainty wrinkling his forehead.

"Sure thing. Don't let me stop you," he said.

Chapter Six

The landscape lights lit the gravel path near the gazebo as Trey and Nat made their way back to the party.

"Now I want to go home and plant a moon garden," said Nat.

Trey let out a soft chuckle. "I thought you said you were more into plastic plants than real ones."

Nat waved his comment away. "Oh, I wasn't serious. Of course I have real plants. Actually, I still have the same little barrel cactus I had in college. How old is that thing anyway?" She stopped in her tracks as if doing the math in her head while they walked was too much of a strain. "That would make it, like, seven years old."

"You're a regular green thumb," he said as he scanned the tent for Farra, but she was nowhere in sight.

Nat clung to his arm with both hands, unsteady on her feet as they crossed the lawn toward the tent again. The ground was uneven, but Trey suspected it had more to do with the two glasses of wine she'd had during dinner than the lawn. He eased his arm away from her, lengthening the distance between them as they walked. The others who'd been interested in the garden opted to call it a night after he talked with them for the last half hour.

"As long as the bar is open and the music is playing, I'm going to sit in the tent. Want to hang out awhile longer?" She looked at him with wide, expectant eyes.

Trey wasn't clueless to the fact that Nat tried coming onto him more than once tonight. She'd hung on his every word, laughed when he wasn't even trying to be funny, and brushed his hand with hers when they stood amongst the flowers, their scent intoxicating, even with present company. Nat wasn't his type though. Too talky, too pushy.

"It's been a long day. I think I'm going to head home," he said, putting even more distance between them in case she tried to ambush him with a hug.

Her expression drooped. "Well, I'll see you tomorrow then."

It was a statement, not a wish.

He stuffed his hands in his pockets while he walked to the truck, thankful to be alone again. His leg ached only a little despite the late night. He'd credit his therapy session after work, the pain pills, and a moderate amount of walking around the last few hours. Now was the time to ramp up his activity level. Summer was on the horizon, the trails were drying out, and his running shoes begged to be used again. He'd ask Cynda if she was up for a modest walk on the Sage River trail in the morning. It would do him good.

As he neared the truck, Trey looked across the lawn toward the house, lit up in all its grandeur. A lone figure sat on the low brick wall of the patio, arms crossed, looking back at him. It wasn't too dark to see it was Farra. Her gauzy light-colored skirt billowed around her legs. He waved, but she didn't notice.

A few minutes later, Trey drove away from the inn, turning onto Highway 61 toward home. Headlights from oncoming traffic cut through the light fog, an unnerving distraction. Last time he'd left Farra at Blueberry Point Lodge in the darkness, it had been the fateful night of the Stetman wedding. Fantastic memories were overshadowed by the sobering ones, and the pain rifling up his leg taunted him now.

If he could go back to that night, there were two things he'd do different. He would have introduced himself a lot sooner, so he could have spent more time with Farra. Trey also would have insisted on driving home.

He and Farra had walked the grounds that night after the band stopped playing and the guests left Blueberry Point Lodge. He considered taking her along the beach—he knew the perfect spot for stargazing. But the beach wasn't a good one for walking on in the dark, full moon or not. Too many cobbles and washed-up driftwood to worry about. Besides, the torrential rains from earlier in the day probably left good-sized puddles on the lawn. It would be like wading through a swamp. Instead, they climbed into the gazebo. They'd kissed too, an unhurried, chill-on-the-back-of-his-neck kind. Farra's slow smile after they'd drawn apart reaffirmed his notion that it might not be the last kiss they shared. But then Ben, his ride for the night, shouted from the back patio that he'd waited long enough.

Ben was a good guy. A little on the unreliable side at first, and Trey had come close to not hiring him last summer, but he'd worked out in the long run. Ben was big, like NBA-player big, so he had a little trouble folding himself into some of the equipment Trey used on job sites. But he was good at muscling the materials around, and he liked to talk. Boy, did he talk. Once Ben started on one of his stories, it could be a good ten minutes before he took a breath and acknowledged someone else might want to say something. Trey interrupted him a lot because talking and working simultaneously wasn't a skill set Ben had mastered yet.

Trey said goodbye to Farra after another hurried kiss. He should have read the signs when Ben dropped his keys three times before he unlocked the door and struggled with his belt buckle for a solid minute. But Ben was in the middle of telling one of his epic stories, and it was funny. Real funny. Trey's gut hurt from laughing even before Ben pulled onto Hwy 61 toward Two Rivers. Something about one of the guests mistaking her husband's shirttail for a napkin at dinner.

He should have insisted Ben pull over and let him drive home when Ben drifted to the shoulder the first time. Trey didn't see it coming the second time; the chain reaction was already in motion before Trey realized what was happening.

"And then she turned about fifty shades of red—hey, isn't that a book title?—and—"

The truck rumbled as it hit the gravel shoulder again. Trey instinctively grabbed the hand bar above his head with one hand and put his hand out to grab the steering wheel with the other. Ben made a gargle sound and jerked the wheel hard to the left. Trey remembered thinking that the headlights coming toward them were far enough away that the vehicles wouldn't collide. But funny things happen to cars when their wheels pass over two very different surfaces at a high rate of speed. The truck shot across both lanes and rolled when it hit the other shoulder. They ended up fifty feet from the road, the truck resting on its roof. When he came to, water dripped into his nostrils. It had started raining again.

He'd spent ten days in the hospital with a collapsed lung and his leg in traction, strung up like a marionette. Two surgeries to put it back together with screws and plates and who knew what else weren't even the worst of it, strangely enough. No, it was laying off his guys after the last of the season's jobs were finished. He'd promised them plenty of work with plowing and wood-splitting contracts, but the accident made getting those finalized out of reach.

His head was so messed up he didn't even think of Farra until after he'd been home a week. Trey hobbled into the kitchen on crutches one night for a glass of water when Sean and Darcy's wedding invitation, still hanging on the refrigerator, caught his eye. Memories of that night flooded his mind, hitting him like a truck.

Call me, she'd said.

Count on it, he'd said.

He'd lied.

It was clear to him that Farra liked to keep moving. Her work demanded it. It was in her genes. So why would a go-getter like Farra, a woman who'd once run a half-marathon on a Saturday morning and the next day hiked down the Kaibab Trail of Grand Canyon, want anything to do with him, he reasoned. Maybe they'd hit it off, and then what? He'd be stuck at home recuperating while she ran and skied and hiked. He couldn't bear to be a burden. And when it came down to it, he didn't want to stand on the proverbial sidelines watching someone do the things he couldn't do himself.

His selfish self-pity held him back and he hated himself for it. As time wore on, his guilt over not calling her snowballed into a greater slight. He'd told her he'd call "soon." But a month later wasn't "soon." Seven months later was even worse. The longer he put it off, the more his embarrassment grew over his lie. He was a man of his word, but not in Farra's case. So his pride kept him from calling her. His silly, unreasonable pride.

Chapter Seven

Farra sat on the bottom step of the trailer, lacing up her running shoes. It looked to be another beautiful day. She woke as the sun inched its way through the cracks of the window blinds in her room, and she decided to get a run in before breakfast.

It had been a restless night despite the luxurious mattress and linens. She wished she could take advantage of them; a sound sleep was something of a rarity these days. But Trey weighed on her mind. Her tendency to stew about unresolved matters was another pesky fault.

If she could muster up the courage to ask him what happened, Farra could let it go. There was no good reason for him not to call her, at least none she could think of, and now that they were back in each other's company, their short relationship—could she even call it one?—bugged her. Maybe he had someone else, an on-again/off-again girlfriend. She'd just caught him in off-again mode.

If he did have someone else, it was just as well they didn't end up together. Not with the way he and Nat flirted nonstop last night. She counted on seeing them take off in his truck together after the party last night, but they went their separate ways. At least she could credit him with a little common sense.

She locked up the trailer and walked the length of the driveway toward the road. Darcy waved to her from the patio. Farra waved back until she lost sight of her friend as the driveway looped to the north before it met the highway.

There was a trailhead across Hwy 61. She'd tried it out for the first time last fall. The rustic pavilion with a map of the two-mile trail was barely wide enough to shelter anyone from the elements, but it had a solid bench that Farra used to stretch out. There was one lone car parked in the gravel lot and fresh footprints in the dirt around the map display. It was such a nice trail to run, and she was surprised there weren't more early risers getting some exercise in before the day began.

Farra took it slower than usual. The trail was rocky, and tree roots snaked over the path in spots. The easy pace gave her time to think. Trey was a runner too. She recalled the moment she discovered that about him. She wasn't intentionally trying to eavesdrop on his conversation with one of the groomsmen as they stood at the bar during the wedding reception that night. Trey casually mentioned he'd like to train for one of the biggie marathons in Alaska. *The Equinox Trail Marathon?* she had asked while standing behind the two men. Trey turned in slow motion, like it was one of those rom-com scenes when the male lead sees his love interest for the first time. He'd stared at her for an uncomfortably long time with his mouth half open until she repeated herself.

That started a conversation between them that lasted the entire night. They'd swapped stories about the races and rivers and ski slopes they'd visited. It was a good-natured competition, she remembered, dropping the names of places they'd been to or would like to see.

I'm working my way up to the Grandfather Mountain Marathon. Heard of that one?

Is that in the Blue Ridge Mountains?

Yes. But my dream is to run one of those big ones in the West.

Like the Red Rock Canyon one? I'd love to tackle that one.

Have you ever been out there? Trey asked.

Yes, several times. Hiked Fossil Ridge a few times with friends. My 10-year-old niece could do that hike though.

Speaking of hikes, Grand Canyon—rim to rim—is on my bucket list. You?

Someday. Next year maybe, she'd said.

His eyes had bugged out and she did the same. Then they cracked up.

Farra smiled to herself as she relived the memory. His passion for adventure was one of the things she liked about him. They had seemed so in sync. Why then?

There was only one way to resolve this.

That was it. She'd ask him. She punctuated the decision with a firm nod. No better time than when she saw him today.

But it was Saturday. He probably had the day off. Her

paced slowed when the realization hit her. Would she even see him again?

Farra was so lost in thought as she ran over the gently sloping terrain that she almost didn't spot the flash of yellow farther up the trail. Ahead, the path opened up on the side of the barren hill until it disappeared into the forest again in another hundred yards. Two people walked briskly along the trail. She'd keep her head down and pass them in the next minute.

When she glanced up again as she neared them, Farra came to a dead stop. The couple, not yet aware of Farra behind them, kept walking.

Funny how it works sometimes. Thoughts can be so intensively focused on a person or object that the mind conjures up that very thing in real time. And here were her thoughts incarnate. One of the two people was Trey.

She'd recognize that dark blond brush cut and the easy swing of his arms anywhere. And he was with a woman.

At first she thought the woman was Nat. She was tall and slim too. But with closer inspection, Farra noticed the long braid swinging against her back. A short wave of relief washed over her until a bigger realization hit her. Trey had someone else.

Farra stood in the middle of the path, thinking. Should she turn before they spotted her? Or forge ahead and give a hurried greeting as she ran past? If she ran ahead, she'd have to eventually turn around. The trail wasn't a loop; it was a dead end at the lake. She'd have to retrace her steps, and then she *would* see him.

No, she didn't want to chance a meeting. Not now. Not anymore.

While she worked this over in her mind, all the while watching them move farther away almost to the point where they would disappear into the trees, she noticed Trey's limp. Even from a distance, it was a pretty pronounced limp. He probably hurt himself cliff-jumping or extreme swimming or bobcat wrangling, whatever he was up to these days.

Farra turned on her heels and jogged in the direction she'd come. There was another trail down the road where she could run in peace. The more distance she put between herself and Trey, the more she fumed. At him for ghosting her. At herself for not calling him out on it when she had the chance. But what did it matter now?

Chapter Eight

Trey felt himself turn a corner that morning.

Maybe the sun glinting off the lake's surface from where he stood atop the bluff had something to do with it. Or the effects of therapy yesterday still lingered, helping his leg feel less wooden. And Cynda's lighthearted banter on their trail walk to Sheevy's Lake sure lifted his spirits. But he'd be an idiot if he didn't acknowledge that he hadn't felt more alive in months after seeing Farra again.

While it might be true, it was ridiculous thought. Not that she didn't have that power over him. But hadn't he purposely avoided her after the accident? Now he was basically calling her his kryptonite. If a few hours with her yesterday had this kind of effect on him, maybe he shouldn't have let his pride stand in the way. Like Bret had a way of lighting a fire under him to get moving, Farra might have helped hasten the process too.

"What are you thinking about?"

Trey literally jumped.

In the passenger seat, Cynda chuckled. "*Wow*. Where were you just now? Because you sure weren't driving this truck. I'm surprised we're still on the road."

He gave her a look. Cynda bit her lip and looked ahead.

"I was thinking about stopping by the inn. I planted some weigela this week and they could use another watering. It'll take ten minutes."

She snorted. Trey could feel Cynda studying him still.

"But you were shaking your head. Do shrubs cause you that much stress?"

Trey shot her another look. "Not at all."

"Then why don't you tell me the truth?" His sister wore that wry smile that meant she had him all figured out. Sadly, she usually did. He couldn't hide anything from her.

"Fine. There's someone I've had...a thing for since last fall."

Cynda shifted in her seat to look at him fully. "Trey! Seriously? And I'm hearing about this now? When do I get to meet her?"

"It's not like that. We're not dating."

"Ah. So, secret admirer status."

"More complicated than that."

She blinked and waited. When he didn't elaborate right away, Cynda threw up her hands. "C'mon. The intrigue is killing me."

He sighed. How could he put into words what he was feeling now, what held him back after the accident? Cynda must have sensed his mental wrangling because her expression grew sympathetic when he glanced at her again.

"In all seriousness now, maybe I can help. Talk to me."

So he did. He filled her in on how he and Farra met the night of the wedding and that he expected to see her again. They discovered they had so much in common in a few short hours that it felt like they'd known each other for years. Then the accident made him rethink starting a relationship with her and how he didn't want to be a burden.

"You basically blew her off, right?"

Trey rested his head against the seat and gripped the wheel tighter. Somehow hearing his reality out loud made it so much worse.

"That's right."

"Maybe you should have let her make the decision."

"I thought about that. But by the time I realized it, it seemed too late. Embarrassingly late."

They pulled into the driveway at the inn. There were a few people on the lawn playing croquet. Another small group was on the beach. Farra wasn't among them. He pulled into a spot near the carriage house and cut the engine.

"So if you haven't seen or talked to her since October—"

"She's here this weekend."

Cynda gaped at him. "In Hendricks?"

"Here at the inn. She's a friend of Darcy's."

The look on her face was so incredulous, he snickered.

"And you didn't know she was coming? You just happened to see her again?"

"That's right."

"Sorry, but this is a no-brainer, little brother."

"She might be seeing someone."

Cynda frowned. "Is he here with her?"

"No."

"Well, there you go." She threw up her hands again. "You have to come clean with her. Tell her what you told me."

"It will just expose me for the idiot I was."

"Are."

"Huh?"

"The idiot you are."

He grumbled. "That doesn't help."

"Worst-case scenario is she tells you to bug off. Which you basically told her last fall, so it would serve you right." Cynda kicked her feet up onto the dashboard and pulled out her phone.

"You're supposed to be on my side."

"I am. But that doesn't mean I'm going to excuse the stupid things you do." She gave him a cheesy grin before she went back to her phone.

"You're right."

"Of course I am. Now go water your weigelas."

TREY SOAKED THE BUSHES SO HE WOULDN'T HAVE to come back until Tuesday. Tomorrow and Monday were his days off too. He'd planned a short trip to fish along the

Temperance River. Nothing too strenuous. Pitch a tent. Keep hiking to a minimum since he was going solo. He just wanted to get out again.

He wound up the hose and shut the water off at the faucet. Footsteps behind him made him pause and turn. It was Darcy.

"Hey," she said. "I brought you some leftovers from breakfast. I'm learning that trying to gauge the appetites of our guests is going to be one of the biggest challenges of innkeeping." She handed him a brown bag.

He smiled. "Happy to help you out."

Darcy looked over the dripping weigela. "Thanks again for coming to dinner last night and talking to that group about plantings. They were singing your praises this morning too."

"No problem at all."

The corners of her mouth dipped when she looked back at him. "We're really going to miss you when you're well enough to start working for yourself again."

Trey leaned against the bed of his truck. "It doesn't mean my time here has to end. I can still take care of the grounds."

She gripped his arm with both hands, almost throwing him off balance. "Really? I was afraid to ask. Are you close to opening again?"

He flexed his leg. "Hope to ease back into it over the next two months. We'll see."

Darcy pressed her palms together and looked to the sky. "You have no idea how good it feels to have that load lifted. Sean will be thrilled that we can check full-time landscaper off the list."

Was he that unapproachable that she couldn't have asked him?

She touched his arm again. "Listen, why don't you come back for dinner? We're having brisket tonight. Sean's been laboring over the smoker for hours already. And there's a bluegrass band too."

His eyes wandered to the patio, to where he last saw Farra. "Who'd you book?"

"Jimmie Monroe and the Iron Horse Boys."

"Nice." Trey nodded with appreciation. He knew the drummer. Their weekends were booked solid months in advance. "I'll be here. Same time?"

"Yes." She looked him up and down. "You're moving better today."

"Cynda and I walked the trail this morning. That loosened me up early."

"It's nice to see you getting back to normal. Farra was on the trail this morning too. Did you happen to run into each other?"

He paused. "No, I didn't."

Darcy gave him a long look as if she wanted to add something. She brushed her hands together. "I'd better get back inside. We'll see you tonight."

Back in the truck, Trey fastened his seatbelt then switched off the radio. Cynda's nose was still buried in her phone.

"Darcy invited me to dinner again."

Her finger glided over the screen for two more

seconds. She stuffed it into the bag at her feet and gave him a gummy smile.

"There you go," she said. "Darcy has practically written the script for you."

"It's not a guaranteed happy ending, you know."

"Here's what you do: wear that pretty blue shirt that I bought you for your birthday and say about twenty 'sorrys' during the course of your conversation with her. You'll be golden."

"Farra's not the type to be affected by pretty blue shirts."

"Then skip the shirt and just apologize. Stop strategizing like it's one of your mountains to climb, and tell her what you told me." She hitched her shoulders to her ears then dropped them. "See? So simple."

Trey looked toward the inn again. A few more people wandered outside, including Nat. Still no Farra.

So, tonight.

Tonight was it.

Cynda was right. He'd messed up big time last fall. Fate stepped in by bringing Farra back to Blueberry Point Lodge again.

Here was his second chance.

Chapter Nine

❧

Farra spent the afternoon talking with a few guests, jotting down their impressions of Blueberry Point Lodge so far for her article. As much as everyone loved the weekend, she'd gathered a page of lackluster quotes. "Nice atmosphere" and "great breakfast" were not exactly winning testimonies for a first-class inn. She'd have to get creative.

Inside the trailer, her fingers flew over the keyboard, a comforting sound because it was a productive sound. Farra loved when that happened—words arranging themselves in her mind faster than she could get them down. Ben and Moira Lansing, business associates of Sean's father, had been talkative and upbeat, probably fueled by sunshine and Darcy's sweet tea and lemon coconut cookies. Their high praise had definitely given her something to work with. Moira mentioned something that

Farra hadn't thought of: the blueberry bushes in the overgrown tract beyond the lawn. Farra wandered over to see for herself and had been surprised to find a faint trail meandering through the lot. Bushes she assumed were blueberries were covered with white bell-shaped blossoms. She'd have to ask Darcy if this was how Blueberry Point Lodge got its name. Now to finish getting her notes fleshed out so she could be on time for dinner. She set the timer for fifteen minutes then she'd head out.

She leaned against the seat, looking through the window of her trailer toward the inn. Torch lights lit the perimeter around the back patio. The tent was aglow again too. A local bluegrass band had come and were warming up, their instruments providing a disjointed but ethereal, faraway sound. Farra found her thoughts drifting as she listened. Memories of the wedding. Bits of conversation from last night. She gave herself a mental shake and focused again on her screen.

Thirteen minutes later, she switched the timer off. There. The article outlined, she'd have three days to fill it in with more details, quotes, and do a little research. Farra closed her laptop, smoothed the front of her shirt, and slipped into her shoes. A soft knock on her door startled her and she almost dropped her water bottle as she grabbed it from the counter.

Trey stood at the bottom of the steps when she opened the door. He looked up at her with a tentative grin.

Wonderful. Just when she'd decided to write him off, here he was again, bursting back into her world.

"What are you doing here?"

He winced at her abrupt question. "They invited me back for dinner."

"That's ni—*aackk*—"

Her gum caught on the roof of her mouth. She tried prying if off with her tongue, but she only pushed it farther back. A series of embarrassing noises happened as she tried not to swallow it. Too late. A coughing fit doubled her over, and Farra gripped the doorframe to keep from tumbling out and into his arms. Wouldn't that be a wonderful start to the evening?

Trey was on the top step in no time. "Are you all right?" His solid grip on her arm was both reassuring and incredibly shiver-inducing.

She blinked at him through watery eyes. The sky-blue shirt he wore brought out the intense color of his eyes, eyes that roved over her before she motioned him to come in while she got a drink of water.

"I will be," she said, clearing her throat. Something snarky was on the tip of her tongue, and she almost let it slip. Seeing him with another woman earlier that morning only reaffirmed he wasn't that into her in the first place. It hurt. But retaliating with a well-timed barb or two wasn't going to get her any answers. And she fully intended to have one by night's end now that he was here again.

Farra filled a glass with water from the sink. Beside her, Trey studied the inside of the trailer. She glanced at him over the rim of the glass while he wasn't paying attention. He looked nothing short of ridiculously hot, but it still didn't excuse him from ghosting her.

"This is really nice," he said finally.

He drifted to the corner where she usually sat to eat, write, and read. On the wall, she'd hung family photos, favorite quotes, postcards, and other stuff that inspired her or made her happy. He stood rooted to the spot for longer than she liked—he didn't earn the right to study her personal belongings so intently!—so she set her glass down. Loudly.

He jolted. "I didn't know you had a sister. You look so much alike." He pointed to the photo.

Farra shifted her weight and squinted at him. "Cousin. And there are a lot of things you don't know about me."

It was a "take that" kind of remark, and it did the trick. But she didn't mean to use such a harsh tone. His throat rippled as he swallowed. Trey stepped away.

She gestured with her glass. "I'd give you a tour, but you can see the whole house from where you're standing."

"It's very...homey." His gaze moved around the tight space, which seemed to have shrunk to half its size now that he was inside.

"I like having everything I need without having to hunt for it."

"And you're not one to be tied down anyway, right?"

His comment hung in the space between them. Trey took a step to peer into the miniscule bathroom.

She wasn't opposed to being tied down with a good enough reason. "There's really no need to be stationary at this point."

Trey scratched his jaw. "I doubt I would fit in there," he mumbled.

She moved closer to him as he studied the cramped space. "It suits me," she said, coming to the defense of her bathroom.

He turned toward her again, and Farra instinctively backed up. The wall with her storage compartments was behind her, so she was momentarily pinned. A surge of heat lit her face on fire as he stood there holding her gaze.

"Of course it does." He lowered his voice. "It's not designed for two people."

Farra stepped aside, opening up a little more room, and her breathing returned to normal. "It could be if they liked each other."

"Oh?" He frowned.

"I mean for a young couple without a family or...a retired couple." She didn't mean for it to sound so personal.

Trey nodded, looking down at his shoes. He opened his mouth to say something, but pressed his lips together instead and made his way toward the door. He ducked his head to see through the window. By now, the party was in full swing under the tent.

"I think I'm going to head to dinner. Are you coming too?"

"Yes." She was relieved this conversation was over.

She nodded and followed him outside. Farra locked the trailer before they walked together toward the tent.

The smell of smoked meat hung in the air and mingled with the sweet fragrance of roses as she and Trey walked past the blooming shrubs on their way to the tent. Already some guests stood near the buffet table, the clanging of metal serving dishes an indicator that dinner was almost ready.

"There's something I've wanted to talk to you about since yesterday," Trey said, still looking ahead.

"Good, because there's something I need to say too."

Trey looked at her, his eyes widening. "Okay. You first then."

No, he wasn't getting off the hook that easy. Farra was certain once she articulated her thoughts, their conversation would go downhill fast. She wasn't the most diplomatic person when she felt she'd been wronged.

"You spoke first. You go."

They walked a little ways, then Trey stopped and looked at the ground.

"I should have said this a long time ago."

There was resignation in his tone. Here he was going to admit that he'd been swept away by the feel-good occasion of the wedding, and he'd made promises he couldn't keep once the night was over. It was hard to stand there silently and take it. Farra focused instead on the firefly that landed on his shoulder, blinking like a yellow caution light. Everything she felt at the moment told her to move on before his words pierced her all over again.

"I wasn't able to finish last night after apologizing," he continued. "There's more to it than that."

"No need to explain any further."

The firefly lifted its wings a few times then flew off.

Farra watched its intermittent blinking until it disappeared in the semidarkness.

"I hope it'll be easier to understand if you let me finish."

Her sharp laugh was a surprise to even her. She didn't mean for it to sound as cynical as it did. Farra ducked her head and stared at her shoes for a few seconds. Get it together. *Let him get it off his chest, then you can ignore him for the rest of the night.*

"I'm sorry. Just…go ahead."

He was quiet, so she looked up and caught the fleeting hurt expression on his face before it disappeared. Over his shoulder, Nat marched across the lawn toward them. Wonderful.

"Hey, guys. Darcy wants to get a group photo under the tent before dinner," she said as she neared. The flouncy white shell she wore was totally inappropriate for the cool night, but it showed off her toned arms. Once her goosebumps multiplied—and Farra totally saw them from where she stood—Nat would go running for a jacket.

Trey let out an exaggerated sigh.

Farra hugged her arms against her chest. She didn't want to be in a photo. Whatever kind of smile she mustered now might look like her stomach hurt. Which it kind of did.

"Oh, did I interrupt something?" Nat planted her hands on her hips, looking like she didn't mind if she had.

"Not at all," Trey said. He looked at the sky momentarily before turning his back on Farra.

Nat took that as an invitation to hook an arm around

his. She gave Farra a pithy little wink over her shoulder as they walked ahead.

"I'll try not to keep him too long." Nat squeezed his arm and leaned into his shoulder, giggling. "Unless Trey has something to say about it."

Farra followed not too closely behind, stewing. It felt silly to hold a grudge after so many months, especially considering she and Trey had spent so little time together at the wedding. Why had one night caused this much angst? Because she had really liked him and she thought the feeling was mutual, that's why. This wouldn't even be an issue if they hadn't bumped into each other here. She had been so over it. A guilty conscience probably obligated Trey to bring it up since he'd seen her again. Farra shook her head as a new round of frustration welled up.

Darcy stood on a chair in the center of the tent with a camera in hand, giving directions as usual.

"Let's have ten in the back row stand and the people in front put your hands on your knees," Darcy said. "And don't be shy."

Farra squeezed into the back, jostling to close the space between her and the women on either side of her. An elbow to the ribs or stepped-on toes wouldn't prompt too many smiles.

"Get closer to each other like you love the one you're next to," Darcy urged again. "We're not going to get everyone into the photo if you're all standing a foot apart."

"I don't have a problem with that," said Nat at the other end of the group. Farra saw her squeeze Trey's arm.

Trey smiled at Nat and gave Farra a neutral look over Nat's head.

"I might be more cooperative if I weren't so hungry," said the woman in front of Farra.

"I'd be more inclined to do what she said if I weren't claustrophobic," someone else mumbled under her breath. That drew chuckles and a prompt to "hurry it up" from Mrs. Claustrophobia's husband.

Farra managed to smile for the photo before she broke away from the group. She wanted to catch Trey before dinner to clear the air.

"Trey?"

There were too many people, too many voices competing for Trey to hear her call out to him. Ahead, Nat looped her arm through Trey's again and led him to a table in the corner of the tent. Nat claimed one seat next to him with her oversized bag then sat in the chair on the other side of Trey.

Farra yanked her sweater over her hips as she made her way across the tent toward them. She didn't care if Nat overheard. Let Nat find out Trey and her had a history, albeit a short one. Farra wouldn't let her emotions get out of control. She wouldn't point fingers. Trey saw her coming because his passive expression morphed into surprise in an instant.

Nat flashed an overdone smile when she saw Farra approaching. "Trey and I were just heading to the buffet. Do you want to sit here?" She pulled out the chair on her other side, well away from Trey.

Farra ignored her, and instead faced Trey.

"How come you never called me? I thought we... I thought..." She swallowed to control her wavering voice. Adrenaline always did that to her. "You asked for my phone number. And I never heard from you after that."

You...you...you

So much for not pointing fingers.

Chapter Ten

This wasn't a conversation to have while sitting in the middle of a crowded tent with an audience and a bluegrass band kicking it into high gear in the background.

"Take a walk with me," he said quietly. "Please."

Nat squeaked in indignation. "What about dinner?"

"You go on without us," Trey said, not taking his gaze off of Farra. Farra stared back. The heat from their confrontation as well as her scrutiny unnerved him.

They walked out of the tent together, heading toward the brick terrace where it was dark and private. Farra folded herself into a chaise lounge, tugging a thick stadium blanket around her shoulders that she found draped over the back of the chair. That simple gesture on her part caused his pulse to quicken. At least she was settling in and had no plans to run off like she did last night. Maybe this time he had a chance.

Trey straddled the end of the lounge chair, facing her. He folded his hands. Unfolded them. Picked at his thumbnail. *Just admit your stupid pride got the best of you. How hard is that?*

"There's something I need to tell you," he started. "Something that happened that night."

"I already know, Trey. Darcy filled me in." She leaned forward to set her hand on his arm. The contact was electric. He was glad for the darkness so she couldn't see the flush that surely was turning his skin a dusky shade of pink at the moment.

"About the accident?"

"Yes," she said. "Don't be mad at her. I pressed her to tell me."

He gave a soft laugh. "You're probably hard to say no to."

"It's both a strength and a curse in one." She smiled. "I'm so sorry that happened to you. I wish I had known."

"It could have been worse. But it's behind me. I just keep looking forward." He clasped his hands together so he could keep them still. "But how did you find out?"

"I saw you today. On the trail. You were limping."

"You were hiking too? I didn't see you though."

"Jogging." She shrugged and looked away. "You were with someone. I didn't want to interrupt."

"You should have. I could have introduced you to Cynda. My sister."

She looked back at him. "Your sister?"

"Yeah, we hike together a lot."

Farra gave a shaky laugh. "Your sister." Did she

sound...relieved?

Somewhere close by an owl hooted. Their attention was drawn to the tall spruce tree nearest them where branches rustled. They listened while Trey silently digested Farra's words. She'd seen him limping on the trail and it had been on her mind until she could find Darcy to ask about him. Why would she do that?

Farra looked back at him. "That still doesn't explain why you didn't call. You're not exactly Mr. Social Media, so I couldn't even stalk you."

Trey shook his head and sighed. "It wasn't that conscious of a decision not to follow up. I—" He stopped. That was another lie.

"So you just didn't think of me? After hanging out together the whole time at the reception? After taking the trouble to ask for my number and calling me two seconds later to make sure the number worked?" The tone of her voice cut into him. He'd hurt her and it was still evident months later.

"Of course I thought of you. After I'd recovered enough to string coherent thoughts together."

"Why didn't I hear from you then?"

Trey hung his head again, thinking how to put his thoughts into words that didn't make him sound like such an idiot. But of course he was.

"I didn't want to be dead weight."

Her forehead wrinkled in confusion.

"What's that supposed to mean?"

"I didn't want to get in the way. To hold you back from anything."

She let out a humorless laugh. "Hold me back? Look at you. You're almost superhuman again."

He chuckled. "And it looks like you found someone else anyway."

"Huh?"

"You mentioned Jack yesterday. Going camping with him."

Farra gave him an incredulous look which morphed into laughter.

"Jack is my *trailer*."

"You named your trailer?"

"People name their boats. Why not a trailer?" She covered her face with her hand, still stifling her laughter.

"I can't argue with that logic."

"Thank you." She shrugged. Case settled.

Trey rubbed his jaw. "Besides, I didn't know what recovery would look like back then. I was not in a good place."

"I wish you would have let me make the choice."

"I know. It was wrong. Then I was too embarrassed to follow up. So much time had passed."

Farra sighed. She nodded. "I probably would have done the same thing. I hate feeling like a burden."

"And I just wanted to be alone and feel sorry for myself in peace."

She laughed again. "We could be twins."

"I'd settle for friends at this point."

Farra dragged the blanket with her as she scooted forward, straddling the chaise too. Her face was inches from his. Her lips curved in a gentle smile.

"I'd like to be friends," she said softly.

Her breath washed over him and smelled faintly of cinnamon. The lights from the tent behind him reflected in her eyes. Farra's look teased him to make good on his words.

"Friends, huh?" He took her hands in his. "Do friends do this?"

Trey leaned closer to brush his lips against hers.

"Good friends do," she said, breathing against him.

Trey pulled away and looked her in the eyes. "I'd handle it much differently if I could have a do-over."

"A do-over sounds good to me," she said, giving his bottom lip a gentle tug with her teeth before she kissed him again. His breath caught when she pulled him closer still. She smiled against his mouth.

"So you forgive me and my foolish pride?" he mumbled.

"Only if you forget what I said about my trailer being too crowded for two people."

"Is that an invitation of some sort?" he asked as Farra's arms came around his shoulders, holding him close.

"Maybe at some point," she said, smiling even wider.

"I'll take that as a yes."

"Do you know what?" Her voice was a throaty purr. "I think this friendship is going to be amazing."

TWENTY MINUTES LATER, THEY LEFT THE PATIO and walked hand in hand back to the tent. The buffet spread was even more sumptuous than the night before.

Trey had never tasted brisket so lean it practically melted on his tongue. There was a snap pea salad that called his name for seconds too. Beside him, Farra barely uttered a word until her plate was nearly empty.

While the meal wound down and people wandered back to the bar, Darcy borrowed the mic to thank everyone for coming for the weekend and explain how it helped her and Sean realize the little things they needed to tweak.

"I don't think they need to fix much as long as the food stays this good," said Natalie, who'd planted herself beside Trey again after visiting the bar. She nibbled on one of the melon- mint-prosciutto skewers while holding a second one in her other hand. "Would you like one?" she asked, waving it in front of him.

It had become more obvious that Natalie's intent wasn't to talk to him about moon gardens or menus. While she might be skirting around her main objective, subtlety wasn't her body language. She leaned into his shoulder, waiting for his answer.

"No, thank you."

"Would you like to dance?" Nat asked, frowning as she looked at his chest.

He wondered why she was frowning until he noticed the firefly clinging to his shirt.

"Pesky things." She brushed it away. "Well?"

Farra made her way across the tent with his and her drinks in hand and slowed when she noticed him talking with Natalie again.

Trey bent over to pick up the firefly where it had fallen

near his shoe. He set it on the table, where it lay blinking and flexing its wings.

"What are you doing?" Natalie giggled like it was ridiculous to rescue a crumpled bug.

"Nothing besides waiting for Farra to come back," he said.

Her frown reappeared. "You two are together, aren't you?"

"I'd like to think so, yes."

Natalie pressed her lips together as Farra approached the table. The two of them exchanged a look. Some unspoken communication passed between them because Natalie got up after giving him another disgruntled look and left. Farra didn't seemed fazed. She set his beer in front of him.

"What happened?" she asked, fingering the blinking firefly. "Poor thing."

"It was on my shirt."

Her brows lifted. "So it wanted to hitch a ride. That's hardly a crime."

"It wasn't me." He lifted his chin toward Natalie's retreating back.

"I see." Farra picked it up and held it in her palm. Its antennae waved. "Maybe it'll recover. I love fireflies."

"I know that."

She looked up at him, surprised. "You do?"

"You wore a firefly necklace the night of the wedding."

Her eyes brightened. "I'm impressed you remember that."

"I saw it when we were in the gazebo. Do you

remember what I said?"

She stared out into the darkness until the realization lit her face. "Maybe?" she said in a faraway voice. Farra rested her chin in her hand, thinking. "Don't tell me. Let me think."

He waited for it to come to her, watching her thought process play out across her features. She puckered her lips slightly when she really seemed to be concentrating. The urge to kiss her again was almost unbearable.

Farra snapped her fingers. "Yes! I do remember. You told me a story about how you used to collect fireflies in the backyard at your grandmother's house. She lived in—" Farra tapped her temple a few times.

"Swalbury, north of the Twin Cities."

"That's right. She told you the more you collected in your jar, the smarter you'd become." Farra slumped against her seat. Her brows dipped. "Sorry, that's all I remember."

Trey folded his hands behind his head and looked up toward the ceiling of the tent. Strands of lights swung lazily in the breeze. Outside the tent and across the lawn, fireflies blinked in the darkness as if competing with their celestial counterparts.

He nodded. "I was one of those kids who drove my parents crazy asking 'why?' all the time. For some reason, I never questioned this outrageous idea that my grandmother held on to until I was well into my teens. Maybe I thought my grandmother wasn't capable of stretching the truth."

"Grandmothers are known for such things," she said

and winked. "Mine was anyway."

Trey chuckled. "Mine did too. I asked her one day and she said the firefly is an ancient symbol for wisdom and guidance. It brings illumination."

The skin around Farra's eyes crinkled as she smiled. "So, do you feel enlightened?"

"I don't know about symbols and ancient wisdom. But I do know this: Seeing you again made me realize I made a horrible mistake. It almost cost me the chance to apologize."

She leaned forward to grasp his hands. "Now is your chance to make it up to me."

He studied their intertwined hands, feeling thankful that fate had brought her back to him. This time he wouldn't blow it. He gave her hands a gentle squeeze. "Where do I start?"

Farra's dark eyes looked like they were full of stars. He could get lost in them way too easily.

"You can start right here," she said, pointing to her lips.

Their kiss was unhurried as he tasted it, luxuriated in it. It was as soft and fleeting as a moth's wings. She drew away slowly to look at him.

"Surely I need to do more than that to get you to forgive me," he said huskily.

Farra wrapped her arms around his neck and rested her forehead against his. "Oh, there is. This is only the beginning."

The beginning.

He liked the sound of that.

PROMISE ME OCTOBER
A BLUEBERRY POINT STORY

D.E. MALONE

Chapter One

Two marriage proposals before the day is over, maybe even three.

That's how many Kiley Byrne counted on getting from Bret Hanning since they were scheduled to work the same bridal luncheon later that day at Blueberry Point Lodge.

"Is he here yet?" Lexi Hollander asked with a wry smile. Her assistant and friend came around to the rear of Kiley's car to help carry the bags of photography equipment into the inn. "I'm surprised he's not standing at the side door waiting for you."

Kiley let out a short laugh. Lexi didn't have to mention Bret's name for Kiley to know whom she referred to. "Me neither."

"If Bret spent half as much time tending his bar as he did trying to distract you, he wouldn't have such a reputation, would he?" Lexi joked.

"Does he really have a reputation, Lexi, or does he just like to flirt?" She'd only heard this from Lexi.

"Would that change your mind about not dating him?"

She gave Lexi a look and pressed her lips together. No way would she answer that.

At a wedding last weekend, Kiley had lost count after Bret's fifth proposal. From anyone but Bret it might be annoying. But Bret was harmless, a world-class jokester, and pretty easy to look at. That might be the perfect combination for a guy worthy of attention from most women. But being around Bret had the opposite effect on Kiley. He set off warning bells in Kiley loud enough to rival a five-alarm fire. Dating Bret, or anyone for that matter, did not fit into her plans.

Still, she secretly looked forward to Bret and his mock proposals. After next weekend though, the propositions and her career as an event photographer would become a distant memory. After next weekend, she would step out of her comfort zone and go back to school for an advanced degree in fine arts. The goal had been a long time coming. First, she had to get up the courage to apply. Then she had to save some money. Even with a generous fellowship from UMD, her monthly budget would be tight. She smiled at the thought as she opened the hatch of her car to sort through her photography equipment. At thirty-three, she'd be a student again.

A drizzle fell on the backs of her bare calves. The damp, warm air pasted stray hairs to the back of her neck. As much as she tried to tame her natural curls in this humidity, Kiley's chestnut hair had a mind of its own. Aside from the showers today, it looked to be a perfect October day for the wedding reception she would photograph here at the inn tomorrow.

Blueberry Point Lodge had only been opened since May, and it seemed like she was here almost every other weekend. Today, Kiley would photograph the luncheon before the group headed to the Twin Cities to continue the celebration.

Kiley opened her red-and-white umbrella, ready to hold it over their heads. "I'll admit his antics help pass the time."

Lexi reached up to shut the hatch and laughed. "I like how you call his flirting with you as just 'antics.' Anyone can see he has a thing for you."

"Well, being the object of Bret's affection is the last thing I need."

Lexi zipped up her raincoat, then reached for the bag she'd set on the ground. "Right. Especially when you're trying to work. And you know how rumors spread."

Unfortunately, Kiley did know. While she'd only lived in Hendricks for three short years, she'd grown up in an even smaller town in the northwest corner of Minnesota. So small that the post office, one of three public places aside from New Life Community Church and Salty Dawgs Grill, had been shuttered since she was in high school thirteen years ago. Rumors bred like the band of feral cats living at the weather-beaten barn next to the *Welcome to Iliola* town sign. In fact, she'd learned of her broken engagement through the grapevine instead of from her fiancé's own lips. But that was so long ago it seemed like another life.

Kiley hoisted one bag over her shoulder and handed another to Lexi, glancing up the driveway toward Blueberry Point Lodge. The stately sandstone inn, overlooking the North Shore of Lake Superior, was majestic. It had been love at first sight when she'd photographed her first wedding here in June. And according to Bret, he'd fallen in love too when he tended bar at that same wedding—with Kiley. Kiley shook her head and chuckled at the memory. Truthfully, she half expected to see Bret peering through the French doors off the dining room, wearing that one-sided grin. It sent a little ripple of anticipation skittering up the back of her neck. But Kiley silently scolded herself for falling for it every time.

She followed Lexi as they hurried up the gravel drive toward the covered side porch. The rain came down heavier now, hitting the heavy plastic tote bags filled with cameras, lenses, and the tripod. Sean Stetman, the inn's owner along with his wife Darcy, held the door open for them as he peered toward the sky.

"So much for clear weather forecasts. This came out of nowhere, didn't it?" Sean said.

Kiley folded the umbrella and stepped into the small vestibule with an intricately tiled mosaic underneath her feet. "I even checked the forecast this morning. I guess we lucked out with the luncheon being inside."

"It wasn't supposed to be, but the bride changed her mind at the last minute," Sean said.

He took their coats to hang in the massive closet, then led them down a long hallway lit with two crystal chandeliers until they came to the oak double doors on the left.

Despite the dreary day, walking into the great room at Blueberry Point Lodge always lightened Kiley's heart. Pocket doors separated the dining room from the living room, and they were always opened for big events. Tall windows lined the opposite wall for a sweeping view of the lake. She loved how the yellow plaster walls contrasted with the blue water and the changing foliage outside. It had to be the prettiest room on the whole North Shore.

"I'll leave you two to get organized," Sean said. "I think I saw the bride-to-be pulling into the driveway when I met you at the door."

Kiley led Lexi over to the small, cloth-covered table set up just for them against the back wall to stow their equipment bags out of sight. It would also be where they sat while the bride-to-be and her guests sat down for the meal. She rarely ate while she worked even though food was offered. These events always left her feeling too keyed up to eat.

She and Lexi went over the details page for the event, planning what shots they'd focus on, and the timetable for each one, during the luncheon. Lexi's expertise in arranging group shots was why Kiley loved having her friend's help. As a newspaper photographer for the *Lakeshore Weekly*, Lexi knew how to line up a football team or a roomful of pint-sized ballerinas in quick order.

Kiley tapped her pen on the table. "I'm going to look

for something to drink before the party starts. Want anything?"

Lexi scribbled on her notepad without looking up. "A water would be great."

Across the room, the small bar where Bret worked was dark and quiet. Maybe he wasn't on duty today after all. Sean and Darcy's kitchen staff were certainly capable of serving non-alcoholic drinks if a small party requested it. She rounded the bar and knelt to peer into the small personal refrigerator that was usually stocked with water and soda.

Rummaging, Kiley spotted one can of diet cola behind the other sodas. She was moving cans around when a pair of brown leather shoes appeared and the familiar deep voice floated down to her at the same time.

"I didn't realize I'd been replaced here."

Kiley gasped and instinctively jumped back.

Except she was holding onto the shelf for balance. Already off-kilter from squatting, Kiley landed on her hip, pulling the shelf and more than a dozen cans with her. One punctured can rolled away, spraying Kiley with a fine, cold mist.

The brown shoes chased the errant can, which was scooped up in a hurry. It clattered into the small sink above her head.

"I'm so sorry for scaring you. Here, take my hand."

So, Bret Hanning is here after all.

There was soda in her eyes, drying on her cheeks, and dribbling down her neck. But she took the outstretched hand because she didn't trust herself not to make matters worse while getting up from the slick tile behind the bar.

His was a large, warm hand that gripped hers, righting her on her feet in no time. Bret was still in a semi-stoop when she went upright and they accidentally bumped noses. His left cheek to her right nostril to be exact. *Could this get any more awkward?*

"Are you alright?" Bret asked, grabbing a hand towel from a short pile of clean folded ones on top of the refrigerator. *Is he blushing?* "I didn't mean for that to happen."

She let out a short laugh. If there was the slightest chance of her tripping, falling, dropping something, or any other way possible to display her knack for clumsiness, Kiley would find it. She brushed at her clothes to no avail; she was soaked.

"Believe me, it's more me than you."

The concern on his face morphed into that sly, one-sided grin that always caused an annoying tingle at the base of her throat.

"Does that mean you'll still marry me?" he teased.

First proposal today. It took less than five minutes.

Kiley backed up another step, almost losing her footing again on a slick spot. His hand shot forward to steady her at the same time she clutched the counter.

"Not if I break my neck first." His eyes were so warm. The laugh lines fanning from the corners hinted at his sense of humor. She wiped her face and the droplets on her neck. Good thing she wore a black blouse today or the soda stains would be visible.

"That's the closest I've ever come to a 'yes' from you," Bret said as he took the towel back. "I should probably not let you out of my sight before our march down the aisle."

"You have your work cut out for you."

He stooped to pick up a few cans at their feet. "A challenge," he whispered, which made his voice even more alluring. Kiley really had to get back to Lexi.

"Are you working all weekend?" he asked.

Kiley nodded. "The luncheon today. A rehearsal dinner at Fernando's tonight. The Aeranelli-Blake wedding tomorrow, of course. You?"

"Just today. I'm in the wedding tomorrow. Paul Blake is my cousin."

Kiley nodded again. Across the room, Lexi caught her eye and gave Kiley a thumbs up and a self-satisfied smirk. Nothing would make Lexi giddier than if Kiley took one of Bret's tongue-in-cheek proposals as an invitation to ask him out.

"I like being on the other side of the bar every now and again for a wedding, don't you?" Bret dropped his gaze to the floor again and picked up another couple cans.

"I've never tended bar, so I wouldn't know."

He chuckled. "Ah, you got me."

Kiley smoothed her shirt hem, feeling dampness around the edge. She'd have to make a quick run to the bathroom anyway to wash the stickiness from her hands.

"I haven't been to a wedding in a while. All of my friends have already married."

He shook his head in mock sympathy. "Better them than you, right?"

She huffed. "No doubt. And I have a small family, so there's not a huge cousin network, either."

Female voices carried through the dining room. Kiley glanced through the doorway into the foyer. That would be the women arriving for the luncheon. She *really* needed to get to work.

"Sorry about the, ah, mess." She took Lexi's bottle of water on the counter.

"Here," Bret said. He handed her the diet cola she'd been searching for before chaos erupted. "I've been saving it for you."

"Thank you." It came out as a garbled squeak. Kiley cleared her throat. "I guess I'll be seeing you around."

Bret wiped his hands on the towel and draped it over one shoulder, eyeing her.

"Looking forward to it as always," he said.

Chapter Two

This was the weekend.

Bret had bided his time long enough, waiting for the ideal time to get closer to Kiley Byrne. Forget the snappy banter and the tongue-in-cheek, marry-me jokes he lobbed at her. It was time to get real. And playing groomsman instead of bartender tomorrow at Paul's wedding gave him an advantage.

Except it didn't. A ticking clock had only made his desperation more acute. And there was nothing cute about desperation. This was the last weekend he'd see her since she announced she'd be hanging up her camera to go back to school in January.

Back outside, he unlocked the truck topper to survey his beverage stock packed into the bed even though his thoughts were still back in the dining room. The load for this afternoon's luncheon and Paul's wedding tomorrow would seem daunting on a normal day. But he'd just been nose to nose with Kiley. An opportunity like that didn't present itself every day. Now adrenalin coursed through him like the Sage River after a spring rain. This truck would be empty in no time.

Bret had parked his truck under the porte cochère since the sky had been spitting for the last few hours. At the moment, patches of blue peeked through in between the thin blanket of clouds, but rain was still in the forecast until late afternoon.

Footsteps crunched the pea-gravel drive behind him. He glanced over his shoulder as Trey Merrick, the inn's gardener, stopped next to Bret and regarded the full truck. Trey clapped him on the shoulder.

"Looks like you're running late today. Need a hand?" Trey asked.

Bret scratched the stubble on his jaw. *Forgot to shave, darn it.*

"I'd appreciate it. My morning jumped to noon in like five minutes."

"Happens to me every day, especially when the leg doesn't give me trouble." Trey was a good guy, always ready to jump if someone needed help. Despite a bum leg from a car accident, Trey found a way to meet the physical demands of his work around the inn's grounds.

Bret hadn't expected the day to start off with a call from his ex. Or that his twelve-year-old son Dalton would end up in the school office with a fever as Geena caught a last-minute business flight to Charleston. No one could say he wasn't a dedicated, loving dad, but he always seemed to be the one to step up for his son's sick days, baseball games, or whenever he needed a ride to a friend's house. There was never a heads-up, this-might-happen-later alert from Geena. Her chaotic schedule affected both Dalton and him.

So, Bret had taken Dalton home to grab some clothes, then drove the twenty minutes back to Dentsen to his parents' house so they could keep him company until after Bret worked the luncheon. Guilt ate at him. Work and this wedding had wheedled their way into one out of two weekends this month he officially got with Dalton. And now Dalton might not even be up for the wedding tomorrow if he was still sick.

Trey trailed behind him as they carried a load of boxes into the walk-in pantry beside the kitchen where he stored his beverage stock until it was ready to use. They made one more trip until Trey excused himself to talk with a delivery driver from Buds N' Blooms.

Back behind the bar, Bret busied himself with unloading ice into the bin, careful not to make too much noise and distract the ladies who mingled at the other end of the dining room. Darcy Stetman appeared, pointed out the bar, and announced it was open if they'd like to get drinks before salads were served. Her throaty voice carried with no trouble. He smiled when she referred to him as "Bret of Beverage Central."

He smoothed his tie and readied his banter as two women sauntered toward him.

"Good morning, ladies."

The tallest woman, wearing a green floral dress, rested her elbows on the counter. She craned her neck to see past

Bret to the back counter where he'd propped the chalkboard with the usual choices plus two custom drinks he'd concocted with the help of the bride-to-be. The woman's many metal bangles brushed together.

"What can you make me that's fruity and non-alcoholic?" she asked.

"Do you like ginger?" He flipped over a flared cocktail glass and set it on the counter between them.

"I adore it."

"Then I think you'll like a Ginger Ovation. It's orange juice, tonic water, and ginger root. I'll even throw on a mint leaf for garnish."

"You're too kind," she said.

A younger woman waiting behind the green-dress lady put her finger in the air. "I'll have one too, please."

Bret nodded. "You've got it."

While he prepared the drinks, he listened.

"I wonder if *he's* on the menu?"

"I dare you to ask him," the green-dress lady whispered loudly enough for him to hear.

The younger woman snickered. "You're wicked, Mary."

"Oh, this is nothing, honey. I would have scored an evening out by now back in the day. Go on, ask him. I'm dying to hear what he says."

He steeled himself in anticipation for the question, but it never came.

Bret was used to flirty comments. He played along, careful not to cross the line into anything too questionable. Sometimes he had to cool his *schtick* down when someone took him too seriously. Once, out of the blue, a young woman came around to his side of the bar and tried to kiss him. He'd barely registered what she was doing before her tongue landed on his cheek when he deflected the kiss. All in the name of making her plus-one for the wedding jealous. It was part of the game, but sometimes a crazy one at that.

By the time he mixed the two drinks, the rest of the party had joined the line. Most of the orders were simple. Sparkling waters, two mimosas, and a few more Ginger-Os once word got around. It was a pretty drink, a little bubbly tinged with gold, and topped with a mint leaf. Across the room Kiley huddled with Lexi over the dessert table. A pyramid of cake platters holding cupcakes was a pretty, if precarious, arrangement to be around for Kiley. She liked to joke about being named "Queen of Disasters Big and Small" by her college newspaper staff. Some story about tripping over the sound equipment cords at a campus music fundraiser topped them all. He'd banged his head on the bar from doubling over to laugh when he'd heard her tell it.

"I have a question for you."

Bret had been so lost in thought for a moment that he startled at the voice. Heat stung his cheeks. It was Green-Dress Lady again. Surely, she wasn't back for her second drink already?

"Shoot."

"My niece Amanda over there." She waggled an arthritic index finger in the direction of the closest table. There, Amanda smiled demurely and gave him a little wave.

"She's wondering if she knows you from somewhere. Did you by chance live in Duluth at one point?"

"I did for about two years." He gave the bar a quick swipe with his towel.

"Maybe she saw you on campus then."

He glanced again at Amanda who looked decidedly too young to be in college when he was at UMD.

"Could be. Or maybe Gellert Park? Spent a lot of time there with my wife and son. That water park was *the* place to be in June and July."

Nailed it. Green-Dress Lady's smile dropped a bit. The wife and son mention never failed. The *ex*-wife clarification was but an unnecessary detail.

"Maybe." She backed away. "By the way, the drink? Fab." She gave him the "ok" sign.

Bret nodded. "Happy to hear you liked it."

He straightened his tie as he watched the two women regroup. Green-Dress Lady shared what she learned. The younger woman frowned and turned pink, glancing at Bret. Another day, another hope dashed. Bret sighed. He squatted beside the refrigerator to run the wet rag over the stickiest of spots on the floor.

He'd suffered through a dry spell himself these last two years. Once Geena made it clear she had bigger aspirations than staying with him, he put himself into a self-induced, no-dating zone. Making Dalton his sole focus took precedence over everything else. And Geena coped with the breakup by going in the opposite direction. More work, more play, less time for Dalton. Luckily, her parents and his folks were hands-on grandparents and lived in Dentsen and Hendricks respectively.

"Bret, I have a request." Kiley leaned over the bar, her eyes wide, blue pools.

He stood. "What's up?"

"The bride-to-be wants a photo with you and her signature drink."

He slid a clean glass across the counter. "With me? Okay." He laughed. This was a new one. "It'll just take me a minute to mix. Then you can shoot 'til your heart's content."

"It's not that simple." Kiley rolled her eyes.

"No?"

She shook her head and leaned even closer toward him. "She wants everyone in the photo holding a drink. And you in the middle."

Oh.

He did a quick head count in the room. Twenty-two drinks, give or take a few. That might wipe out his orange juice supply. Given the cost of that number of drinks, it was a pretty pricey photo op.

"It'll take me about ten minutes. But doable." He flashed a grin and started lining up glasses. "How many do I need exactly?"

"Twenty-three, please." Kiley fiddled with the camera around her neck, squinting down as she played with the lens. "I have to hand it to you. You took that better than I would have."

He played it off with a shrug. "It's not as bad as it

sounds. Mixing drinks isn't as stressful as, say, asking out the girl of my dreams."

Kiley chortled and gave him a quick look before turning back to the camera. "I find that hard to believe. I mean, from what I've seen, you've had sooo much practice refining your delivery."

He scooped ice into the glasses before starting at the beginning again, adding tonic water to ten glasses. Next, the blood orange juice. Kiley stopped working on her camera to watch him. He'd have to skimp on the fresh ginger, too.

"So, you think I'm some kind of charm-slinging Casanova who never gets turned down?"

"You said it, I didn't," Kiley mumbled, looking over her shoulder toward the group.

"As a matter of fact, I can't remember the last time I went out with someone on an actual date." He added a bit of ginger and a mint leaf to each of the red plastic drink skewers. From the corner of his eye, he noticed Kiley had moved the camera, letting it hang at her side from its strap. When he glanced up, Kiley stared at him with a frown tugging at the corners of her mouth.

"That makes two of us. It's so much simpler, isn't it?" she said finally with a flippant tone. She hugged her arms against her chest. "That really is a pretty drink."

"Thank you. And I'm not so sure about that. I feel like I'm missing out." He bit down on his lip, hoping that didn't sound like he was fishing for a date. Even though he kinda was.

At that moment, the mother of the bride hurried up to

the bar. "Are these ready?" she asked as she gathered three drinks.

"I have a tray if that's easier." Bret handed over one of the round, silver bar trays, which the woman commandeered before the words were out of his mouth. She squeezed eight drinks onto it and then realized it was too heavy. Three drinks were promptly unloaded before she scurried off again.

Kiley let out a noisy sigh. "Missing out on what—*this?*" Kiley swept her hand toward the drinks, almost taking one out. Her eyes grew wide with alarm.

He gritted his teeth. "Careful there, Bumblebuss."

Her brow arched as she tried to stifle a grin. "It's *Miss* Bumblebuss to you."

"Now we're back to formalities." The remaining glasses were lined up and filled with tonic water. He could handle this blindfolded. Good thing since his all of his senses were abuzz with the present company.

"Just keeping it professional." She tapped the counter with her palm. "Anyway, if dates lead to all this chaos, no thank you."

"I don't know how you can write it off at your age. Mr. Right may be out there somewhere."

Kiley huffed humorlessly. "I might have believed that when I was twenty, but Mr. Right turned out to be Mr. Way Wrong."

"Uh oh. I haven't heard this story." It might explain a lot.

She waved it off with a hurried flip of her hand. "It's so much a part of the past that I've almost forgotten about him." Kiley looked over her shoulder again. "I'd better get back to the group. Your spot will be saved when you're finished here."

Bret watched her walk back to the group, dribbling what precious orange juice he had left down the side of one glass. If he made it through this weekend without humiliating himself, he hoped to be Mr. Give Me a Chance.

Chapter Three

Kiley checked her watch. Forty-five more minutes and then she could leave this luncheon and take a quick nap. She'd like to look at these photos and maybe send a few teaser proofs out so she could concentrate on the wedding tomorrow.

"I'm ready."

Bret whispered it in her ear as he breezed past her toward the ladies. While he handed out the rest of his drinks, Kiley pretended she didn't notice how most of the women fawned over him. He really ate it up. There might not be a bigger flirt in her life than Bret.

Lexi leaned in. "He's a little insufferable, isn't he?"

"He definitely soaks it up."

"Thank goodness Tom isn't such an attention hog. I mean, he's definitely more outgoing than I am but this"—she gestured toward Bret—"takes extroverted to a whole different level."

Kiley chuckled. "You have to admit he's entertaining."

"And he does have a good heart," Lexi offered.

"But let's not get carried away."

"Or what?" Lexi paused to give her a long look. "You might fall for him after all?"

"I've said it a hundred times. I don't have time for that." She took one last sip of water, set the glass on the table, and brushed her hands together. "I'd better tell him where we want him to stand, or they might rip his shirt off trying to situate him themselves."

Bret held one drink above his head. "Looks like I made one too many," he crowed. "Whoever can reach it, it's yours."

The group surrounded him, clamoring for the drink. Or at least that was the excuse for some of them to get *super* close. Now there wasn't any doubt in her mind. Bret *was* the biggest flirt she'd ever seen.

Lexi gave them directions, and after a harried minute of posturing and chatter, the ladies finally surrounded Bret who beamed in their midst. It was almost the perfect setup for the photo. Kiley checked them in the viewfinder, then looked up at the group.

There were two ladies too near the edge of the frame. She moved out from behind the tripod and walked toward the group.

"Can you scootch together a little more? You two are too far away from the others."

One of the women fanned her face. "I get a little claustrophobic in groups." She blew the air from her cheeks.

"How about moving to the outside, then?" Kiley held onto the woman's arm while she made her way out from the throng of bodies. The woman was almost in the clear when someone's drink knocked into hers with an alarming *clink* of glass on glass. The woman recoiled, except the liquid in her glass didn't stop like she did. It sloshed over the side, soaking the front of Kiley's blouse.

Kiley inhaled. "Ooh! Coldcold*cold*!"

"Your camera!"

Before Kiley registered what happened, Lexi yanked the camera strap from around Kiley's neck.

An ice cube landed on Kiley's neck before sliding into her collar and finally her bra.

"Oh, dear. I'm so sorry," said the woman who'd managed to escape the group.

Kiley patted her shirt, trying to dislodge the ice cube, but it only made it settle in deeper. The cube melted against her skin, dribbling down her stomach and into the waistband of her pants.

"I'm good. A minor snafu." She laughed it off, trying to keep her teeth from chattering. Of course, the ceiling fan overhead was doing a marvelous job of not letting her forget she was drenched to the bone. Kiley picked at the shirt's fabric, conscious that Bret's eyes were on her.

He extracted himself from the middle of his fan club to check on her.

"No one has ever worn one of my drinks better than you." Bret wore a sly grin. "You're having a heck of a day."

"Not funny." What was she going to do? She'd never

thought to bring a change of clothes. Extra batteries, yes. A back-up telephoto lens, definitely.

He looked her over, thrusting his bottom lip out. "I have an extra shirt in my car. Would you like me to get it?"

And what would that look like, her swimming in one of his shirts? "No, thanks. This will be dry in no time." She picked again at the front, pulling it away from her skin. She'd be as good as new in no time if she didn't catch her death from a cold first. "At least it's black. Any other color and it would probably be see-through."

Bret gritted his teeth. "I hate to tell you this ..."

She froze. "It is not."

"Okay, it's not. I'm probably imagining the daisies on your ... underneath there." His eyes dropped again to the front of her shirt.

The sting of embarrassment lit her face on fire. "Are you kidding me?" Kiley looked around, caught Lexi's eye who confirmed the horror with a nod, and crossed her arms over her chest. "On second thought, I need that shirt."

Bret left in a flash.

"If y'all can excuse me for a few minutes. Bret will be back in just a moment and then we can get this photo. Lexi, the settings are good to go." She rechecked the camera just to make sure. Lexi could take the photo while she changed.

Kiley walked into the foyer and met Bret as he dashed back inside. He handed her a black, long-sleeved T-shirt.

"Thank you so much." She held it up to gauge the size.

The shoulder seams would touch her biceps. But with some strategic tucking it might not look too frumpy.

Bret gazed down at her, grinning.

She tucked it under her arm. "What are you so smiley for? I'm in a dire state here."

"I've always wondered how you'd look in one of my shirts. Now I'll know."

Kiley felt her cheeks flame again. "If we weren't in full view of everyone, I'd whack you."

He threw his head back, laughing. His smile flashed. *Such nice teeth.* "You're an easy mark."

"I guess there are worse things you could call me," she said over her shoulder. The bathroom was on the other side of the check-in desk. Now would be a good time to get away before he noticed her turning red like the roses in the vase on the Queen Anne table. "You'd better get back to your photo op."

"My groupies will wait as long as it takes," he called back.

She cringed as she closed the bathroom door. Bret said that a little louder than he should have. The ladies had probably heard him.

As if answering that thought, the group burst into laughter in the other room.

No doubt Bret had rejoined the fray.

Kiley lifted the wet shirt over her head and slipped on Bret's clean, dry one. She gathered the fabric at the neck in one hand and held it under her nose.

Laundry detergent. Citrusy-pine something. She

inhaled again. It was like he was here. With her in this tiny bathroom. A shiver danced across her shoulders.

Again, laughter rang in the dining room down the hall. They loved him. Who didn't?

Kiley bugged her eyes at her reflection in the ornate, gilded mirror over the sink.

Don't answer that.

* * * * *

KILEY TOOK ONE MORE LOOK AROUND THE dining room after coming back for her last equipment bag. She'd have to hurry her preparations for the rehearsal dinner later that afternoon since she'd been asked to stay longer here until the bridesmaids' gifts were handed out. The family had gone all out for custom-designed chokers, commissioned from a local artist. The bridesmaids' reactions were priceless.

She hoisted the bag but almost lost her grip when a clatter behind the bar startled her.

Bret popped up.

She ambled up to the bar and peeked over the counter. "Is my clumsiness rubbing off on you?"

"I'm a butterfingers whenever you're around, you know that," he said with a deadpan look.

"Good thing we won't be working together much longer." She'd never been good at keeping a straight face with him. A smile was already inching its way forward, and they'd only been at it a few seconds.

"Truth be told I'm a little relieved. I'm looking forward to working without distractions." Bret circled a white towel around the inside of a glass, then set it on the shelf behind him. He grabbed another glass from the counter and dried that too. When he caught her eye, Bret gave her a little nonchalant shrug.

"I'm just thankful I won't have to be proposed to anymore." She could give it right back, too.

Bret stopped drying and narrowed his eyes at her. He flung the towel over his shoulder, set the glass down with a *thunk*, and rested his forearms on the bar.

"In all seriousness, maybe we could go out to dinner sometime. You know, as a little retirement, goodbye kind of thing."

Kiley pressed her hand against her chest in mock surprise. "That sounds so serious."

"I'd argue it's less serious than getting married. At least I didn't ask to get hitched again."

She pressed her lips together, thinking. "True," she said. She was done trying to fight the grin.

He must have seen encouragement on her face because an eagerness spread across his features. "*Annnd* ... if you're still opposed to the idea, just think of it as a business meeting," he said.

"A business meeting?"

He cracked the pop top on the ginger ale and poured it into a glass. "Yeah. You know, swap stories. Commiserate."

Kiley rolled her eyes. "As if you haven't witnessed enough of my professional blunders already."

He took a sip, then pushed the glass toward her. "Like I said, we've all been there."

She was parched so she didn't think twice about taking a drink. But when she brought it to her lips, feeling the cold liquid quench her thirst, the realization hit her: she and Bret shared a glass. It was something a couple would do. She set it down and coughed. Kiley hoped he didn't see it that way.

"What have *you* done on the job that you wished you could do over? I thought you were Mr. Perfect."

He grimaced like he had a story to tell but didn't wish to revisit it.

"I don't make mistakes," he said finally.

"Liar! I'm not leaving until I hear this."

Bret cocked an eyebrow. "Good! My lips are sealed, then."

"Seriously? C'mon, one embarrassing moment. That's all I'm asking for."

He growled under his breath. "It was a little more involved than that. We're talking fire, property damage"—he took a deep breath—"I'm feeling heart palpitations already."

"*What*? Now I *have* to hear this."

"I was one of three bartenders at a wedding in Duluth. A group came up to the bar at the reception wanting a flaming tower something-or-other. I've apparently blocked the official name from memory because it escapes me at the moment."

She cringed. "Flaming drinks are never a good idea."

"Agreed. Anyway, we were swamped, so one of the other bartenders told me what it was and how to make it. Basically, you stack a bunch of rocks glasses in a tower, fill the top glass with Sambuca and a schnapps, and light the top on fire."

"Uh oh."

Bret's eyes got big. "An understatement. Well, he got the amounts of Sambuca and schnapps mixed up, and the result was a massive fireball that burned the top of the bar and some lady's handbag."

"Sounds like you got lucky that it wasn't worse."

He nodded as he resumed drying glasses. "Never again."

"Your secret is safe with me."

"Thanks." Bret eyed her. "You changed the subject."

"I did?"

"I asked if you'd like to have a celebratory dinner sometime?"

"Sorry. Didn't mean to."

He shot her a skeptical look. "Uh huh."

"Maybe."

He pointed at her. "Here's a better idea: I have a few friends coming over tomorrow morning. Like a pre-wedding breakfast. It'll be a small gathering. It'll be a good warm-up for the wedding, if anything."

"I don't need a warm-up. I work with people I don't know all the time."

He sighed. "Fair enough. The offer still stands, though."

Kiley repositioned the equipment bag resting on her hip as she looked him over. The muscles of his forearms rippled where he'd rolled up his sleeves, reminding her that she'd already wasted enough of the afternoon dodging his flirty comments.

"I'll think about it. See you, Bret."

Chapter Four

Bret had just finished frying his third pound of bacon when the doorbell rang the next morning. He turned the skillet to simmer and crossed the room, giving the raucous group of guys taking up residence on his sectional sofa an amused glance.

"Almost ready. Give me ten more minutes, then breakfast will be on the table."

Paul, the guest of honor and Bret's best friend, leaned back to rest his head on the couch. "Any longer and we'll have to head to the church for the ceremony."

"I'm skipping the ceremony if it means I'll have to miss this breakfast," said Paul's brother, Rand. The other guys hooted with approval.

There wasn't a better group of guys to spend the day with. And he knew Dalton agreed. His fever gone, Dalton lay in front of the television on the air mattress, still in his pajamas, feet propped up on the entertainment center.

Thankfully Dalton wouldn't have to stay home from the wedding today.

The cold tile in the foyer bit the bottoms of Bret's bare feet as he opened the front door.

"Hey, Bret."

He didn't know who he expected to be standing on his front porch but it wasn't Kiley. And looking especially gorgeous at that. She never wore her hair down. It was always swept back into a full ponytail. He'd marveled many times at how so much hair could be tamed with one tiny rubber band.

She thrust the black shirt at him. "I was going to tuck it into the door handle on your car but"—she paused to look over her shoulder at the sky—"maybe it'll rain again. I washed it."

"Thank you." He took the shirt which she'd folded into a perfect square. Had it been ironed, too? "I'm almost finished making breakfast. Want to come in?"

Kiley took a step back and almost tripped over herself. "I can't. I have to get ready for this afternoon." She hesitated as she said it, like she'd at least considered coming inside.

"But it's not even nine o'clock."

She looked away and scratched behind her ear. "It takes me a while to get organized."

Bret leaned against the door frame. Now he knew she wasn't being truthful. "You forget I've been at many of the same events you have these last few years. I know when you show up."

"Right." Kiley stared at him. "Besides, I've already

eaten. And you have company."

He shook his head. "Are you almost out of excuses?"

Kiley blinked and chewed on her lip. "I might have a few more."

"Oh, c'mon. Have a slice of bacon at least. And coffee. The guys would love to meet you too. You already know Paul."

Kiley let out a dramatic sigh then surrendered. "Fine. But I can only stay for a few minutes."

Bret stepped aside for her to come inside. A few minutes were better than none.

In the next room, the guys shouted in unison at something on television. They talked over one another, drowning out the show, which was already cranked up to full volume. Someone threw a pillow at Paul. Dalton tossed another, knocking an empty pop can onto the floor. Kiley came around the corner with him and Paul saw her first. The domino effect of their mouths snapping shut was comical.

"Guys, this is Kiley Byrne. She's the photographer today."

"Is she gonna take pictures of us now?" Rand asked as he yanked a throw blanket across his bare chest.

Kiley chuckled under her breath and gave the guys a little wave. "I didn't plan to. But my camera is in the car. It'll just take me a minute to get it." She hooked her thumb toward the door.

A chorus of howls rang through the room.

She looked at Bret, grinning. "What happens in your house, stays in your house, I guess."

He gritted his teeth. "If Angelina finds out, Paul's toast. There's so much debauching going on here, it's ridiculous."

"I can tell. Television and lots of clogging of the arteries. Truly heinous stuff for a wedding day." She pushed his arm. "You're the worst influence."

She followed Bret through the room to the dining room table, which he'd simply set with white plates and silverware. A pitcher of orange juice and a carafe of coffee sat in the middle. Bret pulled out a chair for her, so Kiley sat and poured herself coffee into one of the matching white mugs. His bacon still sizzled on the skillet, so he resumed his spot to flip it while keeping Kiley company. He called Dalton into the kitchen.

Dalton was at his side in an instant, fingering a bacon slice that Bret had dropped onto the plate.

"What's up, Dad?"

"I'd like you to meet a good friend of mine. Kiley. She'll be taking photos at the wedding today."

"You already introduced her, though."

Bret leaned a little closer to Dalton. "I know, but she's a *really* good friend and you're my kid, so ... so ... yeah. Show a little manners, okay?" he whispered.

Dalton turned on his heels, waved, then spun back around, trying to nab another piece of bacon before Bret could stop him.

"Save some for everyone else, pal."

"Nice to meet you, Dalton." Kiley said with a grin. She'd undoubtedly heard their exchange. "Can I pour you some orange juice?"

"I'm allergic."

Bret leaned over and whispered, "But say 'no thank you' anyway."

"No thank you anyway," Dalton mimicked, drawing a laugh from Kiley.

Bret threw her an apologetic smile over the top of Dalton's head.

"Can I go back in the other room now?"

He ruffled his son's hair. "Yes, and tell the guys they can start heading this way."

Dalton was out of the room in a flash. He turned toward Kiley as he brought the platter of bacon over to the table.

"He's a pre-teen boy through and through. Sorry for the lukewarm greeting."

Kiley shrugged. "Speaking from my own experience, I was ten times shier at that age."

The oven timer dinged, signaling the egg casserole was finished baking.

"Can I help?" Kiley was out of her chair and beside him before he could answer.

He elbowed the drawer next to his hip. "Hot pads are here. If you can grab the casserole from the oven, that would be great. Set it on the placemat over there." Bret nodded back toward the table.

"Gotcha."

While she tended to the casserole, he took a fruit salad from the refrigerator and uncovered it. For a few minutes, they worked quietly side by side. Kiley slid two muffin pans in front of her, which had been cooling on the counter. Then she went looking for a platter in the cabinets overhead before Bret realized what she searched for.

"We make a good team," he said.

A dimple popped. "We do," she said with a lilt in her voice. She kept her eyes on the plate of muffins she arranged. "Too bad I'm leaving Hendricks."

He nudged her shoulder with his own. "We still have today. If you think you're finished deflecting my proposals, you'd be wrong."

That elicited a heartier laugh.

"Oh, I don't think for a minute that I won't be harassed while I'm on the job today."

He stopped what he was doing and looked at her. "Am I really harassing you?"

Kiley's shoulders dropped. "I'm joking, Bret. You're a little distracting at times, but not a nuisance. Are you getting sensitive on me?" When he didn't answer, she stopped arranging muffins and glanced up at him again.

She was so close to him that Bret noticed a tiny scar on her cheek. He almost reached up to touch it; that's how adept Kiley was at scrambling his brain by being, well, *Kiley*.

"Not at all. I'm testing the waters." Now he smelled her perfume, which overpowered the smell of fried meat in the most tantalizing way. *Help me.*

"For what?"

"To see if I can get away with upping my game. Time's a-ticking."

Kiley laughed.

"Am I missing all the fun in here?" Paul had come up behind them. "Or is that my empty stomach making noise?"

What fun Bret had in mind wouldn't be well received this morning, not with a houseful of half-naked guys and the smell of fried meat hanging in the air. He'd have to be satisfied with what he got—a little banter, a look or two—until later. Telling Kiley how he really felt could wait until tonight. There wasn't a better backdrop than Blueberry Point Lodge to let Kiley know of his real feelings.

Chapter Five

Breakfast was delightful—the food *and* company.

Kiley took her plate to the sink and scooped up a few more empty dishes from the guys at the table in the process. Behind her, whispers and a few hearty chuckles caught her attention. She strained to hear over the running water, but only a handful of words stood out.

... Bret, dude ...

... lucky ...

... a thing?

She could tell from the darting glances and muffled laughter that they thought she and Bret had something going. And Bret didn't dissuade them, either. He doted on her. She got a running commentary from Bret about the buffet as she filled her plate for the first time. *I'm famous for my egg casserole,* he'd said as he stood so close to her, she could smell mint on his breath. Her coffee mug was never close to empty, but he topped it off several times anyway with a wink. When she squeezed onto the end of a wooden bench at the table, Bret brought in a chair from the other room to sit next to her at the corner.

It was a struggle, the decision to come. She'd talked herself out of it a few times, but her curiosity won out. What did his house look like? Was he a good cook? Who else would be there?

They were a chatty, affable group. She knew Paul, of course. Rand was Paul's younger brother. There was Matt Stetman, Sean's brother, a big goofball himself. Paul's father and an uncle with the same salt-and-pepper hair and deep-set eyes were there, too. Kiley couldn't remember his name from the introductions.

"So, Kiley," drawled Stephen, Paul's father. "Bret tells us you're going back to school. That this weekend is your last wedding for a while?"

She had a mouthful of casserole, savoring the maple sausage and the egg's airy texture. Bret wasn't kidding when he said he was a good cook. Kiley nodded and put her finger in the air to give her a minute.

"That's the plan," she said finally.

"Good for you. And you'll live in Duluth?" Stephen asked, pushing his glasses to the bridge of his nose.

"I will. I hate to leave Hendricks, but a two-hour commute twice a week, especially in winter, wouldn't be ideal."

"No, it wouldn't. Did Bret tell you he lived in Duluth for a while?" Wiry and tanned, Stephen reminded her of a distinguished, bookish type. His wire-rimmed glasses that sat on the tip of his nose more often than not sealed her impression.

"He did."

"Maybe he has some insider tips on where to live. Or maybe you already have that settled."

Renting an apartment was one of the few things she'd been able to check off her list. Since she'd be starting her classes in January, finding a rental in the middle of winter made her anxious. The owner of the duplex she'd found was an older lady who lived in the other unit. Kiley got the impression that money wasn't as important as finding the right tenant. The woman agreed to keep the unit empty until Kiley could move in at the beginning of November.

She explained this to Paul. "That's the reason I closed my calendar to new bookings even though I don't start classes until January. I've never excelled at multi-tasking."

"And you've already lined up help to move?" Paul asked as Bret topped off his mug. A few dribbles for her mug too, even though it was full.

Not exactly. Lining up help was still on her to-do list.

Bret set the coffee pot on a trivet and slipped into the chair next to her again. With breakfast winding down, he'd cleared the table while Paul had distracted her with conversation. Now she felt a little guilty for not helping more with the clean-up. She glanced at Bret with an apology ready, but she caught him chewing on a nail. He smiled sheepishly and tucked his hand in his lap.

"Sorry. I could have cleared away dishes instead of babbling away," she whispered.

"Nonsense. I didn't invite you here to do that." His gaze settled on her mouth, and Kiley self-consciously rubbed her lips with a finger, wondering if a bit of egg or a spot of blackberry jam lingered.

"Thank you for this. Everything was delicious."

He smiled. "I'm glad you decided to stay. They obviously didn't scare you off."

She laughed. "Not at all. Your son is especially charming." She put up her hand when Bret feigned shock. "Really, he is. I think he's a budding computer whiz, too. He was asking me all sorts of questions about digital animation that I had no idea how to answer."

"He's a little too smart for his own good sometimes," Bret said. "Geena ... my ex and I have our hands full trying to keep up with his infinite curiosity for technology and how it works."

"UMD has kid classes in the summer. Maybe sign him up next year."

"He's already been through the junior high-level courses even though he's only in sixth grade."

"I hear Microsoft is hiring." Kiley giggled.

Bret blew the air from his cheeks. "No joke. He may be ready for that, but I'm not."

She took the napkin from her lap and set it on the table. "I should get going."

"I'll walk you out." Bret scooted his chair back and stood.

Kiley said her goodbyes to the guys before Bret led her through the house and out to her car.

It looked like Paul and Angelina would have a picture-perfect wedding day. October was in its full glory as Kiley glanced around the front yard. A sprawling white oak dappled the ground as the sun peeked through its canopy. There was still a nip in the air, but it would warm up in the next few hours.

"I almost didn't come." She leaned against her front door and faced Bret. "Workdays make me a little jittery. But I wanted to return your shirt in case I don't see you ... for a while after today."

"Then I'm really glad you got the drink spilled on you," he said, resting his arm on top of her car. "Though it feels a bit strange seeing each other without a camera in your hand."

"Right. I keep feeling that I'm forgetting something."

Kiley was used to them being separated by a bar. Here, she felt small next to Bret. Over his shoulder, the brown brick façade of his house and the barn-red shutters gave it a cottage feel, especially with this majestic tree shading the front yard. The curtains moved in the front window. Dalton and Paul peeked out for a few seconds before they realized she'd seen them. Kiley smiled.

"I heard you talking to Paul about your apartment in Duluth. If you need a moving buddy, give me a call," Bret said.

"Thanks. I may have to do that. Lexi and her husband offered, but his work schedule is sporadic. Your muscles might come in handy."

Bret flexed and laughed. "I usually charge ten bucks an hour per bicep. For you, I'll waive the fee."

"What's the catch?"

He pressed a hand against his chest. "That hurts."

"Oh, wait— 'Marry me.'" She'd used her best Bret imitation for the mock proposal. Bret nodded his approval with a glint in his eye.

He took a step closer. "Kiley, I—"

She put up her hand to stop him. That look set off a warning bell. Thankfully, there was a distraction. "Something tells me you're needed back inside. That's the third time your son has looked out the window."

Bret turned to look, but Dalton had disappeared. Paul stood at the opened door instead. He yelled something, but it was too hard to hear from such a distance.

"What did he say?" Bret asked. He looked annoyed.

"I didn't hear him."

A little red sports car pulled up in back of her car, its brakes rubbing. It came up so fast Kiley thought she'd get hit for a second. *The nerve of some people.* She was about to mention it to Bret, but when she looked up at him again, his frown had deepened.

"Are you expecting someone else?"

"No, I wasn't," he said flatly.

The car door opened. A woman with dark, wind-blown hair and blue-lensed glasses waved and smiled over the top of her car door.

"Did you get my message?" the woman called.

Bret let out a long, loud breath. "Wonderful," he said in a low voice.

Kiley looked back at him. "Who's that?"

"Dalton's mother. Geena."

"Your ex?"

"Yep," Bret said. To Geena, he yelled back, "No, I didn't."

Geena circled around her car and walked up the steep driveway on her tiptoes, her sky-high heels not conducive to navigating an incline, Kiley imagined. She wore a heavy tweed coat, which seemed unseasonably warm for the day.

"Sorry to interrupt whatever you have going on here, but I nabbed two last-minute tickets to the Orpheum for tonight for that paranormal show everyone's been talking about."

Bret shook his head with a perplexed expression. "And that involves me how?"

She laughed more heartily and louder than the situation called for. "Not you. Dalton. He's been dying to see it."

He looked at Geena with his mouth agape.

"Is that a problem?" she asked.

"I thought you had a business trip all weekend? Shouldn't you be in Charleston?"

Geena flitted her hand. "Oh, that? It was canceled."

"And you didn't bother telling me? I had to work yesterday, and Paul's rehearsal dinner was last night. Dalton spent all of yesterday at my parents' house."

"I figured he was already settled, so I didn't want to intrude."

"Intrude? He's your *son*."

Kiley shifted her weight from one foot to the other.

This was embarrassing, but it'd be even more uncomfortable to interrupt. Their heated conversation went on as if they'd forgotten she was there.

"Well, I'm here for him now," Geena said with a quick glance at Kiley. Her bottom lip wavered. Bret had struck a nerve.

"Today is Paul's wedding, Geena. This"—Bret pointed back at the house—"was on the calendar."

Geena huffed and looked away. "What twelve-year-old is going to choose a wedding over holographic ghosts?"

Bret crossed his arms. "That's not the point." As upset as he appeared, Bret had yet to raise his voice. Kiley admired that.

Geena bugged out her eyes. "Oh?"

"No. We made a commitment to be here. And we honor commitments."

"Like I said, he's twelve. Paul won't care if he's not at the wedding."

"*I* care."

There was a pause as Geena clamped her jaw shut. Bret chewed the inside of his cheeks, silent for now. Kiley took advantage to jump in.

"I'm going to get going. Thanks for breakfast, Bret. See you later."

As Kiley walked around to the other side of her car, Geena asked, "Who's that?"

"The photographer for Paul's wedding," Bret said.

Geena laughed humorlessly. "Is the chauffeur for the limo here, too? The organist?"

"Back off, Geena," he said.

She slipped into the driver's seat and shut the door, cutting off Geena's reply midstream. This was one more reason to congratulate herself for not getting involved with Bret. A volatile ex in his life was a no-go, not to mention the distraction that Bret would be as she tried to start off on the right foot for her graduate work.

As she pulled out of the driveway and started down the street, Kiley caught sight of the two of them in her rearview mirror. There was no mistaking the regret on Bret's face as he watched her drive away.

AT HOME, KILEY SAT ON THE STOOL AT HER kitchen counter clicking through some more of the photos she'd taken the day before at the bridal luncheon. She only had twenty minutes before she needed to change clothes and check her equipment before heading to the wedding. Kiley could go through several hundred frames in that time, only a fraction of the photos she took in three hours. But deleting the unusable ones and flagging the photos with potential was actually her favorite part of the process. That, and showing the proofs to her clients for the first time, especially if she happened to meet with them in person. She loved watching their expressions light up when they saw highlights of their special day. Kiley knew she was good at what she did. It was bittersweet she'd have to put it aside temporarily for school.

She smiled when she came across the photos of Bret and the ladies holding up his Ginger Ovation mocktail.

His eyes crinkled when he grinned in the most irresistible way.

Just stop.

Kiley rubbed a hand along the side of her face as she clicked through the remaining photos, trying to concentrate on the images in front of her instead of the mental one which kept creeping into her thoughts—Bret.

The close-ups of the blackberry salad plates and napkin rings decorated with purple aster stems from the garden. The champagne-colored lace overlay of the bride-to-be's dress. The commissioned chokers. Candid shots of the guests after the meal which, unfortunately, had turned out blurry. She'd have to adjust the focus on all of them.

Wait.

She scrolled back to the beginning of the candid photos and looked through them again, slower this time.

Bret stood in the background at the bar in each of the photos, oblivious to her and where she aimed her lens. And he wasn't blurred at all. In fact, she could make out every curl on his head.

In one shot, he'd looked directly at her. Kiley felt a chill race along the back of her neck.

She leaned back against the stool and sighed. For the whole series of shots—seventy-three photos—her lens had zeroed in on Bret.

Scratch that, Kiley. YOU zeroed in on Bret. Don't blame the lens.

She shut off the camera and tucked it into the bag on the counter.

This was her last event for a while. She'd make sure

the photos she took today were among some of her best. Go out with a *bang* and all that. And she'd treat Bret like any other guest at the wedding. Their professional relationship and all that it entailed was over.

Best to keep her head—and lens—focused on the bigger picture.

Chapter Six

Short of calling it a mistake to invite Kiley that morning, Bret wished she hadn't seen the confrontation with Geena. He should have kept it casual, meeting at Two Tree Coffee or somewhere else. Instead, Kiley had a front-row seat to his hot mess of a life where his ex was concerned. Kiley had left in a hurry, but not soon enough.

He stood in front of the mirror in one of the Sunday school rooms at Bethel Lutheran Church later that day, straightening his tie. It fit like a noose, this thing, and he unhooked it behind his neck for the third time. Maybe he was still rattled from his argument with Geena. Either way, he couldn't help noting the analogy. He stuffed the bowtie into his inside jacket pocket. Best to save it until the last minute.

With the ceremony starting in less than an hour, the guys were in high spirits as they waited in the staging area. Bret sunk onto a couch and listened to them rib each other about wedding-related maladies that might keep them from their duties. Their shirt collars pinching their necks, cutting off circulation to the brain. Being blinded by the reflective surface of their rented shoes. Lung damage from the toxic cloud of mingling aftershave scents. With every outrageous scenario, their laughter grew louder.

"Why the long face, Hanning?" Rand asked, nudging Bret's foot with his own. "Liven up."

"Still recovering from breakfast, I guess." He yawned.

Rand, who knew the gory details of his relationship with Geena, huffed. "Breakfast, or what came after breakfast?"

Bret gave him a long look, acknowledging the run-in with his ex had a lot to do with his current mood.

"Put it behind you, buddy. Easier said than done, I know, but Dalton is here. That's all that counts." He plopped onto the couch next to Bret and slung an arm around Bret's shoulders. Rand had always been the more introspective brother compared to Paul. He always had a ready ear.

"I just wish I knew when the animosity would cool down. And when she'd get a clue that the world doesn't hold its breath waiting for her next spur-of-the-moment, inconsiderate move."

"So, your time with Dalton is still unpredictable?"

Bret had to stifle a laugh. "An understatement. On the bright side, he's with me more often than I'm 'allowed.' I can't complain too much."

Paul wandered over with the box of boutonnieres. "My

fingers can't take putting these things on."

"Ah, just the distraction I need." Bret stood and took one of the roses from the box. "Not sure I'm much help, but I'll give it a try."

"Those pins are killers," warned Paul.

Rand looked up at them from the couch. "They can't be as painful as talking with Geena."

Paul's eyes drifted to Bret. "I forbid that woman to intrude on my day. Hey, isn't acupuncture used for stress disorders? Have you heard that?" He strained to look down at Rand while Bret fidgeted with the boutonniere on Paul's chest.

"What are you suggesting, that we use pins to treat Bret right here and now?" Rand asked.

"What have we got to lose? Beats watching him mope," Paul said.

The three other groomsmen overheard the conversation and offered to hold Bret down on the floor.

Bret shook out his hand after accidentally sticking himself with one of the two pins. "I think I get a say in this."

"Nah. You don't," said Paul. He stepped back, leaving Bret with his hands hovering in mid-air. "You're not having any more luck than I did. Maybe she can help."

At first Bret thought Paul referred to Geena since they'd just been talking about her. But Paul smiled over Bret's shoulder like someone stood behind him. He glanced around and found a lens pointing at him. Behind the lens, of course, was Kiley.

"Sorry," she said with a flush creeping onto her cheeks.

"I was going for some candid shots. I didn't mean to surprise you."

"You didn't." Not entirely truthful, but that gave him some time to recover.

Kiley set her camera down on an upholstered chair in the corner and took the boutonniere from Bret. When her fingers brushed his, their eyes met for a second. He wondered if she'd thought twice about the embarrassing episode at his house earlier. A fleeting smile curved her lips until she turned to Paul. He might have imagined it if she wasn't standing so close. Kiley had it attached to Paul's lapel in less than a minute, no joke.

"I think we've found the pro," Paul said. "Thank you."

The other guys were ready with boutonnieres in hand.

Bret stepped aside. His was the last flower in the box. Reluctantly, he picked it up and took his place in line.

"How'd you get so good at this?" Rand asked her when it was his turn.

Strains from the pipe organ in the sanctuary drifted into the room. Next to him, Paul blanched. Fifteen minutes until the ceremony.

Kiley smiled. "I've been to a few weddings."

"How many?" Rand asked.

She looked at the ceiling, thinking, even though her fingers still worked to secure the flower on Rand.

"I think I hit my hundredth in the spring."

"You could probably make a fortune from pinning boutonnieres alone," Rand said.

Angelina's father poked his head into the room. "Are we ready?"

"You guys should line up," Kiley said. "I'd like a few shots in the hallway before you go into the sanctuary." She patted Rand on the chest to signal she was finished with him.

"What about mine?" Bret twirled his own flower between his thumb and index finger when it looked like she was about to follow the guys.

Kiley looked back at him. "How could I forget?"

Bret looked down at her as she took the boutonniere. She slipped one hand underneath the tux's lapel to anchor herself while she slid a pin into the stem and then through the fabric. The pressure of Kiley's hand against his chest made him hold his breath. Kiley must have felt him tense because she looked up and frowned.

"I won't stick you. Have a little faith."

He smiled and watched while she dipped her head to get a closer look at where the pin slipped through his lapel. The job didn't seem like it progressed as smoothly as the others.

Bret cleared his throat. "I'm sorry about earlier. I wish you hadn't heard me and Geena going at it."

After a quick glance, Kiley resumed trying to secure the first pin.

"Don't worry about it. That's life," she said around the pin held between her teeth.

"It's not always like that. You know, us arguing."

She looked up at him again. Her eyes held his for a second longer this time. "So, you two get along for the most part?"

Bret got the feeling something hinged on his answer.

He could tell her he and Geena didn't often share harsh words with each other. But it wasn't because they got along. Geena wasn't very good at keeping the lines of communication open. That didn't quite count as getting along in his book. Kiley would probably agree.

"In the sense that we've moved on from what happened between us. This morning was a miscommunication about our schedules with Dalton." There. That was as diplomatic as he could be without throwing Geena under the bus.

"Relationships get complicated with kids, I imagine." She took the second pin from between her lips and repeated the process. She winced and shook out her hand.

"Careful."

"Better me than you, right?" She winked at him.

He smiled while his heart did a little happy dance. "You said it. I didn't."

Kiley tried again with the pin. "I wouldn't know personally. You know, about sharing custody. Just hearing from friends and family, it sounds stressful."

It was, especially when one partner didn't hold up her end of the bargain.

She straightened and patted his chest, too. "There."

"So, you're accountable if it falls off?" Bret almost laughed when uncertainty clouded her face for a second.

"That depends on what it will cost me." Kiley took her camera from the chair and looped the strap around her neck again.

"Oh, nothing too painful."

"And if it sticks? What do I get?" she asked.

"I'll stop asking you to marry me."

Paul stuck his head in the room again. "It's almost time."

"Coming." Bret said as he looked at Kiley. "After you."

"Wait. Did you just propose to her?" Paul's face lost its peaked expression for a few seconds as surprise registered instead.

"*No!*" Kiley practically shouted it. "He's joking."

Paul was back to looking the part of a shell-shocked groom. "Oh, okay."

Of course, Bret was kidding, but a little dagger of hurt pricked his chest at Kiley's overzealous denial. They walked into the hall together. Kiley stuck out her hand.

"Deal," she said. "If it stays on, no more proposals."

"And if it falls off, I get one dance."

Her smile faltered. "But I don't dance."

"We already shook on it."

Kiley sighed. "Fine. But that sucker is on for good. And you can't sabotage it in any way."

Bret raised both hands. "You have my word."

He watched her walk ahead of him, the gauzy floral skirt she wore swaying around her ankles. An image popped into his head of them sharing a slow dance later on in the dimly lit dining room at Blueberry Point Lodge. His tongue felt pasted to the roof of his mouth by the time Rand interrupted the daydream with a well-aimed elbow in the ribs.

"Wake up. We're heading down the aisle."

Bret knew one thing: this boutonniere was toast before the night was over.

Chapter Seven

ngelina and Paul's ceremony went off without a hitch. The sanctuary had been so packed that they used the choir loft for more seating. Kiley couldn't wait to look at the photos tomorrow. She expected them to be nothing less than stunning, especially since Angelina's mother Sally ran Buds N' Blooms and had an artist's eye when it came to flower arranging. White roses, gardenias, and yellow lilies had taken over the sanctuary. Pops of color came from the garnet ranunculus and asters. Somehow Sally's decorations complimented rather than competed with the splendor of the sanctuary itself, all stained glass and soaring oak buttresses on the ceiling overhead.

Now in the reception room at Blueberry Point Lodge, Kiley got busy with the rest of her photo list. She'd already taken some close-up shots of the table arrangements, the seed packet wedding favors, and Paul's trifle—his version of a groom's cake and his favorite dessert. With the formal introductions over and dinner being cleared, her job was a little more relaxed. She'd focus on the portrait guest shots too, and maybe get a few people on the dance floor. Then she would call it a night.

Sally Aeranelli caught Kiley just as she was about to capture the three flower girls who were sisters, hand-in-hand, dancing in a circle near the head table.

"Kiley? Can you take one of me and my college girlfriends before one of them leaves? It's not very often we all get together."

"I'd be happy to."

"Wonderful. They're over there," Sally said, pointing to the back of the room. "I thought that bare wall would be a good backdrop."

She followed Sally across the room to where the other ladies congregated. With the cake and trifle tables close by, each held a plate or glass compote with dessert.

"Okay, I've rounded her up," Sally announced when they were together.

After a minute of deciding who would stand where, Kiley took a few photos.

Click, click.

Kiley held the camera away from her face. "Hold on a sec. Sally, can you squeeze in a little closer to her?"

Sally moved toward her friend and turned up the wattage of her smile. "How's this?" she asked through her teeth.

"Perfect."

"Watch the table behind you," Sally warned.

Kiley was aware of the trifle table. She'd given herself plenty of room before she started photographing the group of friends. But when she took a tiny step back while sizing up the group, her heel brushed something. She froze, then turned to see it was only her skirt hem. The awkwardness of keeping most of her weight on one foot rocked her back, and it took two more steps to get her balance again.

It was a half-step too many.

Someone gasped as her hip bumped into the table.

Ahead, Sally's eyes popped open, and she reached toward Kiley even though they were a good ten feet apart.

"Wait!"

Kiley spun to catch what she could without dropping her camera, but the disaster was in progress. Glass shattered, the sound echoing in the expansive dining room. The pyramid of compotes stacked next to the bowls of berry trifle wobbled then toppled in slow motion, dishes raining down on top of one another, sending chunks of glass into one of the bowls, onto the table, and scattering on the carpet.

The breath caught in her throat as Kiley surveyed the damage. One of the most important days of Paul's and Angelina's lives, and she'd caused this ... this *mess*.

Darcy had been near when Kiley bumped the table. She stepped gingerly over the broken glass and laid a hand on her shoulder.

"Are you alright?"

Kiley could only nod. She'd pressed the back of her hand against her mouth. Her face had to be on fire.

"I can pay for it all—the dishes, the trifle, getting the carpet cleaned." Her voice shook.

"Don't worry. It was an accident," Darcy said, inspecting the other dessert. It wasn't safe to eat. That one would be tossed, too.

Why she sought out Bret in the most humiliating of moments, Kiley hadn't a clue. But as soon as she locked eyes with him across the room, he excused himself from the person he talked to and wove between the tables to get to her.

Bret stopped in front of the trifle disaster at their feet.

"Looks like we have a little problem here," he said.

Her throat constricted with humiliation. "My foot ... it caught the—"

He guided her by the elbow through the broken glass. Already, two waitstaff were sweeping up glass and picking sponge cake and berries from the carpet.

"Let's go take a breather," Bret said quietly.

Kiley didn't need to look around to know that all eyes rested on her. Bret's hand on her back was the only reassurance that she wasn't completely alone in the world right now. Comforting—that's how it felt, even though alarm bells sounded in her head at being so close to him once again. She'd been trying to keep her distance all day, and was doing a fine job of it. It was just like her to mess this up, too.

"Are you sure you're alright?" He looked her up and down when they stood in the foyer and away from unwanted attention.

"Physically, sure." She groaned. "If you want to pretend you don't know me, I'll understand."

Bret chuckled. "But I like knowing you."

She gazed at his earnest face. Leave it to Bret to say something sweet when she fought to keep her guard up.

Sighing, she leaned forward over the check-in desk and buried her face in her arms. Thank goodness she wasn't taking any more jobs since word would get out after tonight: Kiley Byrne knew how to ruin an event in grand style.

"It's not the end of the world. Trust me," he said. "There's a back-up trifle in the refrigerator. Paul was worried there wouldn't be enough left for him to enjoy tomorrow. And the next day, and the next."

She glanced sideways at him. "Really?"

Bret nodded. "And look at it this way. At least it didn't happen before it was served. It's just leftovers at this point."

"Oh, give me time. There's still plenty of chances for me to ruin another moment or two."

"It was an accident, Kiley. Most of them have already forgotten about it, guaranteed."

Kiley looked down at her camera, scrolling through the shots she'd just taken of Sally and her friends. At least they'd turned out well. She deleted the dozen or so that came afterward of the blurred ceiling and chandelier, hard evidence of the catastrophe-in-progress.

"I have a proposal guaranteed to make you forget the trifle," Bret offered.

She narrowed her eyes at him. "Are you reneging on our deal?"

"Nope." The spark in his eyes hinted that whatever he had in mind would definitely take her mind off the accident. It wasn't a given that it would be a good thing. What did she have to lose, though?

"I'm all ears."

Chapter Eight

"What do you say we disappear into *that* for a while?" He cocked a brow and nodded to the garish pink-and-purple photo booth behind her, rented for the occasion.

It was one of the few ways he could think of to spend a little alone time with Kiley. He hadn't given up on the idea of turning their professional relationship into something more even though timing was running out. So far, she hadn't committed to seeing him after tonight.

Kiley turned around to look at it. Since she didn't give him a "no" right away, Bret held out hope it at least tempted her.

"That sounds dangerous," she said, giving him a half-smile.

"It's only as risky as you want it to be. I was only suggesting you get on the other side of a lens for once."

"Then I apologize for thinking the worst," she said as she swept back the black cloth curtain to peek inside

"Besides, I need a photo of us. For posterity. Since you're abandoning me."

She laughed. "Right. Never mind my lifelong ambition to get my MFA. Shame on me for leaving you behind."

He cocked his finger at her. "Exactly! You've finally seen the light."

"The only light I see right now is the exit sign on the back wall down the hall. My time here is almost up. And I wish it was sooner rather than later."

"Like I said, I need you in the photo booth." He snapped his fingers and patted the kitschy booth. "C'mon, it'll be fun. How many have you actually sat in?"

She made a circle with her finger and thumb. "Zero."

Bret gave a decisive nod and grabbed her hand. "Tell yourself this is a bucket-list moment if you need to."

Again, she laughed. "It's so not, but okay."

Yesss! He mentally rubbed his hands together. Something bubbled into his chest as he pulled Kiley into the booth.

Of course, the bench seat inside was smaller than expected. They couldn't be any closer unless she sat on his lap. Kiley tried maneuvering away to put a little space between them, but photo booths were designed to get everyone up close and personal.

"You okay?" he asked when he heard her let out a breath.

"Me? Oh, yes. I'm just debating on whether I'll look better with cat ears or a clown nose," she said, examining the assortment of props on a little shelf in front of them. The purple feather boa caught her eye. She wrapped it around her neck before donning the cat ears, too. "In case I start taking myself a little too seriously."

"I'm going to press that button, and that will start the countdown on the screen here." He tapped the black frame in front of them. Their reflections looked back at them. He waved. Kiley giggled and waved back.

"There will be four flashes with about five seconds between them."

"And we just smile, or what?" she said, still staring at his reflection in the dark glass.

"The 'or what' is the fun part. Just be spontaneous and weird."

"What does that mean?"

"It means get creative." He pushed the button to start the countdown. "No sense in overthinking this."

5 … 4 …

"Wait, it's going! What do I do?" She clutched his arm.

"Smile, maybe?" He glanced down at her hand. *Oh, this is going to be good.*

Kiley groaned. "I'm no good at this."

3 … 2 …

Their reflection was still visible while the numbers flashed on the screen. He nudged her in the side. "You don't look even remotely happy."

1 …

She showed all her teeth in response. "How's this?"

"It looks like you're going to bite me."

Kiley giggled.

The booth lit up when the camera clicked.

"Oh gosh, that was bright," she said. "I think I'm blind now."

He made a face. "You're being more dramatic than I ever imagined."

"It's started again. Four seconds," she said, grabbing a miniature plastic guitar from the shelf.

He followed her lead and took the plastic microphone with a sequined head. Kiley fake-strummed; he sang a garbled line of "Hey, Jude." The camera flashed.

They both threw down their props at the same time and turned to each other simultaneously. The shock of uncertainty registered on her face, and she let out a horse laugh, which Bret decided right then and there made Kiley the most beautiful woman he'd ever seen.

Flash.

"We just wasted a photo," she said, shaking her hands in mock panic. "What do we do for the last one?!"

He threw his arm around her, pressing his cheek against hers. Only she had something else in mind—he didn't know what exactly—because she was halfway onto his lap when the last photo registered. *The End* lit up on the screen.

"That's it?" She gaped at the now-darkened screen.

"Afraid so." He cleared his throat and wondered how long they could sit here with her leg draped over his before she realized it.

Kiley noticed right away and practically threw herself to the opposite side of the bench, shaking the booth.

"Sorry," she mumbled.

"Uh oh."

"I know," Kiley said with a groan. "That went by way too quickly. We *maybe* got one decent photo."

"Not that."

"What?" One big chunk of hair was flipped to the opposite side of her head when she looked at him. She could pass for a rooster with a malfunctioning comb.

Bret tapped the floor with his foot as a signal to look down.

Kiley was raking her fingers through her hair when she froze, staring at the floor. "That didn't just happen," she said.

Wilted and forlorn, the boutonniere lay at their feet.

"Oh, I'm afraid it did." A laugh escaped him. "You owe me."

Chapter Nine

Kiley unscrewed the lens and tucked it into an inner pocket in the camera bag. All of the couple's portraits were finished. She'd tried to get every face in the room before people started to leave. Over three thousand frames later, Kiley would bet she hadn't missed more than a handful.

Across the room, Bret sat at the head table with Rand Blake and another groomsman. Bret threw back his head and laughed, and the sound carried across the distance. Kiley found herself smiling, too.

Bret had yet to claim his dance for his boutonniere falling off. She'd taken him semi-seriously, but apparently Bret was only joking. Once they left the booth, he'd grown uncharacteristically quiet. The dispenser outside the booth spit out the four photos in one long strip. He'd looked long and hard at the photos before showing her. They'd laughed over their awkward poses before he tucked the strip into his jacket pocket and disappeared into the reception room again.

What had she expected? Trying to keep Bret at arm's length had been her modus operandi up until now. Why all of a sudden would she feel a hint of regret that this was their last night together? The nostalgia of photographing her last wedding for a while must have hit her. Yes, that was it. Her melancholy had nothing to do with Bret Hanning.

There was a tinkling of silverware on glass, and the room quieted.

At the head table, Bret held a glass aloft.

"I'd like to make a toast to Kiley Byrne, out intrepid photographer tonight, who will be retiring this weekend to return to school."

A murmur lifted as guests put their heads together and pointed her out to others. Kiley flushed. She almost gave Bret the cutting motion across her throat for him to knock it off before she remembered everyone in the room was looking at her. It was just like him to call attention to her this way. Kiley wanted to hide behind her hands. Didn't he remember that the trifle disaster was probably still fresh on everyone's minds?

"I've been lucky to work in her vicinity these last few years. Going forward, events on the North Shore just won't be the same without her."

Now she was sure her face registered every shade of pink. Glasses clinked together as hearty shouts went up in salute. Bret locked eyes with her and gave her a lopsided grin. He loosened his tie while still holding his glass in the air. The lights above his head illuminated his dark hair, giving him a halo effect. She raised her camera and snapped a quick photo because that was the sort of thing Bret would get a kick out of. King Bret, life of the party.

"How long have you two been dating?"

The voice came out of nowhere. Kiley turned to look over her shoulder. There was a gray-haired man across the table, peering around the flower arrangement. He stood and moved over to the empty seat next to her. She realized now that everyone at the table had scattered, leaving them alone.

"Oh, we're not. We just work together a lot. You know, as a photographer and a bartender."

"That's how I met my wife. We worked together," the man said, a wistful little smile ticking up the corners of his mouth. "I'm Joe."

"Hi, Joe. I'm Kiley." She leaned against the back of her chair. "Where did you work?"

"At Rainbow Candy in Milwaukee. She worked as a line inspector. I came in for second shift as a machine mechanic," he said, folding his hands around a water glass. "We only got to see each other in passing, but a smile here and a 'hello' there did the trick."

"A candy factory. How sweet."

His smile broadened when he got her joke. "Indeed. And she's been my sweetheart for almost sixty years."

The man seemed like he wanted to say more. Kiley wasn't in any hurry to leave him. As soon as she finished her cake, she might take a few more candid shots around the room. Then she'd call it a night.

"How long did it take you to propose?" She loved proposal stories. They were filled with such hope. As ill-fated as her own engagement turned out to be, her fiancé had proposed at the site of their first kiss—on the swing set of their grade school playground. Kiley had to give him credit for such a sentimental gesture, even if it was one of only a few admirable traits.

"Seven years." He shook his head. "I had my work cut out for me initially."

"How so?"

"All the single guys had their eyes on her. She was charming, witty, lots of smarts up there," he said, tapping his temple. "I didn't think dim-brained me had a chance."

Across the room, Bret had sat down again at the head table. One of the bridesmaids brought him a slice of cake, and they talked with another groomsman while they ate. Bret did a double-take when he noticed her looking again. An electric charge tickled the back of her neck when he grinned.

"But then I got called in to work the day shift one week. One of the guys went on vacation, and I was the only one with a flexible schedule. The first day she asked me what time I took my break. She took hers at the same time that day. And the next, and the next ..."

"And then you started dating." Kiley had all but given up hope she'd find her happily-ever-after. Those kinds of relationships were few and far between.

"My dream came true. Six months later we married."

"Seven years, though. She held you at arm's length for seven years? You must be persistent."

"The Korean War was mixed in there. Got drafted," he said and made a face. "Put a little kink in my plans."

Bret got up from his spot at the head table and gathered the cake plates from the other two. He tossed them into a garbage can near the bar and then disappeared, the crowd swallowing his retreating figure as he walked into the foyer.

Kiley sighed. Their photo booth session from earlier seized her thoughts again. The sensation of his body pressed against her side lingered and made a shiver crawl up her spine. Now she half hoped they'd see each other again after she stopped working these events. But when, Kiley had no idea. The realization made her heart ache a little.

"But she was worth the wait," Joe said, cutting into Kiley's daydream.

"Where is she? I'd like to meet her." Kiley looked around. There were plenty of older couples here. She'd taken portraits of most of them, but she didn't remember taking one of Joe and his wife together. "And I'd like to get a photo."

Joe's bottom lip sagged. "She passed last year. All that I have left is in here. The memories." He pointed to his head and tapped the spot over his heart simultaneously. "And here."

"I'm so sorry."

"A life well-lived. We went all over together. And had a beautiful family."

As heartwarming as Joe's story was, it made her feel even more down.

Joe smiled. "I'd do it all over again in the blink of an eye if I could," he said as if sensing her doubt. "It's part of the dance. And a glorious one at that."

"Uncle Joe, are you trying to steal my girl?"

Bret had snuck up on them when Uncle Joe had her attention. Pulling out a chair, Bret sat. When his thigh accidentally brushed against hers, he mumbled an apology and scooted it farther away. His complexion matched the rosy hue of the blossom on his boutonniere when she snuck a look at him.

"I thought you told me you weren't dating this rascal?" Joe rasped in a voice that seemed incapable of whispering.

"I'm ... we're not!" She looked at Bret for back up, but he'd only crossed his arms and adopted an innocuous expression.

Joe gave them a knowing smile and shook a crooked finger between the two of them. "Just friends, huh? That's the basis of any relationship worth its salt."

"I keep trying to talk her into it, Uncle Joe. She's too stubborn." He gave her a wink, and Kiley's heart did a backflip.

"The stubborn ones are worth the wait," said Uncle Joe.

Across the table, Bret's gaze bore into her. His head bobbed in agreement. The edges of his mouth ticked upward.

Someone laid a hand on her shoulder.

"Kiley?"

It was Angelina. Her face was flushed from dancing.

"Now that it's dark, Paul and I are wondering if you

might be able to take some shots of us in the moon garden," she asked. "I'm really hoping the flowers will show up. Can you do that?"

Kiley rose and set her camera bag on the table. "Of course. What a stunning backdrop that will be. Let me change lenses, and I'll meet you outside by the gazebo in five minutes."

It was perfect timing, really. She was no match for Bret *and* Uncle Joe. Between the talk of proposals, Uncle Joe's matchmaking attempts, and Bret looking dangerously handsome in his tux, she wasn't sure if her resolve would carry her through the end of the night.

Chapter Ten

The reception was in full swing when Bret saw Kiley return from taking the gazebo shots with Paul and Angelina. She popped into his field of vision across the dining room, pausing inside the doorway and scanning faces until she settled on him. It was clear she sought him out like she'd done so many times this weekend, first at the bridal luncheon yesterday, and at the wedding and reception today. Maybe it was wishful thinking, but the tension in her shoulders seem to ooze out of her when she spotted him. He leaned against the bar, talking with Matt Stetman, but Bret lifted his chin when she caught his eye.

"I hear you bought the old Peterson place," Matt said. "Let me know if you need a hand. I think Darcy and Sean won't be roping me into any more projects around here for a while."

"Thanks. I might take you up on that," he said as Kiley

met up with Angelina and Paul as they still circulated among the tables. If he had to guess, Kiley was probably calling it a night.

"What are your plans there?" Matt asked.

"I'm gutting the inside." He shrugged and made a face. "Not much to salvage. It hasn't been well-loved. But I'm in no hurry. It will be a slow and steady process, I think."

"I've heard about the condition it was left in," Matt said, bugging his eyes. Matt gleaned insider knowledge whenever he could about all the homes around Hendricks, Bret had learned from his brother Sean. "Like I said, I can help if you need it."

He'd bought the tract home on five partially wooded acres just outside of town last month. It was a sight, the house, but the property sat high on a hill with a small view of the lake over the trees on the other side of Highway 61. Sage River Creek ran through a corner of the lot. To Dalton, that was everything.

"The floor has a little slope to it. Might need a hand with that." Bret was handy, but when it came to big stuff like leveling floors, he hired out. And Matt Stetman moved a mile a minute. That was one reason Matt was one of the most sought-after carpenters around. Great guy, too. He'd lend you any tool he owned even if it meant he had to buy another for himself before you finished the job.

When he looked for Kiley again, she'd disappeared. Angelina and Paul had resumed circulating. She couldn't have left without a goodbye.

"Is something wrong?" Matt asked.

"Just looking for someone. But I think she left." He

craned his neck to see over the dance floor. Had he missed her somehow, sitting at a table or talking with someone in a shadowy corner?

Panicked, he excused himself from Matt and hurried into the foyer, looking first down each of the hallways toward the kitchen and side entrance.

No Kiley.

A hot desperation made his heart pound. He crossed the foyer to the front door, ready to hunt down her car outside. Hopefully, he wouldn't see a pair of taillights snaking down the driveway toward the highway when he opened the door. Kiley couldn't be gone just yet, not without saying goodbye.

"Hey, Bret."

His hand on the doorknob, Bret closed his eyes and exhaled. *Close one.*

"I was hoping to catch you before I leave," she said when he turned. Kiley's eyes were wide, searching. Her restless curls looked under control again, like she'd snuck into the powder room to fix her hair.

"I thought I'd missed you."

Kiley wore a wistful smile but didn't say anything.

"You weren't planning to leave without paying up, were you?"

"I thought you might have forgotten about that," she said.

"No way." Bret held out his hand. "How about one dance?"

She nodded.

Back in the dining room, the deejay had transitioned

into a quieter string of songs. Couples swayed together under the dimmed chandeliers. Bret led her to the far corner away from the speakers, where it looked a little more private.

The jarring sensation of feeling her arms draped over his shoulder for the first time gave him a chill as they moved to the music. Kiley must have felt it too, because she stiffened for a few seconds before leaning into him again, this time resting a hand against the back of his neck. He exhaled shakily. They spun slowly for the span of one song. When the next one started, Bret leaned back to see her face.

"Let's get married."

She shoved his arm and laughed, breaking the spell. "You promised no more proposals."

"The bet is over. We're back to normal."

"There is no normal with you, Bret."

His arm tightened just the slightest bit around her waist, drawing her closer. "Ah, a compliment."

Kiley snort-laughed so loud a woman wearing a beaded sheath dress and dancing with her husband gave them a scornful look.

"Okay. I'll cancel my plans for the foreseeable future." She waved a dismissive hand. "The newborn photo shoot next weekend? Forget it. The engagement session? They're out of luck."

"I'm serious. But next weekend isn't good for me, either."

"Well, I'm not serious. I don't even know you really."

"That's not true. We've worked together for almost three years. You know plenty about me."

"But not enough to get married," she said. Her eyes caught the light overhead, and they practically danced with her merriment. He fought the urge to kiss her.

He scoffed. "What do you want to know? C'mon, shoot me some questions."

"How about ... have you always been this obnoxious?"

"I've been told I'm kind of charming."

Kiley squinted at him.

"How about sometime in October, then?" he offered. "Still warm enough for an outside event, but cool enough that we don't have to worry about the ice sculpture melting too soon."

"If and when I get married someday, I will definitely not have an ice sculpture," she said.

"Okay, scratch that. They're too pretentious anyway."

"Amazing. We actually agree on something."

Kiley zeroed in on him with such an intense look that the hair on Bret's arms stood at attention.

"Okay, here's one. I'd like to know if I'm the only person you're currently proposing to." She raised her eyebrows, waiting.

"Yes."

She nodded and looked away. After a few seconds, she whispered, "Good."

Well, this is something. "Promise me October, then," he said. "That gives us a whole year to get to know each other."

Kiley laughed. "'Promise Me October' sounds like the title of a country love song."

"It could be," he said and cocked a brow. "*Our* love song. I'll write it."

She sighed, still smiling. "Seriously, why would you want to associate with such a klutz? I'm bound to ruin any important occasion."

"I'm willing to chance it."

She pulled away slightly to look him in the eye.

"I'm serious, Kiley. I'd like nothing more than to be around for any mishap you cause in the foreseeable future."

"But I'll be in Duluth soon." The smile had disappeared.

He held her a little tighter. No more joking now. This was what he'd been hoping for. "All that means is we can take it slow."

The slight nod of her head was all he needed. Bret cradled her face in his hands and brushed his lips against hers. The effect was immediate. His pulse galloped when Kiley wrapped her arms around his back, falling deeper into the kiss. They clung to each other for a few magical moments, Bret feeling his pent-up longing grip his core and take his breath away.

When she released her hold on him finally, Kiley still leaned against his chest, looking up into his face with a sleepy grin.

"Then we'll hold off on the wedding and take it one day at a time," she said. "But I'll miss the constant proposals."

"I don't see why I can't keep it up."

Kiley pulled away, looking puzzled.

"What is it?"

"Say years down the road we decide—"

"Yes?"

"To, you know, *get married*." She rolled her eyes.

"Now you're talking."

"How will I know a fake proposal from a serious one if you're propositioning me all the time?"

"Oh, you'll know." Bret loved their easy banter. He could do this all night if Kiley was game.

She looked skeptical. "How?"

"Because it will be a spectacle. A hard-to-miss, ridiculously elaborate proposal."

"I know something about hard-to-miss spectacles. I create them all the time."

"That's one of the reasons I like you."

She scrunched her shoulders and grinned. "I can't wait."

His mouth found hers again for an even deeper kiss.

"Neither can I," he said against her lips.

HER NORTH SHORE CHRISTMAS
A BLUEBERRY POINT STORY

D.E. MALONE

Chapter One

ucy Riggins tucked her chin and studied the basket of greenery on the counter with a critical eye.

Peppermint candy picks stuck here and there—check.

Two flocked reindeer suspended mid-prance—check and check.

And finally, one taffeta tartan bow attached front and center. The customer insisted on the candies and the reindeer. It wasn't what Lucy would have chosen—what was the connection between candy and forest animals anyway?—but the customer wasn't paying for Lucy's opinion. It was a nice arrangement. Not stunning or even whimsical. Just *nice*. In other words—generic. She'd have to up her game if she wanted credit for decorating the tree that earned the highest bid at the Holly Days Christmas Tree Festival. This arrangement might earn her a participation award at best.

With a heavy sigh, Lucy attached the order slip to the basket and placed it on the shelf behind the counter for pick up sometime tomorrow. She wouldn't be here. Instead, she'd set her alarm for seven o'clock, stop at Debi's Donuts for a pastry and coffee, then spend the morning at Del's Auction House, setting up the tree in time for the festival. If the day went as planned, she'd crown the tree with the handmade birch bark star and be home in time to finish decorating her own house. Then she'd have most of the afternoon to get ready for the sponsor's dinner at Blueberry Point Lodge later that night.

There were fifteen more minutes before she could lock the door and finish cleaning the flower shop. She glanced around the store, taking in the holiday decor. Lucy loved this time of year in Buds 'N Blooms. The sun had tucked itself into the horizon an hour ago, letting the night color the windows. The trees were lit, reflecting themselves a thousandfold in the surrounding glass, the scent warmers sizzled with cinnamon wax, and Christmas songs play on repeat over the store's sound system.

The sleigh bells above the door jingled. Lucy looked up.

A man locked eyes with her even before he'd closed the door behind him.

For a split second she was worried. It was dark. The only other customer she'd had in the last hour was pulling out of the parking lot onto Highway 61. Lucy didn't like the way he stared at her as he came toward the counter, but then she saw the hint of recognition on his face like he knew her. And sure enough, as he dodged the table displays and came into clear view, she realized she knew him too.

"Can I help you?" Lucy's smoothed her hair. She was sure she looked like she'd been caught in a windstorm. Unloading boxes from the truck and then unpacking them had probably taken its toll on her appearance; she's been too busy to even glance in the mirror during her six-hour shift. Lucy peeked at the dark flannel shirt she wore underneath the florist's apron. Tiny white dots of Styrofoam stuck to her sleeves.

He flashed a grin. "Just looking for an arrangement." He stood there with the smile pasted on, looking at her like...like he expected something more than an offer to help.

She picked at her shirt, suddenly self-conscious. Guys this good-looking usually didn't wander into Buds 'N Blooms. She wished she hadn't finished with the arrangement so soon. Now she didn't have anything to keep her occupied. Well, besides staring at him, trying to make the connection.

"There are plenty around the shop. If you don't find something you like, I'd be happy to do a custom one. Just let me know."

"Will do."

He stood there for a few seconds longer than necessary with slight amusement twisting his lips. He opened his mouth to say something else but must have decided against it because he tucked his hands in his pockets and turned away. Lucy wracked her brain trying to come up with his name. She'd met him last spring; she did remember that.

While he wandered around the display tables, Lucy snuck looks at him. He had the kind of face you don't forget. Prominent chin with a cleft. Deep penetrating eyes underneath heavy brows. And hair so black it melded with the darkness outside the windows. His gray tweed overcoat fit him well enough that it must have been custom made. He looked like he could afford custom tailored clothes, because only the most expensive merchandise in the store caught his attention so far.

Lucy huffed and shook her head, scolding herself for being so judgmental. *But the guy was certainly good-looking. No one would argue that.*

He studied the table of small trees hung with felted strands of balls. They were Lucy's personal favorites, little gumdrop trees. Finally he turned to her, scratching the back of his neck, and sighed loudly.

She couldn't help the smile she'd been fighting. Hopefully he wouldn't think she was laughing at him. "What's the occasion, if you don't mind me asking?"

"The occasion?" He looked at her blankly.

"Yes, is it for a birthday? Christmas? Is there a theme you're following?"

He rubbed his temples like she'd asked one question too many. His gaze wandered to the collection of felted Santas on the shelf against the wall. His eyes widened. She could almost see the exclamation point in the thought bubble pop up above his head. He was that readable. Funny.

"It's a hostess gift." He stood in front of the shelf, looking at them as if he'd found the holy grail of hostess gifts. "Actually, one of those would be perfect." He picked up the largest Santa, the most expensive one, and cradled it in the crook of his arm like a babe. Arletta Arbuckle, a local artist, would be over the moon if he bought it.

"Do you need a card to go with it?" She pointed to the small rack of cards at the end of the counter.

"I, uh…"

"And I'll wrap it for you if you'd like. Or would you like to take it with you as is?"

He set it on the counter. "I'll take it with me." He looked at her with earnest, then down at the plush figure, frowning. "Actually—"

"Have you changed your mind?" Arletta didn't have to know she'd almost sold the crown jewel of her Santas.

"No. I mean, yes, I want it. Can you wrap it for me after all?"

Lucy squinted at him. He seemed so flustered she almost felt sorry for him. *How did she know him?*

While Lucy cleared the counter for the wrapping paper, he watched her. His scrutiny made her feel like she had four hands instead of two and none of them were cooperating with tucking the Santa into a box of tissue wrap. When she wrangled the wrapping paper around the box, she misjudged the amount she needed and had to start over. It took her twice as long to tape up the box. When at last Lucy knotted the ribbon across the top and pushed it across the counter toward him with relief, he didn't move.

"You're Lucy, right? Lucy Riggins."

"Yes, I am." Now she really felt dumb. His name still escaped her. "I thought you looked familiar. We met in April, I think. At the small farms conference, right?"

His smile broadened, lines framing his eyes. Gosh, he was handsome. *Please don't make me ask your name.*

"Yes, that's right." He stuck out his hand. "Trec Kingston."

Phew.

His grip was all-encompassing, warm. She didn't want to let go just yet, but how pathetic would that be if he had to drag his hand from hers. "You were...are an investment banker."

That sparked an even broader grin. "You have a good memory," he said.

Lucy shrugged. "It comes with the job. Customer service and all."

His grin faltered a bit. "Of course. That's a great skill." He unfolded some bills from his wallet and paid for the gift.

Lucy tucked the hundred-dollar bills into the drawer and gave him his change. "Someone is going to be really excited about that gift. The artist lives in Hendricks, you know."

"Really? Maybe they already have it."

Lucy shook her head. "No. Arletta Arbuckle's Santas are one of a kind. And the one you bought?" Lucy didn't quite know how to tell him that not many people in Hendricks could afford the gift he just bought. "Trust me. Whoever gets that will be very happy."

"You're the expert," he said, slipping his wallet into the folds of his coat. His eyes lingered on hers before he gave her a tight-lipped smile.

The way he said it sounded a little patronizing. An expert of what exactly? Holiday decor? Impatiently, Lucy swiped at the loose curl that fell over her eye. Good looks aside, Lucy was ready for him to leave. It was time to close anyway.

"It's nice to see you again." She hoped he'd get the hint.

"Is it?" He admired her wrapping job, not looking at her.

Did she hear him right? Was he…teasing her?

He gave a short laugh. "I'm sorry. That was rude." He picked up the gift and backed toward the door. "Thanks for your help."

"You're welcome. Watch out for—"

Too late. He'd bumped into the table of pom-pom trees. Lucy held her breath. They wobbled like earthquake victims, but thankfully there weren't any casualties. Those would have been a nightmare to untangle before she headed home.

"I'd better get out of here," he said, opening the door.

Lucy breathed a sigh of relief. Seeing Trec Kingston again was not something she'd counted on. She smiled as she turned the lock on the door and glanced at his retreating figure in the dark. But sometimes the best surprises happen when you're least expecting them.

Chapter Two

The night was like flint, except for the scattering of snowflakes shushing against his windshield as Trec drove along Highway 61. Thankfully it wasn't far from the garden center to the Flint Hills Motel. He congratulated himself on beating the storm out of the Twin Cities, but it didn't bode well for Amelia, his assistant, who couldn't leave town until later. It was no matter; he'd just have to treat her to dinner some other time.

His thoughts returned to Lucy Riggins, and he caught himself grinning. He'd be lying if he told himself his visit to Buds 'N Blooms was solely to buy a hostess gift. It was the perfect excuse to see her again after all these months. And she'd remembered him too; he wasn't sure she would. Lucy was as pretty and unpretentious as she was during the short time they were together at the Small Farms and Sustainability Conference last spring. When she'd walked into the kickoff breakfast that first morning in that look-at-me oversized alpaca sweater and her luminous doe eyes taking everything in, he knew he had to meet her. She was a free spirit, the outfit, the light in her eyes, the way she stood out like a single flame in a dark room. He liked that. He ended up meeting her sooner than he'd expected. She spotted the empty seat beside him and dumped her shoulder bag onto the floor, letting out a loud sigh like she'd just let go of the weight of the world.

They'd exchanged small talk during the breakfast. He'd kept his eye on her during the presentations that morning. The breakout sessions in the afternoon sent them in different directions, him mentoring a small group of new business owners and her leading a hands-on workshop. When the conference attendees gathered in the inn's common rooms for dinner, Lucy was with another man. Later, Trec found out through some discreet snooping that they were dating. So he'd backed off. Not that he would have asked her out, but whatever hope he held of getting to know her better flickered out.

A few minutes later, Trec unlocked his door on Room 12 at the Flint Hills Hotel as his phone buzzed. He fished it out of his breast pocket and shouldered the door open at the same time. Inside the hotel room, a sparsely-decorated space, he dropped his bag on one of the chairs and sat on the edge of the bed.

"Hello?"

It was Amelia, his assistant.

"Trec, thank goodness! I've been trying to reach you for an hour." Her voice was breathy, uneven.

"Sorry. Reception is spotty in town, especially in this weather." He brushed the snow from his hair, the shoulders of his coat. The white flakes dusted the dark carpet for a few seconds before melting. "What is it?"

"Bad news. I'm at the hospital."

He froze. "Are you all right?"

She let out a short laugh. "Not really. Totally wiped out on the ice. Stitches, a cast, the works."

He slumped. "You're kidding?" He shook his head at the stupid comment. "No, of course you're not. How about 'I'm so sorry' instead?"

"Not as sorry as you're going to be in the next minute." The humor didn't leave her tone.

"Don't tell me I left the check there."

"You have the check, remember? I gave it to you this morning and watched you tuck it into your leather portfolio. You took that with you, right?"

It sat on the passenger seat next to him all the way from St. Paul. "Yes, I did."

"Good." She paused. The sound of a blood pressure monitor hummed in the background. Muffled voices filled the silence. Amelia cleared her throat. "You can do this, Trec."

"I can do *what* exactly?"

"Put together a nice-looking tree."

That hadn't even occurred to him during their conversation so far, that he'd have to decorate a full-sized Christmas tree now that Amelia was four hours away. In a snowstorm. With a cast and stitches no less.

She must have smacked her head too, because the

thought was crazy. "You've got to be kidding me." Embarrassment coursed through him just thinking about it.

"I believe in you," she said flatly.

"That's *your* problem. There's a reason I deal with numbers for a living. There is not a single creative bone in my body."

She laughed.

"I'm serious."

"The center is counting on us to sponsor a tree."

He shook his head. "The check will have to do. I'm not decorating the tree. No one will bid on anything I make."

"You're selling yourself short." She sighed. "I'm sorry I'm letting you down—"

"You're not, Amelia. You had an accident."

"But I don't want to let the organization down either. You know it's near and dear to my heart."

She got him. Now he'd have to come through for her. The Great Lakes Center for Disabilities was the charity of choice for the Holly Days Christmas Tree Festival. Businesses all along the North Shore were sponsoring trees to bid on. It was a huge moneymaker for the center, which had been relying on less and less state and federal aid for years, instead staying afloat with private donations.

And Amelia's younger brother had been a recipient of the center's services for years.

He dropped his forehead into his hand, looking at his shoes, still with the phone to his ear. He had no choice. It would be selfish if he refused.

"Fine."

"You'll do great, Trec. Thank you. And again, I'm so sorry this has all fallen to you."

He knew she was sincere. Amelia took her work seriously; she was the best office manager he could have hoped for when he opened his business four years ago.

"No problem." He couldn't quite erase the drone of resignation in his voice.

"I'd enlist my mother to help, but she's flying in from Denver tomorrow. Her plane will probably be delayed with this weather too."

"I can handle it. I think."

"If you get in a bind on Saturday, she'll be in Hendricks by then. She wouldn't miss this for the world."

Trec closed his eyes. Where would he even start?

Amelia cleared her throat. "So you have the tree, correct?"

"Yes, it's in the Jeep." They'd picked out a six-foot artificial one the other night after work. Her tiny compact car couldn't hold much, let alone an unwieldy box. Unfortunately, Amelia had the decorations with her in the Twin Cities.

"I'll text you some ideas for what you can buy at the store in town, simple things that even you'll be able to throw on the tree to make it look festive."

"This is going to be humiliating."

Amelia snickered then gave a short gasp. "Oh, that hurt. My stitches will open up if you make me laugh too hard. Then I'll have to claim workman's comp."

"You're not at work."

"No, but I'm consulting." She snorted into the phone. "Kidding, of course."

Trec sighed long and loud. "Just take care of yourself. I've got it under control." He rose from the bed and walked to the window, pushing the curtain aside. Lazy snowflakes fell under the streetlamp across the parking lot. His truck was already covered. "I think."

She wished him luck again and said she'd keep the phone close in case he had questions. Or needed moral support.

He'd been looking forward to this weekend for the last couple months. Another trip to Hendricks, the chance to see if Lucy remembered him, maybe have dinner together, the festivities at Blueberry Point Lodge and the festival— all things to lure him out of the office for a much-needed break. But here he'd gone from president of an investment group to Christmas tree designer in the span of five minutes, and he wasn't quite sure he'd survive the weekend now.

Chapter Three

Red ribbon...silver stars...ornament hooks. Lucy only needed three things. She wouldn't linger like she always did. It would be a grab-and-go stop inside Maisy Day's General Emporium since she was already behind schedule. Lucy tucked the list into her bag, pulled her collar tight around her throat, and opened her car door against the bitter wind.

Mill Street was deserted. It wasn't exactly good shopping weather, even if it was three weeks before Christmas. The plow had cleared the streets earlier, but more snow had accumulated. Judging by the radar on her weather app, snow was in the forecast until tomorrow afternoon. Another storm system wasn't too far behind.

Inside the store, it was quiet too. Maisy, the silver-haired owner, was bent over a crossword book at the front counter, her pencil tapping on the surface.

"Good morning, Maisy." Lucy stopped on the doormat to wipe her feet.

"Is it? I can't tell since I've been busier than a beaver on the moon." Maisy straightened, pressing her hand against her back.

Maisy and her jokes. Half the time they were so off the wall. But that made them funnier.

"I'm sure it will pick up. People can't stay inside all weekend."

Maisy's look was skeptical. "What brings you out?"

Lucy took her list out and gave it a little wave. "I need some last-minute things for the tree festival."

"I hope you find what you're looking for. I had another shipment of Christmas things coming in this afternoon, but it looks like the weather will have a say in whether it gets here."

"If not, I'll make do." She shrugged. "I probably have these things at home somewhere, but I was too lazy to dig through my Christmas stuff this morning."

Maisy pressed her lips together. "Don't tell me your tree isn't up yet."

Lucy shrugged again. "Too busy."

"You young people. Always running," she said. She looked down at the crossword book and her brow creased. "You should do more crosswords. They're very relaxing."

Lucy laughed. "Really? But you've been frowning at it since I came in."

Maisy's eyes widened at the realization and she laughed. "You got me."

With some searching, Lucy settled on a patterned red

ribbon to work with the rest of the tree's ornaments. Luckily, the silver stars that caught her eye last week were still in stock too, though she had to dig through piles of tiny bagged pinecones to find them. No hooks, though, but it wasn't a big deal. Paper clips would have to do.

She wandered into the office supplies aisle, her eyes on the stars in her hand, when she bumped headfirst into someone's shoulder. Someone's very *hard* shoulder. It didn't budge a bit.

"Excuse me, I—" she started before she realized who it was.

"Hi, Lucy."

Snowflakes crowned Trec Kingston's hair and dusted the shoulders of his overcoat like he was Father Christmas in business attire. His gaze swept over her from head to toe in bewilderment.

Lucy's heart raced. "I'm so sorry. I didn't see you coming." Her face must be in flames. It wasn't only because she was surprised to see him. It was his all-encompassing look, almost like he knew what his presence did to her insides. Almost like he *liked* it too. But that would be foolish. Guys like Trec didn't bother with women like her. They were as different as the sun and moon.

He laughed. "Obviously. No worries. But your head took the brunt of the collision. Are *you* okay?

"Just a bruised ego is all." She marveled at the dark fringe of his eyelashes and how they complemented the shape of his eyes. Merriment still lit his face. *Look away before you get lost in them and say something ridiculous.*

"So"—he looked at her basket filled with ribbon spools then at the stars in her hand—"it looks like you're decorating?"

"Yes. I'm doing a tree for the festival. I ran out of a few things so I need to restock."

His smile wavered. "I'm sure it will be one of the prettiest."

"I hope so. With the price they set for the lowest bid, bidders deserve the best." There she went putting her foot in her mouth, showing her frugality like that was all that mattered for a benefit. She ducked her head, taking the time to look at his basket. He'd picked the same patterned ribbon she had. The star ornaments too. That wouldn't do. "I should have made the connection with you and the festival. Your company is sponsoring a tree too, right?"

His eyes widened. "We wouldn't miss the opportunity."

"I wondered why you'd come all this way just to buy a hostess gift."

"The gift is for the Stetmans. Since they're hosting the sponsor dinner tonight. You'll be there too?"

She'd thought of not going. Lucy avoided big gatherings. She could hold her own in a crowd, but it always drained her. There wouldn't be too many people she knew. John and Sally, the owners of Buds 'N Blooms, would be there to represent anyway. But when she'd called Darcy Stetman to tell her she wouldn't make it, Darcy begged her to reconsider.

"Against my better judgment, yes." She shifted her weight and looked toward the register, where Maisy was back to concentrating hard on her puzzle book. Lucy hitched her shoulder. "I'm not really a fan of parties."

"You and me both." Trec paused and his magnificent brows dipped. He seemed at a loss for words. But the front door opened, bells jingling, and the blustery wind blew a magazine from the rack near the front counter. He shook his head like his concentration was broken. "I should let you get back to shopping."

Lucy wasn't about to trade her ribbon in for another pattern. It complemented the ornaments and pom-pom strings she'd already bought. *He'd* have to exchange his, but how could she change his mind?

"So are *you* in charge of the decorating?"

"Oh, ah...no. I'm picking up a few things for my assistant. She'll do the honors." *Was he blushing?*

"Can I give you some friendly advice?"

His brows shot up. "I'm all ears."

"I saw a nice patterned ribbon that will go with the other things." Lucy hooked her finger at him. "Follow me."

His smile was wistful as they made their way through the store back to the Christmas aisle. She brushed his arm at one point, as they walked side by side, a tickle of pleasure dancing up the back of her neck.

"Here we go." She rummaged through the spools, picking a dark pink-and-red plaid with metallic green threads crisscrossing the ribbon. "This will go perfectly with what else you have."

Trec turned the spool over in his hands. "I see what you're doing."

She froze. "What?"

"You have the same ribbon. You don't want to compete with me."

"I-I don't think there's much—"

He snorted derisively. "Much competition?"

"I was going to say 'much choice.'" She snatched the spool from his hands and tossed it back into the box. "I was trying to be helpful."

His teeth flashed with a grin. "No worries. I was only having fun."

Now that he'd stirred her up, Lucy was more embarrassed than ever. She had to get out of there before it set the tone for her whole day. "I'm sure your assistant will do a wonderful job with whatever ribbon you choose. Good luck with your tree."

His laughter followed her as she met Maisy again at the front counter and quickly paid for her things, not wanting to chance another meeting with him before she left the store.

Of course he didn't need her advice. He managed million-dollar portfolios. His clients were probably some of the wealthiest people in the Twin Cities. While he dealt with numbers, multiplying earnings into unimaginable wealth, money she couldn't dream of earning during the entire course of her career as a floral designer, she played with silk flowers and baskets. How hard was it to choose between plaid versus polka-dot ribbon anyway, for heaven's sake?

Chapter Four

Trec adjusted his tie as he stared at Blueberry Point Lodge through his windshield, lit up like a holiday diorama glowing from the inside out. He counted five Christmas trees in the windows on this side of the house alone.

Christmas trees.

If he never saw another artificial fir for the rest of his life, he'd count himself a happy man. For the better part of the afternoon, he battled lights and wired ribbon, glitter balls, and dollar bills that he painstakingly folded accordion-style and tied with red yarn. He could take credit for that idea at least. Amelia thought his dollar bill birds were brilliant.

Still, the tree looked sad compared to the twenty or so other trees inside Del's Auction House. People clearly took decorating for the benefit seriously. He'd never paid attention before. Amelia had always taken care of it. This was the first year he'd cleared his calendar to come, agreeing with Amelia that it was good for business. Some joke. Now he'd probably lose business once everyone got a look at his pathetic tree.

Lucy had already finished the floral shop's tree and left by the time he arrived. Of course it was stunning. And of course his company's tree was assigned the spot right next to hers. His humiliation was at an all-time high as he was forced to add the generic decorations right next to her work of art.

Trec closed his car door and followed the walkway to the porte cochere. Darcy and Sean Stetman greeted him and the couple ahead of him. A doorman in a red velvet vest took his coat while reciting what the evening would entail—cocktails, a buffet, and then a short slide presentation about the Great Lakes Center for Disabilities. The house smelled of fir and sweet scents. He followed the couple into one of two large sitting rooms showcasing period furnishings. The overstuffed sofas and armchairs looked comfortable, arranged in small groupings. People lined up before an immense bar for cocktails. A harp player sat in one corner on a tufted yellow chair, gliding her fingers across the instrument as music drifted through the rooms. Trec joined the cocktail line, surveying the room with his hands in his pockets. A gigantic tree stood in the farthest corner of the room. He couldn't begin to guess how many strands of lights it took. Metallic gold balls the size of small cantaloupes dangled from the boughs. What were those crocheted-looking ornaments? If he could get a closer look—

Stop. He could quit obsessing about his failed decorating job. Amelia had tried helping him over the phone, patiently critiquing the flurry of photos he sent her way. In all, it had taken him two hours to add the lights, ribbon and garland, stars, and dollar-bill ornaments. Now Trec caught himself frowning as he studied the huge tree in the Stetmans' house. Whoever had decorated this tree had serious talent.

"Don't you clean up nicely."

Trec turned to find James Werth, one of his clients, giving him an overly dramatic appraisal.

"I go all out once a year. Your timing is impeccable." Trec straightened his tie. "But seriously, it's for a great cause."

James rocked back on his heels and surveyed the room. "This place is really something, isn't it? It was on my radar back when it was for sale."

"It's stunning, and probably in the best hands. You don't have time for a place like this."

James threw back his head and his meaty jowls shook with laughter. Along with an obsession for filling his garage with Bugattis and regular trips to his homes in Belize and Nice, James also indulged his appetite. Often.

"You think you can manage my calendar as well as my portfolio? Let's play it safe and leave that to my wife." James paused. "Speaking of which, any idea who the pretty little package is in the red dress?"

Trec winced at James's question. He liked looking just as much as any other man, but the demeaning remark was beneath him. When he spotted the one who'd drawn

James's interest, he bristled even more. Lucy had come into the room. She spotted him, giving him a small wave and a lopsided grin.

"No one that would interest you." Trec glanced pointedly at James's wife across the room. "Or Mary, for that matter."

James caught his meaning and a twinkle brightened his already glassy eyes. "Am I stepping on toes?"

Trec threw back his shoulders and watched Lucy work her way across the room in a graceful, unobtrusive way. If only he were so lucky. The red dress, satin with a lace overlay, hugged her curves and complemented her fair skin. His blasted tie seemed to have tightened since he spotted her. He dug two fingers into his collar to relieve the pressure. "Not at all. I'm only saving you from yourself."

They ordered drinks and moved away from the bar, taking an unoccupied spot near a grandfather clock against the far wall. While James droned on about the Stetmans lack of taste for decent wine, Lucy monopolized almost every minute of Trec's thoughts. The room had become more crowded as guests poured into the house, but he'd developed tunnel vision. Lucy stood next to the giant tree, having a very earnest conversation with another woman about it. Every hand gesture, every cock of her eyebrow, every twitch of her lips as she listened held his undivided attention. He'd better stop or she'd catch him staring like a pubescent teenager in the throes of his first crush.

"Either I'm boring you deaf or the scenery on the other side of the room is a major distraction," said James while simultaneously clinking his wineglass against Trec's tumbler.

"I'm admiring the tree." He lifted his glass toward it, pointing. "I had to decorate one of those things today. Amelia had an accident and couldn't make the trip. So the job fell to me."

"Sorry to hear that." James snorted. "But I would have bowed out. Don't have the patience for such things."

"That was my thought too," Trec said, shrugging. "The Center has helped Amelia's brother a great deal. I did it for her more than anyone."

James clapped Trec on the shoulder. "You're a good man, Trec."

"Except I ran out of time before they closed the auction house this afternoon. As of right now, it's nothing short of awful."

"I'm sure it's not that bad." James sipped his drink, surveying the room. "You've always amazed me. Down to earth, humble." He laughed. "All the things I never could wrap my head around."

Trec wasn't about to agree with him, but what James said was spot on. "I didn't hear you say 'creative,'" he joked.

James rubbed a hand over his bald head. "Maybe not in the decorating sense, but you're a creative genius when it comes to building portfolios."

On that he could agree with James. He'd worked hard to make that a reality.

"Listen. If this tree is as bad as you say it is, why don't you get back in there and tweak it before tomorrow?"

"Can't. The auction house is closed."

"Do you think I'd suggest it if I didn't have a solution? Del Arbuckle and I are good friends. I can get you in early tomorrow morning before it opens."

He could at least redo the ornaments. It wouldn't be an exaggeration to say he'd thrown them on. After one of the festival volunteers gave him a thirty-minute warning that the building would be locked, he'd panicked. He'd wrestled with the lights and ribbon way too long.

"How early?"

"How long do you need?"

"An hour tops."

"It'll have to be around six o'clock then," said James. "The festival opens at eight o'clock with a breakfast with Santa. You'll want to be out of there well before the volunteers show up again."

"That will work." He swirled the liquid in his glass, clinking the ice cubes together before he downed the drink, glancing at Lucy over the rim. Trec felt better. Maybe his company's tree wouldn't be the worst-looking one after all.

His confidence boosted, Trec excused himself from James and made his way over to the decadent buffet. Two eight-foot tables were covered with platters of artfully arranged hors d'oeuvres. A four-foot-high planter of fir branches and silver and gold balls stood on a center table, and smaller mirrored vases held birch twigs entwined with fairy lights. There were crystal bowls of caviar, platters stacked high with white-chocolate strawberries and fresh mint leaves, and at least a dozen silver trays of canapes, skewers, and pastries, all with accompanying name cards written with a calligraphic hand.

Trec's plate was filled in no time. He picked one of the delicacies and sampled it while he found Lucy amongst the crowd. Darcy Stetman held her by the arm while the two of them looked to be sharing a joke. Even though Lucy's back was to him, he wasn't disappointed with the view. He popped the rest of one canapé into his mouth and plucked another. After a few of these smoked trout canapes, he might work up the nerve to talk to her again.

A few minutes later, Lucy let him off the hook by approaching him first. Of course she headed his way right when Trec stuffed a lobster roll into his mouth. The pastry was dense, chewy; he couldn't quite swallow it fast enough.

"Hi there," she said simply, grinning up at him like she knew the difficulty he was having swallowing the blasted thing. "Enjoying the party?"

"Of course. You?" He hoped the bread wasn't pasted in between his teeth.

"As parties go, it's wonderful."

He ran his tongue discreetly over his teeth while she glanced around the room until he felt confident that smiling wouldn't reveal what had just been on his buffet plate. "But don't tell me: You'd rather be at home in sweats, watching cheesy rom-coms, and drinking chamomile."

Lucy opened her mouth. The corners of her eyes crinkled in amusement. "How did you read my mind?"

He shrugged and tried not to marvel at the way the

skin above her neckline flushed. Did he embarrass her? "I have three sisters who love to FaceTime me from the comforts of their couches."

She laughed. He must make her self-conscious; she couldn't look at him for long without glancing elsewhere. A gold filigree earring dangled prettily from her ear.

Trec handed his empty plate to one of the waitstaff then brushed his hands together. "So you decorated your tree for the auction in no time. You were gone before I showed up."

Lucy exhaled loudly. "It's been a crazy day. I had to put some finishing touches on that tree before I could start on the auction one." She lifted her chin toward the opulent tree in the corner. "I was so efficient I finished in record time."

No wonder the Stetmans' tree was so stunning.

She looked back at him. "How did your tree turn out?"

Trec resisted the urge to complain. No pro wanted to hear a beginner whine about his lack of skill. He should know. His father had little patience with teaching him the ropes of the business. What Trec had learned was because of his own determination.

"I surprised myself. It's not too bad." It wasn't quite a lie. Tomorrow morning James would let him into the auction house and he'd spruce it up. No pun intended.

"I can't wait to see it." She waved at someone behind Trec. Her fingers drifted down his shoulder, taking them both by surprise. His throat tightened when she held on to his forearm, her pale, delicate hand in sharp contrast against his dark jacket. "Listen. Darcy wants to introduce me to someone. I'll see you tomorrow, right?"

"You bet. Bright and early."

As Lucy joined Darcy across the room, Trec wondered what tomorrow would bring. He didn't count on drawing a high bid for his tree. What he did hope for was Lucy agreeing to dinner after the auction. That would be worth more than winning some tree-decorating contest.

Chapter Five

As soon as Lucy stepped outside the next morning, she regretted her wardrobe choice. Snow swirled in undulating patterns on the sidewalk. The twin firs on either side of her porch bent over, bowing to the wind. Her fleece-lined sweater and wool leggings were no match for the cold, not to mention the knee-length buffalo-check skirt. But she'd bought it for the festival and it was too late to change anyway. Resigned, she pulled her collar tight against her neck and hurried to her toasty car. Thank goodness for automatic start.

Debi's Donuts was abuzz when she entered the shop a few minutes later. She'd grab a pastry and a drink then be out the door. But it was crowded as usual, a line snaking among the tables to the door. Behind the counter, Debi Thomas and her two employees darted back and forth filling orders.

Lucy breathed in the sweet scent of sugary yeast and freshly brewed coffee. Debi's was the go-to place in Hendricks if one wanted pastries with a side helping of gossip. There were only six tables in the place, way too few for the amount of business it drew but the shop was small. Still, Debi made the most of it with a decor that was eclectically cozy. Vintage bakery signs decorated the yellow bead board walls. Her ceramic cookie jar collection sat high on the one shelf encircling the entire shop.

Lucy was checking her phone messages when her ears perked up at the words "drama this morning." She glanced to the two women in front of her who were deep in their conversation as they waited in line.

Someone was at the auction house earlier before the volunteers showed up. A few trees were vandalized.

Vandalized? Who would do such a thing?

Apparently they know who it is, but it's hush-hush.

Someone local?

The other woman shrugged.

Trees vandalized? It better not be hers. She'd put three hours into that tree. The festival was opening in an hour. There wouldn't be much time for repairs if hers was the unlucky tree.

While these thoughts ran amok in her mind, the line in front of her grew shorter.

"Hey there, Lucy. What can I get you?" Debi drummed her fingers on the counter, waiting. She wore her ever-present smile and a Christmas-themed apron. Debi's apron collection was impressive and envied among the locals.

"A latte and a cinnamon roll, please." She dug into her bag for her wallet.

Debi took the five Lucy handed her and tucked it into the drawer. "I'm hoping to come to the festival after work. I heard there's a record number of sponsored trees this year. That's great."

"It has gotten bigger each year, but I think once word got out that the money would benefit the disabilities center, it exploded."

Debi slid the container with the roll across the counter toward Lucy. "Speaking of explosions, did you hear about what happened at the auction house this morning?"

"I just heard someone mention it. Any idea what happened?"

"I've picked up bits and pieces. One of the sponsors broke into the auction house super early. A big-time banker from the Twin Cities is what I heard. Used decorations from other trees like the place was his own personal shopping mart or something." Debi waved dismissively. "But you know small-town gossip."

A banker from the Twin Cities? She could make a pretty good guess who that might be. But stealing ornaments? No way.

"Lucy?"

Lucy was so engrossed in the idea that Trec sabotaged the festival trees she almost forgot her change.

Debi handed it over. "I hope the rumors aren't true."

Lucy dropped the coins into the tip jar. "Yeah, me too. I guess I'll find out soon enough."

The auction house was a few blocks away on the

corner of Mill and Rimrock. Parking was already scarce. Lucy left her car at the public lot next to D & G Grocery and hoofed it the two blocks. The snow had grown heavier since she'd left home. It crept over the tops of her boots and dampened her leggings. The weather forecast called for six more inches at least.

There must be some truth to the gossip spreading like wildfire in town, because when Lucy walked into the auction house, a group surrounded a few of the trees. Trec was in the middle of it all. While he talked with Agnes DeLina, the festival's organizer as well as the owner of the auction house, Del Arbuckle, Trec's face registered embarrassment and anger. When he spotted Lucy coming toward him, it flamed.

Lucy came up behind the group and everyone turned to her, opening up the circle. That's when she got a look at her tree. Her exquisite mess of a tree.

"What's going on? What happened here?"

It had clearly fallen over, but someone had pulled it upright again. Two other trees were still lying on their sides. A few glass ornaments were shattered on the floor, their shiny fragments glinting from the overhead lights. Ribbon and lights tangled together like a Christmas-themed spiderweb. At least her birch bark star survived. It sat atop the tree, like it was relieved to be surveying the damage from a safe distance.

Agnes clucked under her breath. "That's what we're trying to figure out."

"For the last time, I'm telling you James Werth let me in. He's a good friend of yours." Trec was nearly shouting and appeared like he wanted to jab his pointer finger into Del's chest if he didn't check himself in time.

Del's expression was one of incredulity. "James Werth? I've talked with him twice and that makes us good friends? He was supposed to be showing the building to a potential tenant, not sneaking his buddies in here during off hours."

"It didn't occur to me that he wasn't telling the truth." Trec ran one hand through his hair. He wouldn't look at Lucy. "And I was hardly sneaking. I'm one of the sponsors!"

Agnes looked at the mess over the rims of her glasses. "Well, you're certainly not going to bring in any bids for your tree with it looking like that."

Trec gave a short, humorless laugh. "I need some air." He stormed off without another word and disappeared through the foyer doors.

Lucy turned to Agnes. "What happened exactly?"

Agnes bent over to help Del pick up one of the two fallen trees. "Some mishap. Honestly I was so mad I didn't pay much attention to his bumbling attempt at explaining himself."

Del stood again, red-faced with the exertion. He kicked the green extension cord with his foot. "He said this was the problem."

The three of them studied the cord as if it should offer more of an explanation.

"I'm so sorry, Lucy," said Agnes. "Is it fixable with only"—she checked the clock on the wall across the room —"fifty minutes until the doors open?"

Lucy rearranged the lights closest to her. "Yes. It's doable." She looked down at the other tree, which still lay on its side. "Is that Trec's tree?"

Agnes sighed. "I'm afraid so. It wasn't very inspiring before. Now..." She shook her head. "We should probably just move it to the back room. I'm not sure it's salvageable, especially if it's at his mercy."

Lucy laughed while she untangled a portion of ribbon. "I'm sure his assistant will be able to work some magic."

"Assistant?" Agnes wore a confused expression when Lucy looked over at her again.

"Yes, his office assistant. Didn't she do the decorating?"

The older woman gave Lucy a skeptical look. "No. This was all him. It was almost funny watching him struggle with it yesterday. I had to kick him out the door at four o'clock. I think he would have stayed all night fighting with that thing if I'd let him."

Now Lucy felt bad. She thought he'd had help. No wonder he looked so frazzled. And to be interrogated by Agnes and Del like that. It still didn't explain why three trees had suffered such devastation.

Agnes gave a short whistle and signaled to someone across the room. "I'll get his out of the way and leave you alone."

But Lucy stopped untangling for a moment and touched Agnes on the arm. "No. Leave it."

"Honey, this isn't worth the trouble."

She smiled at Agnes. "I'll see what I can do. I'd hate for

the Center to lose the income from one less tree to bid on. I'm sure he's mortified."

Agnes sighed. "I was probably a little too testy with him."

Lucy bit her tongue.

"If he comes back inside, I'll talk to him. I'd hate to lose his support." Agnes gave the tree one last look. "If anyone can save this pathetic thing, you're the one."

Chapter Six

The distance from the auction house to his snow-covered Jeep was far enough to cool his temper. Trec unlocked the door, climbed in behind the steering wheel and let out a loud sigh. The snow blanketed the windows, cocooning him inside the dark interior. It was the perfect place to collect his thoughts, away from prying eyes and loose tongues.

He leaned against the headrest, watching his cold breath cloud the air in front of him. What a complete disaster. They'd accused him of purposely destroying trees, wouldn't even listen to him explain that it'd been an accident, like he was some common vandal. Why would he do that? It would be a total blow to his reputation with his business name all over the publicity for this event. The only thing he could be accused of was being clumsy. He'd been rushing around so blindly this morning trying to fix the tree that his foot caught under the large extension cord snaking across the floor. His tree was the first casualty. And while unwinding the cord from his ankle, he'd pulled it too hard and took out two more.

Trec groaned, replaying the scene in his mind. Having grown up in a small town, he knew rumors ran rampant. What did it matter? He was an outsider. He'd be gone by tomorrow and then the locals on the gossip circuit would find someone else to fire them up. If he left now, he could take it slow through the storm and make it back to the Twin Cities well before dinner. Or at least get as far as Duluth. But even before the thought fully formed, he shut it down. That would mark him a coward and make him look even more guilty. He ran a reputable firm. Hundreds of clients entrusted his company with their retirement nest eggs. He wouldn't run out of town like a shame-faced deserter, his image in shreds. No, he would use this self-imposed time-out to craft a sincere apology and then work double time to undo the damage to his tree.

Lucy.

What kind of impression did she have of him now? No doubt Agnes DeLina and the auction house owner were filling her in on his crime. She'd want nothing to do with him after today. If he put himself in her shoes, he couldn't blame her.

As his anger subsided, the cold crept into his Jeep. Trec turned on the car, cranking the heat way up, and took out his phone. He should check on Amelia.

"I was just thinking about you," Amelia said after she picked up on the second ring.

"Don't tell me: You had a premonition of me

accidentally strangling myself with strands of Christmas lights."

"Not exactly..."

"Or did I bleed to death from a paper cut after folding all those dollar-bill dove ornaments? I could probably fold the things in my sleep if I had to."

There was silence on the other end. Then, "Trec, you sound kind of bitter. Did something happen?"

He didn't mean to unload on her. He needed a reset button. "I called to see how you're doing."

"I'm fine," she said slowly. "My foot is propped on a pillow, there's a holiday soundtrack playing on repeat, and I'm finishing my Christmas shopping online. Plus, these pain meds help the aches I didn't know I had until now. Tom has been wonderful, of course."

"I don't doubt that for a second. Sounds like the perfect Saturday. Well, minus the cast and stitches."

She laughed. "How's *your* day going?"

"Not good."

"I can tell. What's happened?"

He filled her in on his early morning plans, which had spiraled out of control. "I can handle millions of dollars in a volatile market, but these prickly festival organizers are ruthless."

"You'll just have to go back in there and make it right."

"That's the problem. I have to redo the tree. It was hard enough the first time."

"Don't worry. Once you hand them that check, they'll forget everything."

"I sure hope so."

"How's what's-her-name? Lucy was it?"

He paused. "What do you know about Lucy?"

Amelia laughed long and loud this time. "You had me call the floral shop last week, remember? You wanted to talk to her about a custom arrangement and needed to know her schedule."

"I did, didn't I?"

"Yes." She paused. "So?"

"I was going to ask her to dinner tonight. But after the tree debacle, I'm probably the last person she wants to be seen with."

"Don't sell yourself short. Go back in there and pretend it never happened."

"Impossible."

"Don't make me defy doctor's orders to come bail you out of this."

It was Trec's turn to laugh. How'd he get so lucky with an assistant like Amelia?

"If I'm not at the office on Monday, you'll know it didn't turn out well."

He said goodbye and tucked the phone back into his pocket. Heat continued to pour out of the vents, blasting Trec with hot currents of air. He switched it off, sweating profusely. It might be nothing compared to the heat he'd feel in a few minutes when he walked back into the auction house. Feet to the fire, he'd try to make right his mistake. He'd also find out if Lucy would take him up on his offer of dinner out or if his chance with her had gone up in flames too.

Chapter Seven

Lucy slipped the hook of the last ornament over the branch tip, adjusted another, and called it finished. Her tree hadn't suffered much damage after all. The lights and ribbon took the worst of the assault, but she'd put up enough trees in her thirty-one years to win the lightning round of tree decorating if there were such a thing. Thankfully, the tree sponsored by Northshore Insurance and the third victim of Trec's clumsiness wasn't in bad shape either. Someone had already stepped in to fix it.

Trec's tree was a different story. He clearly didn't know what he was doing. Either that or impatience got the best of him. Some boughs were wrapped with lights more than once, others not at all. He'd skipped half of one side, the part of the tree that faced the wall. And then tripping over the extension cord pulled the tree over, finishing it off. Luckily the red balls were plastic and the dollar-bill dove ornaments were hardy enough to withstand the accident. She checked the time on her phone. Twenty minutes before the doors opened. She'd have to work quickly.

His voice interrupted her thoughts moments later. Lucy dug into her duffel bag for more hooks, using the opportunity to glance at him talking with Del near the concessions. His words were muffled, lost in the commotion of the festival preparations, but his tone had lost its edge from earlier. Its deep timbre was soothing and exciting at the same time. How would it sound as a whisper in her ear?

Stop.

The lack of sleep must be getting to her. Daydreaming about someone she'd talked to less than a handful of times was crazy. After today, she wouldn't see him again until next year when he sponsored another tree. *If* he sponsored another tree. Lucy moved to the other side of his tree, out of sight. She didn't want him to see her just yet, not until she'd finished. Maybe it was silly, but she didn't want Trec thinking he owed her anything for doctoring his tree. Lucy stole another look at him through the branches. She hummed along with Mariah Carey's version of "All I Want for Christmas" playing throughout the room. The way his shoulders filled out the folds of his overcoat was nothing short of intoxicating. He was so tall she'd have to stand on her toes to link her arms around his neck for a kiss. And what might that first kiss feel like, soft and lulling? Like sinking into a warm bath? Or filled with heat, scorching her lips? Lucy let out a soft snort, smiling. Maybe a daydream or two wasn't *that* crazy if it made her feel this lighthearted.

She wasn't going to finish in time. Trec shook Del Arbuckle's hand and the auctioneer pointed to Trec's tree. Lucy didn't miss Trec's look of surprise when he noticed most of the decorations already in place. Maybe she should duck into the restroom to compose herself. A few steps backward and she'd be out of sight in no time.

"Lucy!"

Too late. He crossed the space between them in long strides, a smile lighting his face.

She couldn't look him in the eye. Her face must be on fire; it certainly felt like it. "This really wasn't in that bad of shape. I just tweaked the ribbon, put the bird ornaments back on and—"

His mouth hung open in disbelief. "You did more than that. This looks amazing!" he said. "Where did these come from?" He touched a beaded silver snowflake, sending it spinning.

Lucy shrugged. "They were extras that didn't fit on my tree. Just last year's stock from the shop. Not a big deal."

"I owe you then. Your business doesn't need to cover for my lack of talent and supplies."

"Really, it's nothing. I have a few more to put on. Here, you can pay me back by helping." She gave him a handful of snowflakes. Her fingers brushed his palm, and a tingle sent a charge up her arm.

The touch didn't escape Trec either. His eyes lingered on hers for a few seconds before he tried to separate the first snowflake from the rest. The struggle resulted in one snowflake shedding its beads onto the floor, scattering in every direction. He laughed, shaking his head. "I'm so out of my element it's not even funny."

Lucy had never met someone so clumsy who looked so decidedly unclumsy. "If it's any consolation, you look perfectly at ease."

"Seriously? I feel like I have octopus tentacles for arms and three left feet."

Gritting her teeth, she chuckled. "That's not a good visual."

While Trec hung the snowflakes, he kept glancing at her. His expression was passive except for his eyes. They were studying, judging, questioning. Seducing too. Okay, maybe that was her *thinking* he was trying to seduce her. She'd had a wild imagination all her life.

He'd opened his mouth a few times as if to say something. Each time Lucy held her breath. Being near him had started to affect her breathing. She cursed herself for having so little control over herself.

"Okay, this should do it," he said. Trec took a step back and stuck his hands in his pockets. "Looks pretty good for what it suffered this morning."

Lucy clamped her lips together when she saw what he'd done. Oh boy.

He grimaced. "What's wrong?"

Just say it.

"All of the stars are on your side. It needs to be...balanced."

His expression went from pleased to solemn in a second. "I can see that now."

"Sorry."

"No worries," he said, plucking a few ornaments off to redistribute them. His arm brushed hers as he came to her side of the tree. She inhaled the woodsy scent of his cologne as he stood next to her. "If it means getting a higher bid, a little extra work is nothing. I'm just glad I have connections." Trec winked at her.

"These were a nice touch." She touched one of the dollar-bill birds. "Did you make them?"

Trec chuckled. "I'm a little embarrassed to admit it, but yes."

"Embarrassed?"

"I didn't expect it to be so cathartic after stressing about decorating a tree."

She smiled. "At least you found something to enjoy during this whole ordeal, right? They're very cute."

He worked in silence for a few more minutes while Lucy consolidated the packing materials and boxes, trying to think of something interesting to say. They had nothing in common. What could a floral designer talk about that a big-city investment banker might find interesting?

He brushed his hands together when he placed the last snowflake. "Now what?"

Lucy glanced toward the judge's table near the front door. Agnes had donned her festive sweater, the handmade one by her sister Arletta Arbuckle, owner of Handmakery Studio and Del's wife. It had bows and jingle bells and appliquéd poinsettias as big as salad plates. A person could hear her coming from the other side of

Broman County. Agnes hugged a clipboard to her chest, a sure sign the auction was starting soon.

"They'll start the bidding process any minute now. They'll auction the first tree, then do another tree every fifteen minutes." She looked back at Trec. "You don't have to stay. It's a long process if...if it's not your thing."

Trec took a step back, hand to his chest with mock offense. "Not my thing? What do you mean? All this jolly jingle holiday mingle stuff gets me in the spirit."

Again, Lucy laughed. "Suit yourself. I didn't want you to feel obligated."

"As long as there's fresh coffee and those cinnamon buns I saw over on the refreshment table, I'm good."

"So that's what drew you back to Hendricks, Debi Donuts."

Something sparked in his eyes, but his smile faltered a bit. "How'd you know?"

The room felt smaller then, the walls closing in on them. Her eyes were drawn to his lips. "You have that look about you."

One corner of his mouth curved upward. "Tell me more about this look."

The dark lashes hooding his eyes mesmerized her until the skin crinkled around them again like he knew how they affected her. Words ping-ponged around in her mind. *Irresistible. Mischievous. Heartbreaker.*

She'd almost come up with an answer to his question when an arm slipped around her shoulders, squeezing her tight.

"Why didn't you give me a heads-up this morning? I could have helped with...something."

Sam Campbell.

Her ex-boyfriend had the annoying habit of sneaking up on her from behind and giving her one-armed bear hugs. She didn't like it when they were dating, and she liked it even less now. Lucy eased herself out from under his arm, sidestepping away from him.

"Honestly, there's nothing for you to do. I've already finished." What Sam was doing here was anyone's guess. For one thing, it was too early in the morning for him to be awake. Secondly, she hadn't spoken to him in weeks. It was just like him to pop in, acting like he was an important part of the action when in reality he avoided work like it was a disease.

"Sam, you remember Trec Kingston. He gave the financial presentation at the small farms conference in April." Keeping the annoyance from her tone wasn't easy.

"Of course," Sam said, grabbing Trec's hand, pumping it like a well handle. "Are you giving Lucy tips on managing her wealth?" He emphasized "wealth" then laughed.

Lucy snorted at the insult. "*Sam.* Really?"

"Sorry. Just joking." He hooked his thumb at her, looking at Trec. "She's always taken herself too seriously."

There was a slow rise and fall of Trec's chest. His smile tightened. "I may be a bit biased, but thinking about one's financial security at any point in your career is a smart thing to do."

Sam shrugged it off. "I suppose."

She cringed at Sam's coarseness. She'd never noticed it with such clarity until now. How could she have dated him for three months without seeing it? It was three months too long, that was for sure.

Trec straightened and looked like he wanted to escape. He'd lost the playful expression from a moment ago. "I'm going to grab one of those rolls while they're fresh," he said to her. Then more curtly, "Sam, take care."

He made his way over to the refreshments where pastry boxes were lined up, lids open.

"Is that the guy you broke up with me for?" Sam asked incredulously. "If so, he's a total step down for you."

He also fabricated the most incredible scenarios, if only to paint himself the victim.

Lucy crossed her arms. "I'm not even going to answer that question."

"Because it's true, isn't it?"

She squared her shoulders and looked Sam in the eye. "I'm busy today. There's nothing for you to do, so I'd rather you find someone else to help."

"Whoa. Get to the point why don't you?" He threw up his hands and walked away.

Lucy sighed, watching Sam amble into the kitchen, probably hoping to find an unattended box of donuts. He gave Trec a look when he passed him and shook his head in an exaggerated show of disbelief.

She condensed the last of her boxes. At the bottom she found one last star ornament she missed hanging. After looking for an empty space on Trec's tree, she found the perfect spot. Across the room, she caught Trec's eye.

Alone, he leaned against the wall, watching her. He shook his head slowly, wearing a crooked grin, as if making fun of her precision. His look was electrifying.

Sam's accusation of her dumping him for Trec was partially right, she mused. If dating Trec had even been an option, then yes, she would have broken up with Sam in a heartbeat.

Chapter Eight

Six hours later, the festival committee had moved steadily through the trees, announcing the highest bidder for each one. Trec was relieved when his tree went for well over the minimum bid. It was a small amount compared to most entries, but considering the near-disaster with decorating, he called it a win.

All morning he'd caught that weasel Sam shooting him looks as if he were competition for Lucy's attention. At one point, Sam openly glared at him while Trec presented Agnes with the $1,000 donation from his company. Trec was on his way to have a few words with him when a potential client sidetracked him. It was just as well. Causing a scene at a Christmas tree festival probably wasn't in his best interests. But Trec didn't like Sam's backhanded comment about Lucy's income, and Trec *really* didn't like how Sam had slung his arm around her shoulders when he'd first appeared, claiming Lucy like she was his property. But Trec wasn't one to step on toes, no matter how unworthy those toes might be.

Trec listened to the auctioneer begin his call for bids on the last tree—Lucy's. She was across the room, almost lost among the number of people still here. To him, a spotlight might as well be shining on her from above. Lucy was a heady mixture of indifference and poise. Her wardrobe spoke of confidence, but she hung back as if she didn't like attention. The crossed arms were a sure sign. He couldn't take his eyes off her.

The bidding began at three hundred dollars, which quickly escalated to five.

"Do I hear five fifty? I have five fifty," the auctioneer called, pointing to the back of the room.

"How about six hundred? Six hundred it is." He signaled to the woman standing near Trec.

With each increment, Lucy's eyes grew larger.

"There's seven hundred over in the right corner.

"Let's see if we can get seven fifty. There's a seven fifty."

Trec glanced at the woman next to him, waiting for her to up the bid. As if on cue, she raised her hand.

"There's eight hundred over there," Del called as he pointed to the woman again.

"Do I hear eight fifty? Eight fifty?"

Trec scanned the room. No hands were raised. Lucy's open-mouthed expression was pure delight.

Del's voice cut through the silence. "Sold for eight hundred!"

There was a collective gasp, then applause. Lucy's

hands flew to cover her mouth. Her expression alone was worth the four-hour drive through a snowstorm.

DURING THE TIME THAT FOLLOWED THE winning bid on Lucy's tree, Trec refilled his coffee, grabbed another donut and enjoyed the scene. He lost Lucy in the crowd as people swarmed to congratulate her. Then she appeared again against the backdrop of a handmade quilt hanging on the wall. Time for photos of the winner.

Of course Lucy's tree won. He smiled for her when Agnes presented her with a golden tree trophy a few minutes later. Lucy hoisted it high for a photo, then tucked it discreetly in the bag on her shoulder when the photographer moved away.

With the crowd finally thinning, Trec took the opportunity to catch her alone.

"Congratulations."

"Thank you," she said before averting her eyes. "I can't believe someone paid that much money for it."

"I can. It's beautiful. You're very talented."

She smiled again, but this time she winced.

"What's wrong?"

Lucy looked around then back at him, amping up her smile again, even though it looked forced this time. "Not a thing. My tree won the highest bid. What could possibly be wrong?"

Trec scanned the room. "I don't see what's-his-name. Did he miss your big moment?"

"Sam misses a lot."

"Not much of a boyfriend if you ask me." He mumbled it, but she looked sharply at him. Instant regret sank his heart. "I didn't mean that. It was rude."

She gave a little wave. "It's not—

"I hate to interrupt, Lucy," said the woman whom Trec recognized as the owner of Buds 'N Blooms. They'd met at the sponsor dinner last night. "We need to get another photo of you with the center's board members and one with the lady who bid on your tree."

Lucy gave him an apologetic grin. "I'm sorry. I'll talk to you later?"

"Of course."

He watched her go. This was her day. He didn't feel right keeping her away from the attention she deserved. And what was he thinking bringing that buffoon Sam into the conversation again? Did he want to elevate Sam by sounding boorish himself? Trec thrust his hands in his pockets. His time in Hendricks was winding down. If he didn't act fast, his chance of making a deeper connection with Lucy would disappear.

With one last glance over his shoulder toward Lucy, he wandered in the opposite direction to find Agnes and took out his wallet.

Chapter Nine

Some of the trees had already come down, the sponsors and the winning bidders working simultaneously to pack them and the decorations into tubs for transport. Lucy would wait until tomorrow. Thankfully, the woman who bid on her tree wanted to pick it up at Buds 'N Blooms on Monday morning. That gave Lucy an extra day to dismantle it.

Lucy's attention turned to her pile of boxes and bags she'd set against the wall. Sam had offered to come back to help at the end of the day, but she'd grown to understand he just liked to hear himself talk. He was probably at his apartment with his feet up, clicking through the channels, and had no recollection of his empty offer. She surveyed the mishmash of stuff. Now to get them into her car. Then her day was done.

"Do you need help with those?"

That smooth voice was instantly recognizable, even

when she hadn't seen him coming. Trec should be well on his way back to the Twin Cities by now. There wasn't any reason for him to stick around the auction house. The surprise left her speechless for a few seconds.

As if reading her mind, he said, "I decided to stay another night. It's dark, and the roads may not be all cleared." He shrugged.

Lucy looked down at her boxes. "That's great! I mean, the help would be great." She took a deep breath. *Don't make it personal. He didn't stay because of you. He's only being kind.*

"Listen, I still owe you for what you did for my company's tree. If you hadn't fixed it, no one in their right mind would have bid on it." He picked up most of the load.

Lucy shifted her weight, tucking a box under her arm. She stifled a smile. He was right about that. "Maybe you can make me one of those little bird ornaments sometime."

"That's too easy."

"It's enough."

"Are you busy tonight?" he asked as they made their way to her car. "We could grab dinner at Red's."

Was this a date? Lucy's heartbeat quickened. Her free hand moved absently to her hair. Stray wisps had come out of the hairband. She was afraid to look in a mirror.

His eyes widened. "I mean, unless you have other plans. I don't know about you, but concession food only goes so far."

They stopped in front of her car and she opened the

hatch. Lucy laughed. "I've always felt concession stands would make a killing if they offered salads during the second half of the day."

He smiled. "So, then dinner is a yes?"

"I'll load the rest of my things into my car and meet you at Red's in fifteen."

Lucy closed the hatch and hurried to get the rest of her things inside. The snow had finally tapered off. A few errant flakes floated down from the darkened sky. The parking lot was busy with people leaving, red brake lights reflecting off the newly fallen snow. A few rows over, Trec's dark head ducked into his car. Her nerves fluttered like a moth's wings in her chest. Dinner with Trec? How would she be able to eat?

For the past forty-eight hours she'd been daydreaming about him since he walked into Buds 'N Blooms. Now here she was second-guessing herself for accepting a dinner invitation. Of course, he didn't mean anything by it. Trec owed her like he said. A business courtesy.

But that wasn't fair. He'd been nothing short of kind. Charming, actually. It was her own insecurities bubbling to the surface, refusing the notion that maybe he wanted to spend more time with her. The Twin Cities were close to four hours away though. How many long-distance relationships developed after one little dinner date?

When they arrived at the restaurant, Red's had a line waiting outside the door. It was a Saturday night after all, and there were people in town for the festival.

She stopped in her tracks when they neared the building and looked at Trec. "This is an hour wait at least," she said to him as he held open the front door. She felt his hand on her back as they went inside.

"It won't be a problem."

"What does that mean? Do you have a FastPass or something?" Warmth spread through her when he clutched her arm to his side so they could squeeze through the throngs of people.

He chuckled. "Something like that."

Inside, the foyer was shoulder-to-shoulder people. The waitress, Mindy, saw them coming and stepped away from the hostess stand. She already had menus under her arm.

As they were ushered through the restaurant to the small room in back, Lucy whispered, "How did you do that? You're not a local."

Trec looked down at her with raised eyebrows. "Sometimes it takes a little more than just knowing the right people."

She chuckled. "What's that supposed to mean?"

When he didn't answer and only raised his brows higher, she caught his meaning. He'd *paid* to get a table. Heat rose to Lucy face. This was more than a reciprocal dinner for taking care of his tree.

They settled at their table near the stone fireplace. There were only four other tables in this small wood-paneled room. The dim lighting lent a cozy cottage feel to the space.

He folded his hands in front of him. "Okay, let's see the hardware."

At first she didn't know what he meant. Then it

dawned on her: the trophy. She dug it out of her bag and set it on the table.

"Impressive."

She shrugged, looking at the little golden tree on the marble base. An inscribed plate on the base read, *Highest Bid Award, Holly Days Christmas Tree Festival.*

"What? Your tree won the highest bid. A *very* high bid."

"Bidding on the trees is more about donating to the center than shopping for a Christmas tree."

"Don't downplay your talent," he said. "Besides, it's where I'd shop for a tree."

She shrugged again. "It's just decorating. It's not like I'm performing heart surgery." She paused. "Or helping someone with their retirement portfolio."

He threw back his head and laughed. He had nice teeth too. Lucy tried not to stare too long.

"What you do is just as important," he finally said.

She shook her head and looked into her lap. "Plugging plastic flowers into pots? Hanging stars on fake trees? I don't think so."

He rested his elbows on the table and leaned forward. The lit candle in the golden glass votive between them made his eyes dance. "You create beauty."

Her throat was dry when she swallowed. "It's superficial."

"It makes people feel good."

That was true. It made her happy at least.

He cocked his head to the side, grinning. "You're not denying that."

Lucy leaned back in the chair. "You got me."

Their waitress came for their drink order. Trec asked Lucy what she'd recommend for an appetizer, but the only appetizer she'd ever ordered was the mozzarella sticks. They were the cheapest. When she suggested them, Trec didn't hesitate.

"Good choice. Mozzarella sticks are vastly underrated," he said which made Lucy smile.

When the waitress left, Trec cleared his throat. "So, now that the festivities are over, what will keep you busy between now and Christmas?"

"Mostly work." She was taking extra hours during the week since Sally closed the shop for two weeks around Christmas and New Year's. It hurt financially, but luckily she had a little in savings to tide her over.

"Of course."

"And I'll have to dismantle the tree tomorrow. The person who bought it will pick it up at the shop on Monday morning."

"That's a lot of work. First the decorating, then undoing it."

Lucy shrugged. "I don't mind. It's what I do." Again, the self-consciousness crept up. Why did he make her feel so inferior? He'd done nothing to encourage it.

"You probably don't have to bring home work at night, do you?" he said. "That must be so nice. To be able to rest your brain."

She bristled. It must have registered on her face because Trec straightened in his seat.

He lay his hand on the table in front of her. "I didn't

mean anything by that. It came out a little more awkward than I thought it would."

"It's nothing. Really."

"All I meant was I'm on call until I go to sleep, and even then my mind doesn't turn off right away."

Lucy swallowed. "Lucky for me, artificial flowers don't give me that much grief."

He smiled, but it was crooked, unsure.

It set the tone for the rest of the dinner. Lucy couldn't shake the feeling that he was out of her league. All of the real-world problems he solved during the day seemed so much more important than working as a florist in a blip of a town four hours from the big city. She tried to keep the conversation lighthearted, but her tone sounded flat.

The bill came and Lucy thanked him profusely when he paid. Before he put his wallet away, Trec held out one of his business cards.

"If you ever need financial advice—"

Lucy deflated. Of course. That was all she was to him, another potential client. She took the card and studied it, afraid to look at him for what her face might reveal. Lucy just wanted to leave.

His gaze rested on her face. "Or if you want to, you know, meet for dinner again. I hear Sego's is nice."

Sego's was nice. Nicer than any restaurant she could afford.

She walked ahead of him out of the restaurant. "We'll see," she said over her shoulder. It was an easy out, him living so far away. There wouldn't be any chance of them bumping into each other. It was just as well.

They were in the parking lot. She didn't want to drag out the goodbye longer than she had to. Her car was in the opposite direction as his.

"It was nice seeing you again," she said, sticking out her hand.

His expression was unreadable as he looked at her hand. Then he shook it.

"Yes, very nice," he said. "Lucy, I..." he started to say, still looking at their intertwined hands. "Well, I guess it's goodbye."

Lucy could only manage a nod. She hurried to her car, wondering if her relief was greater than the regret tugging at her heart.

Chapter Ten

S o many custom arrangement orders had come in that morning. Even with her and Sally working straight through until closing for the next ten days, Lucy wondered how they would finish on time before Sally closed Buds 'N Blooms for the last week of December and first week of January. Sally blamed Lucy for the influx of business. "Once everyone got a look at your festival tree, they wanted something like it on their table for Christmas dinner," Sally had said earlier. Sally wasn't complaining, of course.

Lucy placed the newly completed centerpiece on the wire rack behind her, attached the name tag, and plucked the next order ticket from the book. She sipped the hot chocolate Sally had just made her.

White chrysanthemums, red roses, magnolia leaves, pinecones.

Plaid ribbon and a silver container.

Lucy gathered the flowers and other supplies from around the workroom. She turned the radio volume up, letting the strains of Brenda Lee's "Rockin' Around the Christmas Tree" set the pace for getting these arrangements finished. She'd made so many centerpieces since Thanksgiving that her mind easily wandered while her fingers plucked and tucked, twisted and tied the arrangement together. Her thoughts returned to Trec as they had constantly since she'd said goodbye to him in the parking lot at Red's Saturday night. As usual, she'd read too much into his kindness. His attentiveness to her the whole weekend—at the sponsor dinner, at the auction, then Red's—could be explained by his pure professionalism. To him, she was like a business associate, someone to repay for a favor or transaction received. She helped him after his tree debacle, so he bought her dinner. Simple as that.

She shook her head as she stuck the pinecones into the florist's foam.

But she'd liked him. *Really* liked him. He didn't seem insincere. In fact, once she could see beyond those mesmerizing eyes and his self-deprecating humor, she found him very down to earth. That was the trouble. Obviously he didn't think of her the same way. Passing off his business card and then the quick departure proved it.

Sally poked her head into the workroom.

"Lucy, someone is here to pick up the auction tree."

Lucy wiped her hands on the apron. "Okay, I'll be right out." The boxes were already waiting by the door. She'd just help load them.

She picked bits of floral foam from her sweater sleeves then washed her hands. The stuff stuck everywhere.

Sally was at the counter when Lucy walked into the front of the shop. Lucy looked around, taking another sip of her hot chocolate and a cookie from the plate of gingersnaps she'd brought in earlier for Sally and their customers. At present, they were the only ones in the shop.

"He's loading the first box," Sally said in answer to Lucy's puzzlement.

Lucy could see through the front windows that snow had begun to fall again. The world outside was shrouded in white. "Will it ever stop?"

"I'm not counting on it until April," Sally said, separating silk poinsettia stems for another arrangement.

Lucy passed the counter, admiring Sally's work. "That's really pretty."

"I feel like they're all starting to look the same to tell you the truth."

Lucy giggled and squatted to lift a box of ornaments for the tree. She froze.

She retraced her steps to the counter where Sally worked. There on the counter next to the silk flower stems and the green wire was a bird. Its dollar-bill wings and white paper cutout head tucked into the center crease looked decidedly amateurish surrounded by the mass-produced Christmas decorations. She picked it up by the red pipe cleaner hook and twirled it slowly between her fingertips. Her breath caught.

"Where did this come from?"

Sally stopped what she was doing as if she noticed it for the first time. "He must have brought it in."

"He?"

The front door opened as if to answer her question. A gust of wind set the tiny bell ornaments on the nearest tree tinkling in harmony. Lucy turned.

"You asked me to make you one. I thought I'd deliver it personally," Trec said. His dark overcoat was dusted with snow. He brushed it from his hair. "Since I had to pick up my tree anyway."

Lucy wondered if he could hear her heart pounding beneath her sweater. It was at least loud enough to drown out his words, because she didn't hear him correctly. "*Your* tree?"

Trec came toward her. "Yes, the tree I bid on at the auction. And won."

"You bid on my tree? But I thought...the woman, Helen."

She couldn't remember the woman's last name, even though she'd written it on a slip of paper along with her phone number to coordinate a time to pick up the tree. Lucy was almost too flustered to remember her own name at the moment. Beside her, Sally's smile was nothing short of euphoric.

"Helen is my assistant Amelia's mother. She comes to the festival every year." He took a step closer.

"But...why did she bid on it?" She put her hand on her chest, hoping to still the mad beating.

"Because it's a beautiful tree, and I don't have one."

Lucy couldn't keep the smile from her face. He'd come

all the way back from the Twin Cities for her tree. Or had he even left Hendricks this past weekend? A little spark of hope wriggled its way into her heart. Had he come back for *only* the tree?

"Of course I know nothing about decorating trees." His eyes burned into hers, a little smile having lit them on fire. "Light strings might be the death of me."

"That's true."

"So I'll need help setting this one up again."

Lucy shifted her weight and glanced toward the windows, feigning indifference but felt herself grinning like a goon. "I might know someone. Her specialty happens to be stringing lights." The hot chocolate felt as if it ran through her veins, sweet and warm.

"And I suppose I'll have to take you to dinner again," he droned with an equal measure of boredom.

Lucy looked at the remaining boxes by the door and then at Trec. His expression was so anticipative and bright.

"Dinner would be wonderful."

She bent down to retrieve one of the two remaining boxes. Trec lifted the other under his arm and opened the door for her. Outside, fat snowflakes surrounded them like they were walking through their own personal snow globe. Lucy slipped the box into the back of his Jeep. When he'd shut the hatch, Trec turned toward her.

He was so close Lucy could smell mint on his breath. The smile disappeared, and he grew serious. "Unless you'd rather keep it…more professional. Instead of dinner,

I could compensate you for your time, for gas. You could send me an invoice." His eyes searched hers.

She lifted her hand to brush the flakes from his shoulder and his fingers were there in an instant to take her hand. Trec's touch was firm yet gentle. His thumb caressed her palm, sending a steamy river of delight running up her arm.

"Compensation and invoices? That takes all the fun out of decorating," she said, smiling up at him. "Let's stick to dinner."

He nodded, drawing her closer, tilting his head ever-so-slightly to conform to hers. When he brushed his lips against her mouth, Lucy melted. They were warm and soft, and despite not wearing a coat herself, Lucy was far from cold. Trec's arms pulled her into the folds of his dark overcoat, cocooning her from the elements, while their kiss deepened.

"I was hoping you'd say that," he whispered.

A Special Note to Readers

I hope you've enjoyed the stories of these special couples as much as I loved writing them. If this was your first time in Hendricks, I hope you'll visit again soon. One way to enjoy the series is through the exclusive Blueberry Point goodies you'll receive when you sign up for my newsletter, *Welcome to the Sweet Life*. You'll get access to free content, monthly giveaways, a sneak peak at what I'm working on, and notice of special sales events. I'd love for you to receive the inside scoop on my author news so we can stay connected.

Chocolate Oatmeal Dream Drops

A simply delightful cookie to make, eat and/or share. Darcy doesn't mind at all when Grace decides to make a double batch to give away!

1/2 stick margarine

1/2 c. evaporated milk

1 tsp. almond extract

1 3/4 c. quick oatmeal

3 T. cocoa

1 c. sugar

1/2 c. nuts

Blend margarine, cocoa, sugar and milk in a large saucepan. Bring to a boil then cook for one minute while stirring. Remove from heat and add flavoring and oatmeal. Drop onto wax paper, one at a time, then sprinkle with nuts. Keep refrigerated or freeze them.

Lazy Days Lemon Coconut Cookies

A staple at Blueberry Point Lodge for summer events, these delicate cookies taste like sunshine.

3/4 c. butter
   1/2 c. sugar
   1 egg yolk
   1/2 tsp. lemon extract
   1 tsp. vanilla
   2 c. flour
   1 1/2 c. coconut

Preheat oven to 350 degrees. Cream butter and sugar together. Beat in egg, vanilla and lemon extract. Mix in flour and coconut until well-blended. Shape into one-inch balls and place on a greased cookie sheet. Flatten with a fork. Bake for 8-10 minutes. Cool completely before frosting with Lemon Butter Frosting.

Lemon Butter Frosting

1/4 c. butter
   1 tsp. grated lemon peel
   1/8 tsp. salt
   2 c. sifted powdered sugar
   4 tsp. lemon juice

Beat butter, lemon peel, salt and powdered sugar together until creamy. Add lemon juice gradually. If necessary add a drop or two of water for desired consistency.

Kiley's S'mores Bars

These delicious chewy bars are the perfect end note to dinner on a fall night.

- 2 c. flour
- 2 c. crushed graham crackers
- 1 tsp. baking powder
- 1/4 tsp. salt
- 1 c. unsalted butter, room temperature
- 1 1/2 c. packed light brown sugar
- 2 large eggs
- 2 c. marshmallow topping
- 1/2 c. semi-sweet chocolate chips

Preheat oven to 350 F. Grease a 13x9 glass pan. In one bowl, combine flour, graham crackers, baking powder, and salt. Set aside. In another bowl and using an electric mixer, beat butter and sugar together on medium speed until well combined. Beat in eggs. Slowly add flour mixture on a low speed.

Press 2/3 of dough into pan with your fingers until even. Spread marshmallow topping evenly over the dough. Sprinkle chocolate chips on top. Drop teaspoon-sized pieces of remaining dough on top of chocolate chips. Bake for 30 minutes or until top turns golden brown. Cool on a wire rack for 30 minutes before slicing into bars.

Not-So-Snappy Gingersnaps

Melt-in-your mouth chewy is a better way to describe these buttery sweet cookies. We enjoy them year round too!

3/4 c. Crisco
    1 cup sugar + extra to roll in
    1 egg
    1/4 c. molasses
    2 c. flour
    2 tsp. baking soda
    1/2 tsp. salt
    1 T. ground ginger
    1 tsp. cinnamon

Preheat oven to 350 degrees. Grease cookie sheets. Beat together Crisco and one cup of sugar. Add egg and beat until light and fluffy. Add molasses and mix until combined. In a separate bowl, stir together the flour, baking soda, salt, ginger, and cinnamon. Add these dry ingredients to the first mixture and beat until smooth and well-blended. Roll dough into one-inch balls and roll in sugar before arranging on the cookie sheet. Bake 9-11 minutes until the tops begin to crack. Makes about 40 cookies.

Also by D.E. Malone

Hearts in Hendricks series

Love Like Water

Love Like Fire

Love Like Air

Love Like Forever

Blueberry Point Romance series

Love, Lies and Lavender

Love, Lies and Mistletoe

Love, Lies and Lullabies

Love, Lies and Lemon Pie

Love Between the Lines, a free novella

Silver Leaf Falls Novella Series

A Forever Kiss in Silver Leaf Falls

Middle Grade (writing as Dawn Malone)

Bingo Summer

The Upside of Down

About the Author

D.E. Malone writes contemporary romance and is the author of the Hearts in Hendricks and Blueberry Point Romance series. She also writes for middle grade audiences as Dawn Malone. Her work has appeared in the Chicken Soup for the Soul series, *Highlights for Children*, and other magazines and newspapers. When not writing, she loves spending time outdoors in the garden, hiking, and exploring places off-the-beaten path. She lives in Illinois with her husband and a lab-mix rescue. Sign up for her newsletter Welcome to the Sweet Life for new releases and other bookish news. She's on Facebook, Instagram, and Goodreads as dmalonebooks.